THE NEXT LIE

OTHER TITLES BY CAMDEN BAIRD

The Last Morning

THE NEXT LIE

A THRILLER

CAMDEN BAIRD

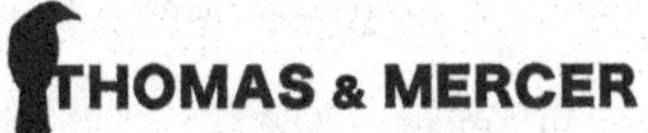

Published by Thomas & Mercer, Seattle

www.apub.com

Amazon, the Amazon logo, and Thomas & Mercer are trademarks of Amazon.com, Inc., or its affiliates.

EU product safety contact:
Amazon Media EU S. à r.l.
38, avenue John F. Kennedy, L-1855 Luxembourg
amazonpublishing-gpsr@amazon.com

ISBN-13: 9781662530265 (paperback)
ISBN-13: 9781662530272 (digital)

Cover design by Lisa Amoroso
Cover image: © Robert Brook, Christopher Stevenson / Getty

Printed in the United States of America

For S.J.
for being there

SADIE
THE WIFE

Now

My neighbor's dead and my husband's missing. He didn't take anything, not even his phone. It's charging on his nightstand, still plugged in, as if Allen might reappear at any moment to check the latest stock market reports and basketball scores. Tell me about the storm, the one that's raging. Our bedroom's eerily quiet, except for the droning rain, and I'm soaked to the bone, my pajama pants and T-shirt serving as a chilly second skin.

Lightning crackles across the sky illuminating Allen's dresser. His key ring and his wallet remain untouched. I rub my upper arms when I shiver, not wanting to face what this means, not wanting to take that mental leap. After all this family's been through, it's hard not to imagine the worst. No. I've got to pull myself together and stay calm for Emma. Work out what's happened and why, so I can fix this for our family. A terrifying thought occurs. Maybe whatever's happened is so heinous it can't be fixed.

My open suitcase rests on a chair, loaded with vacation outfits. A cute new swimsuit and a pretty hibiscus sarong lie on top of neatly folded sundresses, sandals, a wide-brimmed hat. Allen's packed suitcase stands in the corner, ready to go. But we won't be going anywhere, will we? Not if Allen's done the unthinkable. Not if he doesn't come home.

What if he's fleeing the country? Abandoning me and Emma? Leaving us both behind? The wind moans and lashes out, shakes the windows in their casings, sends tremors throughout the house. Until I feel like I'm sinking in quicksand, getting slowly sucked under.

I gasp and break free, dash into our walk-in closet. Squat by our fire-proof safe and quickly work its keypad. It hums through a series of numbers then clicks open and I fumble around inside, locate our passports: Allen's and mine. Grasp them both with shaky hands.

"Mommy? What's happening?" Emma stands in the doorway, dressed in her nightie and holding her worn Night Doggie. The stuffed lovey is brown and white with stubby legs and arms, floppy ears and a cute puppy snout, but no tail. I return the passports to the safe and lock it. She was probably awakened by the sirens.

"It's okay, sweetie," I say. "It's too early to get up. Let's get you back in bed, hmm?" My breath goes rough and ragged, as if I'm still outdoors and under assault from the elements, *as if* I'm in a vault trapped by fear.

Emma's pout tugs at my heartstrings. "Why are you all wet?" My hair's plastered to my face and neck and dripping on the carpet. It's pretty clear I've been out in the storm, but I can't tell her the truth or anything close. This is Emma's last day of school before her weeklong spring break. She's going on a trip herself—or was supposed to. I stare at our unmade bed, my pulse racing, but I steel my nerves and usher Emma along.

She frowns and hugs Night Doggie closer. "Is someone's house on fire?" she asks peeking over her shoulder.

"No, sweetie," I say. "Everything's all right."

But, deep in my soul, I know it's not.

I think of Allen and how he's run, and the dark implications of what that means. Of the lies upon lies he seemed to tell during Emma's kidnapping, and the way I initially doubted him, before foolishly believing I could take him at his word. I had so many questions but I set them all aside, wanting to save our marriage at any cost, and so I did.

But now, there's everything that happened last night.

Dread swoops down on me like a raven, digging in with sharp claws, and clutching my heart in its talons—tighter and tighter—until it weeps.

And I know whose house is burning.

It's ours.

SADIE
THE WIFE

Before

The commotion in Cass's driveway drags my attention from my morning coffee and across our drenched backyard, past Emma's play set and over the fence. I set down my mug and stand from the breakfast nook table, peering through the window. The gray morning rises in the mist and rain drives down harder. My God. Something's happened to Cass.

I dash to the patio door and step outside. Hurry in my pajama pants and T-shirt across the lawn, as my slippers squish, soaking up moisture, spewing out flecks. Muddying my pajama pants up to the knees. But I don't feel the rain pounding my hair and racing down my cheeks, sopping through my T-shirt until it clings, damp against me.

Emergency lights beckon, turning and turning and casting their eerie glow. I spy a fire truck, two cop cars. My pulse skitters. An ambulance with its rear doors left open wide. A police officer spots me approaching the gate and strides over, tugging at the brim of his hat. Rivulets stream from its brim, race down his nose. He wipes them with his uniform sleeve. I see from his name tag his name is Brady. "I'm sorry, ma'am. You can't be here."

"But Cass?" My voice quakes when I ask, "My neighbor, is she all right?"

I get a sick, sinking feeling she's not.

"This is a potential crime scene, ma'am. We have to keep this area clear."

Crime scene? No.

The police officer motions me back toward my house. "Ma'am?" He closes the gate between us and its latch catches.

I nod, though it's like I can't hear him, his words competing with the noise in my brain. I'm overcome with fear because of what happened yesterday. I know how that could look and what that might mean for me, for Allen, for Emma. I grip my arms around myself and peek past the officer's shoulder surveying the scene.

"Ma'am?" He nods me away and I comply with his stern look.

I hurry back into the house and grab a couple of dish towels in the kitchen, patting down my wet clothes and hair, and mopping up mud splatters. Save light creeping in from the breakfast area and kitchen, the den is dark. So are the adjoining living room and my office, with its partially open pocket doors.

This house has two staircases, a steeper one in front descending to the foyer and this back staircase with a landing three-quarters of the way up, leading alternately to Emma's playroom over the garage on the left and the upstairs hall on the right. I check the garage door in the kitchen at the base of the stairs. Allen's SUV is parked beside mine, so he obviously hasn't left for work. When I came down for coffee, he was sleeping soundly. He must still be in bed, or showering—getting ready.

I take the steps two at a time, my hand on the railing. I have to tell Allen what's happened, let him know about Cass. But when I reach our bedroom, he's gone. The duvet's pushed back on our bed and no steam clouds the bathroom mirror. Not a single light is on.

I dart into our walk-in closet.

Empty.

Race through the upstairs hall and check Emma's room. She's snuggled under her covers, stirring lightly. I hope she sleeps through this. This is too much for a child. Too much for me. I dash into Allen's office and hunt around for clues. His laptop's open on his desk, its screen saver whirling with multicolored coils accordioning over one another.

Flashing emergency vehicle lights pour in from the window behind his desk and I look out through the slanting rain. My heart pounds as a group emerges through Cass's back door. EMTs flood her rear deck, ducking their heads against the rain. Firefighters wear shiny black hats and slick yellow coats. Two police officers appear. And then, a third. A gurney comes next.

Covered.

Bile rises in my throat and I cup my mouth.

Cass.

I turn from Allen's office window, my stomach churning. Where did he go? Why would he run? Unless he himself had something to do with Cass's murder. For months and months, Allen claimed he'd barely known Cass Thomas. Now, I know that was a lie. Fear settles in my belly like a lead weight, makes my chest heavy and my breath catch.

A framed photo sits on Allen's desk. I grasp it tightly, staring at the family portrait. Allen, Emma and I laugh at the beach, dressed in flip-flops, shorts and T's. Allen snapped the selfie with one of his long arms. Emma's got my lighter hair and dark eyes, but her straight-across eyebrows are Allen's. I set down the photo, my world spiraling. Slipping away from me like sand threading through my fingers. Faster, faster . . . than my galloping heart.

Oh my God.

What has Allen done?

SADIE
THE WIFE

Before

"Happy birthday to you! Happy birthday to you!" Allen's and Emma's voices ring out in a joyful chorus as Allen sets my beautiful birthday cake on the table. It's got thirty-eight candles on it and they're all glowing brightly.

"Make a wish, Mommy! Make a wish!" Emma sits up straighter in her chair wearing a cute panda sweater. It's February second and snow lightly drifts outside the breakfast nook window, dotting the darkened sky.

I smile at our precious girl, all big brown eyes and grins, and up at Allen who's standing beside me. "Thank you," I say, "the cake is beautiful." He got it from a bakery and its cream-colored frosting and pink fondant roses look luscious—and yummy. It's a special order white chocolate cake with a raspberry filling, my favorite. Allen gets one for me every year.

"You're welcome." He's tall with dark-blond hair and is still very handsome at nearly forty. In some ways he's better looking than when I met him, but maybe I believe that because I love him more. He takes his seat at the table beside me. "Now blow out your candles. Go on."

I laugh and close my eyes and press my hands together, but it's so hard to think of a wish that would make my world better than it already is. The terror of what happened eighteen months ago hasn't left us completely but we're finally moving on from those dark days. At first it was in baby steps and then by leaps and bounds. Now we're holding hands and running into a very bright future. My heart's so full.

I laugh and open my eyes and tell Allen, "I can't think of anything to wish for. I already have everything I want." I dart a sunny gaze at Emma and she giggles.

"Why don't you wish for a pony?"

"Ha!" I thumb her nose. "I bet you'd like one too."

The candles are dripping on the cake, burning down quickly. "How about a trip?" Allen suggests with a glint in his eye.

"What?"

"Wish for a couple's getaway."

My husband's up to something. "Allen?"

"Your cake's going to catch fire!" Emma warns and I chuckle.

"Okay, okay!" I squeeze my eyes tightly shut and imagine me and Allen under a palapa on a tropical beach. Open my eyes and blow, blow, blow. Oops. Three candles are still burning. I extinguish them just in time. Each candle's melted down to a waxy nub.

"Yay!" Emma bounces in her seat and claps her hands. She's been in a great mood since learning about *her* trip. Her aunts Pat and Gayle are taking her on a kid's dream vacation: a theme park character cruise in the balmy Caribbean. They're whisking her away over Emma's spring break as an early treat for her seventh birthday.

At first, I was reluctant to let her go, but Allen insisted it would be good for our girl, a wonderful adventure and a way to build additional happy memories. That's something we learned about in family counseling. Creating more positive experiences helps put the difficult times behind us by making them seem farther away.

"I made you something, Mommy." Emma hands me a small package wrapped with lots of tape and a crooked bow.

I wait to cut the cake and open her present first. "What a lovely gift! Did you wrap it yourself?"

Her grin reveals two missing front teeth. "Uh-huh." She's so darn cute, adorable. She's grown her hair out and wears it in a high ponytail most days. It's what the other girls do in first grade, and we're so happy to see her making friends and fitting in.

"Impressive! I bet I'll love what's on the inside even more."

Emma watches expectantly as I remove the wrapping and open the lid of the box. It's a pot holder made on a child's loom in lots of vibrant colors. "I *love* this." She beams at my reaction and then I tease, "It's just what I wished for."

Emma cackles. "Is *not*."

"Maybe not." I lay it against my chest in a display. "But I'll use it proudly. Thank you, sweetheart." I lean over and give her a kiss.

"Now, my turn." Allen lifts something he's hidden on the chair beside him. It's an envelope.

"Thank you." Our fingers brush as I take it from him and my heart flutters. Still in love with my husband after all these years. I sigh and break the seal of the envelope, wondering what it'll be this time. Allen often gives me outings, like a visit to a fancy day spa or tickets to a fun event. But these aren't event tickets inside the card. I open it and stare at the printed email. It's a travel itinerary confirmation. I gasp and look up. "Aruba?"

"Emma will be in good hands, so I thought why not take a little vacation ourselves?"

My heart thumps happily. I've always wanted to travel to the Caribbean and Allen knows that. We've talked about going for our ten-year anniversary, but that's two and a half years away. "Allen? Are you sure?"

He winks. "Better start shopping for that bikini."

My cheeks warm and I shove his chest and laugh. "This is too much."

"Nope." He takes my hand. "It's just enough."

"Kiss Mommy!" Emma insists. So he does.

"Thank you," I say softly.

His blue eyes twinkle. "We're going to have a great time."

Allen passes me the cake cutter, then asks Emma, "Now who wants cake?"

O'REILLY
THE COP

Now

I shut my cruiser's door and press through the sea of first responders swamping Cass Thomas's driveway. It's been storming on and off all morning and a heavy drizzle masks the scene. EMTs roll a covered stretcher toward the open ambulance hull. I raise my hand to flash my badge, and one guy nods as I reach for the blanket holding it high at a protective slant to examine the corpse. Thomas's face is sallow beneath the series of blond ringlets framing her high cheekbones and forehead. Her eyes are closed and bluish circles rim them. A trickle of dried blood pools in her right ear. When I lift the blanket farther, I note bruising on her arms above the elbows. She's dressed in casual clothes: jeans and a striped, fitted top with a scoop neck and cap sleeves. "What happened?" I ask, glancing from one EMT to the other.

The lead guy speaks. "We found her in the living room. She seems to have tripped and possibly hit her head on the coffee table."

"Accident?"

"Inconclusive, though it appears she had a visitor."

An officer standing close by chimes in. I know her as Bev Johnson, a fresh transfer from the precinct in Durham. "We got a call this morning from a concerned neighbor." Johnson squints and shields her eyes, as rain's blown beneath the brim of her hat. "Said she heard shouting yesterday evening, voices. Cass and someone else. This neighbor heard glass breaking too." Johnson jerks her head toward a window overlooking the deck, and I observe its spider-web-like pattern. The glass is smashed from the inside as if someone rammed into—or was thrown up against—it hard. A forensics team carefully examines the damage. One person wearing gloves uses tweezers to extract fibers from the glass. A second gloved individual holds open a sterile evidence bag into which the nearly invisible fibers are deposited.

I remove my hat and rub my temples, wipe away the rain with the back of my hand. "What time did the call come in?"

"A little after six a.m.," Johnson answers. "The neighbor didn't phone it in until she got up this morning. Said she worried last night she'd misheard things and didn't want to interfere once the noise calmed down. Since Cass is an early riser, the neighbor decided to check on her first thing, but got no reply to her texts. When no one answered the front door either, she came around back and saw the busted-out window. She phoned the police then."

"Where's this neighbor now?"

"Down at the station giving her statement."

I nod and make a mental note to talk to her myself later.

Our forensic pathologist Libby McMann walks up to me removing her thin blue gloves and tucking them in her rain jacket pocket. She carries a medical bag in one hand and wears a slicker over her scrubs, and requisite sterile booties. Raindrops speckle her square eyeglasses. She's in her sixties with short silvery hair.

"Any guesses?" I ask her.

"We'll know more after the autopsy, but from the state of the body, I'd say blunt force head trauma. Could have been an accident but judging by the window . . ." McMann shrugs.

"Right," I answer, getting her drift. "Maybe not."

"There was clearly an altercation," McMann ventures. "Could be domestic."

"Except Miss Thomas's ex-husband and son Bobby are dead."

McMann scans my face, wondering how I know that.

"Former case," I explain. "The Wilson girl kidnapping."

"Ah yes," she replies. "I was glad not to be involved."

I smile at the older woman. "That one had a happy ending."

She zips up her raincoat. "Wish they all did." McMann stares back at the house. "She could have a new boyfriend," she relays about Cass. "Or, an old one, who's resurfaced." She lets the innuendo hang. Certain men can't take no for an answer, don't know how to leave a woman alone. Yeah, I've seen a lot of that. Too much, for my liking.

"Right." I catch a glimpse of the Wilsons' backyard. Allen had a history with Cass, but that's decades old, or so he says. I wonder if he and Sadie heard anything last night, and if there's any connection?

I approach Felipe Gomez, the cop guarding the back door. He's a veteran on the force and a former Marine like me. I appreciate the way he stands at attention, his eyes surveying the area. He's cautious, observant. The type of officer we need. "Mind if I have a look around?" I ask him.

He nods and steps away from the door, letting me in. The wooden picnic table I walk past collects rainwater on its warped surface. The drizzle's getting harder now and I scoot into the house, shake out my hat through the open door, then seat it back on my head.

Cass's kitchen is as barren as I remember containing a card table with two folding chairs in its breakfast area, and not much else. A built-in desk claims a third folding chair and holds a kid-size baseball mitt along with an adult one, a stack of magazines and a notepad, a coffee mug full of pens. There's bound to be a fourth folding chair around here somewhere.

I spot Chief Claremont in the front hall coming down the stairs. I fell out of her good graces once, but no more.

"Anything up there?" I ask her.

Claremont shakes her head. "Nothing appears to have been disturbed. No signs of forced entry either. Cass evidently knew her visitor and invited them in."

"We did find this." Val Rodriguez appears from the living room wearing thin blue gloves and holding a half-empty wine bottle. "It was on the coffee table." Her curly hair's pinned back but I remember how it looked this morning, fanned out around her pillow.

Her birth name's Valentina but her family calls her Val. Now, so do I when we're in private. Though I haven't hidden our involvement from the chief like I did my relationship with Kate, I respect that Val likes keeping things professional on the job, and I do the same. After Val helped break Emma's kidnapping case, Claremont promoted her to captain and she heads our domestic crimes unit now.

"We'll send it to the lab," Claremont says, speaking about the wine. There should be prints on the bottle, and the wine itself could have been tampered with. "What were they drinking out of?" she asks, musing aloud.

Val sets her hands on her hips. "I'll poke around."

"Upstairs is clean," Claremont volunteers. Although I trust her, I want to have a look myself. The master bedroom's sparsely furnished and the double bed's made. The en suite bathroom's light is on, its door left open.

I scan the master bath and peek behind the sliding glass shower door, but don't spot anything unusual. The large mirror over the vanity highlights my drawn expression. Despite its positive outcome, Emma's case took a toll on me. I've never fully stopped beating myself up over my blindness with regard to Kate. Maybe if I'd been more astute we'd have gotten that kid home sooner. Claremont tells me no, and that she's forgiven me. Now Val says it's time for me to forgive myself.

I check the medicine cabinet to my left. Shaving cream. Perfume. A few over-the-counter meds. All seems in order.

I reenter the bedroom and open and shut a few dresser drawers but find nothing of interest. Lots of athletic wear. Cass is—was, Jesus—a gym teacher. The closet doesn't reveal much either. A couple of dresses, nice slacks and tops, assorted shoes and fashion boots.

There's nothing in one of the bedrooms at all. The third holds a small cot and has a teddy bear leaned against its pillow. Aha. The fourth folding chair. It's got a storybook on it, like the kind you read to an older kid, one old enough to appreciate mildly spooky chapter books. But there is no kid. Tragic.

I return downstairs to find Val staring into the dishwasher. She slides out the top rack and points to something inside. Two wineglasses nest one beside the other. Both are sparkling clean. The dishwasher ran so no chance of fingerprints, dammit.

Still, one thing seems clear.

Cass wasn't drinking alone.

TERESA
THE EX-WIFE

Now

A breaking news report flashes across my television screen as I'm fixing breakfast. One poached egg, a dry piece of rye toast and black coffee. Cass Thomas is dead under unclear circumstances. I'm shocked that her death is being made public before too many details are known and wonder how Allen's handling it. Are he and Sadie huddled together while consulting with the police? Presenting a united front? They're bound to be questioned as neighbors, and considering their prior history with Cass. The police are asking the public to come forward if there's anything anyone knows.

Forrest ambles into the room in his lanky twelve-year-old body, all elbows and knees beneath baggy clothing, and stares at Cass's work photo on the TV. "Some of my soccer friends go to her school." I know the ones he means: Matty, Paul and Brian. "Said she was a nice lady." They've already been talking about it. Good news travels fast. So does bad.

I consider which type of news this is. Though it's wicked to speak ill of the dead, I never liked Cass Thomas, to be honest. Some would say she got what she deserved. Others would lock me away for even thinking that. But no one here's the mind police, least of all Forrest.

His dark-blond hair hangs at an angle on one side. The other portion of his skull sports a buzz cut. For the past three months, I haven't seen him wear any color other than black. He's in black jeans and a black T-shirt now.

Allen warned me not to make a big deal and I haven't. Middle school's a shitshow most days, and my son does what he must to look cool, so I pick my battles. I've also treaded very carefully when it comes to reprimanding Forrest since early last year. Each time I scold him, he throws Emma's kidnapping back in my face, acting like I'm one to talk about misbehavior. Even though *I didn't do it*, it hurts like hell that he believed I could have.

I motion to the box of cereal on the counter and the bowl I've set out for him. "Breakfast?" Forrest doesn't like eggs and rarely eats in the mornings, but I still try.

Forrest shakes his head and grabs his backpack, which is—yes, you've got it—black. "Not hungry. I'll get a snack later at school." The thick strap of his duffel bag's over his other shoulder. He drops it in the hallway by the front door and it hits the floor with a whack. "Here's my stuff for Dad's."

"You're not going to your dad and Sadie's." That's our routine: two weeks here, two weeks there, but sometimes routines are amended. "They're going on their trip tomorrow, remember?" No, clearly he doesn't. I swear that kid doesn't listen to half the things I say and I've spoken to him about this a dozen times. "You're going up to Northern Virginia to spend time with your grandma." I get that the notion doesn't thrill him, but she's taking him to the air and space museum in Washington, and to a baseball game besides, making an effort.

"Uh, yeah." He rolls his eyes. "And Emma's getting a cruise out of it." He says this sullenly, but I can tell he doesn't actually resent his younger half sister the way he used to. I've seen the two of them acting chummy, when I've gone to pick him up from Allen's house. If I were an empathetic ex-wife, their sweet relationship would warm my heart. But I'm not, so . . .

Forrest leaves without saying goodbye and I think about other things, like how my life might have been different if Allen and I had never broken up. I tried to fill up his world as best I could but then he left us for a larger universe, one inhabited by Sadie and Emma, and now I'm standing in such a narrow space it's like he no longer sees me at all. As if I'm invisible and mean nothing to him. Like I've been swallowed by a giant black hole.

It's lonely in this darkness, and cold.

KATE
THE EX-CON

Now

I'm trying my best to be an upstanding citizen, I really am, but some people get on my every last nerve. Like this guy here, walking back toward the counter to complain about his double-shot caramel macchiato, even though I made it expertly. I didn't acquire my barista skills in prison. I learned them on the job. I was lucky to land this one, thanks to Beau.

The shortish man quickens his steps. Button-down shirt under an argyle sweater vest, khaki pants, and round wire-rimmed glasses, slightly balding on top with a paunch hanging over his belt. I peg him for fifty and a college professor, but not full fledged and tenured. An associate at best and he resents it. He therefore resents me and the rest of the world. He stares straight down at my latte art—pretty swirls forming a heart—then up at me. Sets his cup on the counter and it clatters—startling *her*.

I ignore the rumbling in my brain like slow-rolling thunder. Oh fuck. I had so much on my mind this morning with the breaking news story, I forgot to take my pills. Big mistake. "Can I help you?" The garage door is open at his back, letting in a cool spring breeze and the telltale scent of lingering rain. It stopped raining about an hour ago and the dark clouds are lifting, giving way to a sunny day. A colorful row of tulips borders the outdoor patio area, their petals glistening with raindrops.

His mouth puckers in a frown. "This isn't what I ordered."

This café used to be an automotive shop, not a cool gathering place near campus. Squat tables hold students typing on laptops and townies sipping their lattes. A tapestry of denim and colors, tattoos and body piercings. It's beautiful in here. *Was.*

My eyebrows arch innocently. "Double-shot caramel macchiato?"

"Yes, but." He licks his thick lips. "I said 'no whip.'"

The thunder inside me grows louder, pooling in my ears like sticky blood.

"That's not whipped cream, sir," I say. "It's steamed coconut milk." I keep my tone mild, though the secret storm rages, grows stronger. *Dumb prick,* Katherine snarls, *wouldn't know his dick from his asshole.*

Shit.

"I *asked for* coconut milk," he says. "But I'm quite sure this is soy."

We're quite sure it is not.

Lightning bolts of pain singe my eyes.

My heartbeats quicken, palms sweat.

It hurts like motherfucking dammit.

Katherine leans against my pupils, peering out into the room.

Throw the whole damn thing back in his face!

I blink to rein her in, take a deep breath. Envision a calm, glassy lake.

Beau's hand is on my arm, muscles tensing below his ink sleeve, green ivy and twisting vines. "Everything okay here?"

He glances from me to the customer, who's happy to inform him, "She made my coffee wrong." My eyes sting and burn, but I won't let *her* take charge. Not today of all days. Not in light of what's happened to Cass. Too risky. I consider going to the police with the information I have, but no, best not to get involved. With my luck that will only somehow put me in the frame, and if we go back to prison, we'll crack. Once was more than enough.

"It's okay," Beau tells me, "I'll take care of it." His smoky gray gaze calms me, helps me know there are better people in this world. Good people like Nick at the soup kitchen, and like Shane used to be before he disappointingly let me down. First a cop, always a cop, and cops like Deputy Chief Shane O'Reilly don't like having girlfriends around who bend the law, much less break it. It's a bad look at the precinct, I guess.

"Why don't you take a breather, all right?" Beau says. "You're due for your break anyway." That's a lie. It's only eight thirty in the morning and I'm not due for a break until eleven. Still. If Beau's offering, I'm taking. Beau's a handsome guy in his early thirties with shaggy dark hair that makes him look like an A-list actor. If he wasn't married, I'd want him for myself. Sometimes, I still do. Not that Beau would be interested.

Just ask him, Katherine growls, low and sexy.

She purrs like a cat and I snap, "*Fuck off.*"

Shit. I didn't mean to say that out loud. The customer cocks his head at Beau, speaking about me as if I didn't exist. "Maybe her break should be permanent?"

For an instant, I'm lightheaded, sick, and the whole room is wobbling, walls melting like big jelly blobs, the floor going soft beneath me, a shroud closing in.

Beau hitches his chin, telling me to go. But not in a mean way. Gently. So I do, moving past Ginger, who's making a nonfat mocha—with whip. The jerk watches me leave, sending bad juju chasing after me like vermin on little skittery feet. Katherine wants to teach that guy some manners. Knock those ridiculous-looking glasses off his smug-ass face. But no.

We've had enough trouble with the law to last a lifetime.

We turn and walk away.

SADIE
THE WIFE

Now

The orange school bus drives off and I wave goodbye to Emma, my heartbeats slowing to a crawl, until I can't breathe, my stomach knotting painfully. My personal counselor calls this PTSD as a result of Emma's kidnapping, and she's arming me with strategies to combat it. These past eighteen months have been all about building trust. Trust that the person who took Emma is securely in prison and no longer a threat to our family. Trust that Emma's recovering and blossoming, despite her harrowing ordeal. Trust that—although we can't always keep our children safe—Emma is home safe with us now.

"Ready for spring break?" Mandy asks. She's the mom of a fourth-grade girl named Amelia.

"Yeah," I say, although I'm far from ready to do anything but scream. I can't believe what's happening, how my whole world's been turned upside down. I feel like I'm in a snow globe that's been shaken and is hanging by its base, like the ground is above me and I'm walking on the sky. "You?"

Mandy smiles broadly. "We're heading to the beach. Got a rental for the week."

"Nice."

"How about you guys?" Mandy's about my age and also works from home. Does computer malware consulting while I'm an actuary for an insurance firm. We've talked about it some but only in passing. We're not really friends, not really close. Then why do I sense her silently assessing me, like she can tell something's wrong? Like she knows something dark has gone down at my house? But she can't know, can she? No.

I paste on a smile and say conversationally, "Emma's going on a cruise with her aunties." The next words stick in my throat. "Allen and I have planned a couple's getaway." I try to sound enthused about it, although my grin's way too tight, like a clown's in heavy makeup, someone who looks ridiculously fake. A strand of my hair slips from my ponytail and I tuck it behind my ear.

"Oh nice!" Mandy responds but then her forehead wrinkles. She notes my trembling fingers and her eyebrows arch. "Hey, are you all right?"

"Yeah," I lie because I can't think of anything but Allen being gone. Should I notify the police? Could he be a victim of foul play himself? My nerves churn anxiously because I know he's not. He's hiding somewhere, but why? I don't like the answers to that question that form in my brain. "I think maybe I've had too much caffeine."

"Did you eat breakfast?" I shake my head and Mandy frowns sympathetically. "Then maybe have something to eat."

The other moms have left now. So has the one dad who's always here. He teaches chemistry at the university, and says he knows Teresa. Everyone knows Teresa with her pixieish haircut and doe-like eyes. I'm not jealous of her, or Cass. Anger boils up inside me but then it relents, remorse taking hold.

I'm not in competition with a dead woman, much less Allen's ex-wife. Doubt trickles through me, makes my face hot. What if Teresa's gone missing too? She did that once before, but by herself. Could she and Allen be together? No, that would be insane. I could call her to ask but would I get a straight answer? Or would my questioning her only fuel the fire of accusations she'd make to Allen about me later, driving him right back into her arms?

I don't trust Teresa and I never have. When I was at the depth of my despair, miserable during Emma's abduction, I had the strangest feeling that she was sneakily manipulating the situation to her advantage. That her big weepy eyes and sympathy were all for Allen, and not an ounce of it for me.

"Thanks," I say before I go. "I'll do that." Then I realize maybe I stayed silent too long, and didn't respond to Mandy's suggestion about eating something in a timely way. She'll note that I'm distracted and not behaving much like myself.

I hug my arms by my elbows and stride toward my house, self-conscious that Mandy's aware of my frazzled state. That she can somehow sense my worries and intuit I'm on edge. That, once she learns about Allen being gone, she'll express her concerns to the police by saying I was acting jittery, then the police will think I'm in on it too. *That I had something to do with Cass's death.*

I expect to hear Mandy walking away, but there's a noticeable dearth of footsteps on the pavement behind me, a strange silence on the street as I amble toward my house and a mourning dove calls. And, when I pause to glance over my shoulder, she's watching me.

O'REILLY
THE COP

Now

The chief's expression is urgent, fire in her bright-blue eyes. "We'll learn more once we get the forensics reports. In the meantime, we're going to assume that Cass Thomas's death is suspicious." We're in a windowless briefing room at the station going over what happened this morning and where we are. White cinder block walls trap a mildewy smell in this two-story brick building, only steps from the historic courthouse ringed by a roundabout.

Claremont rakes a hand through her short red hair. She's a small-framed woman but tough, in her mid-forties. "There were signs of a struggle in the home, a smashed-out window. We pulled fibers from the broken glass and we're hoping to get something from them."

Claremont continues as officers take notes, some on paper and others on their phones. "Thomas clearly invited someone in," she says, "so we're looking for a person she knew, and not some random stranger. The two of them were drinking wine. It won't take long to run the prints on the wine bottle. Unfortunately, the wineglasses went through the dishwasher, so we'll have no luck there. We do intend to analyze what's left of the wine in the bottle, but that will take a little longer.

So will Cass's autopsy, though McMann," she says naming our forensic pathologist, "suspects Cass died from blunt force head trauma. We're waiting to have that confirmed."

"Could it have been an accident?" Cole Brady asks.

Claremont folds her arms. "It's possible Cass fell and hit her head on the coffee table but if someone else was with her when that happened, they didn't stick around to help—or call nine-one-one.

"According to the neighbor, Cass and somebody else were loudly arguing right around six thirty p.m., and we're going to want to find out who that person was and what they and Thomas were arguing about. We released news about Cass's death to the media in hopes that someone will come forward who knows or saw something."

Department transfer Bev Johnson raises her hand. "I understand that Cass Thomas's neighbor, Allen Wilson, was implicated in some prior deaths, but then later exonerated."

The chief views her appreciatively. "Yes, that's right." Johnson looks like she has more to share and Claremont motions for Johnson to stand and address the room.

Johnson straightens her spine, shoulders squared. "I've been reading through the files on Emma Wilson's kidnapping, because it seemed a little odd to me that Thomas, a potential murder victim, had also been connected to that case. Cass Thomas was initially named as a person of interest in Emma's kidnapping but was ultimately cleared.

"During that investigation, a few interesting things about Allen Wilson popped up. He'd been tied to two prior accidents, both resulting in untimely deaths. Allen's parents died unexpectedly in a drowning when Allen was in his teens. So did his first girlfriend, Diane." She shrugs. "And now, a neighbor's suddenly dead under suspicious circumstances too? Someone Allen knew from high school, and who was previously suspected of taking his daughter, Emma?"

"You could be onto something," Claremont concedes. "Where you smell smoke there's often fire." Val and she and I discussed the possibility of

Allen's involvement in Cass's demise privately in Claremont's office earlier. "It's Allen's motive that's unclear."

Val wants to add something and Claremont nods for her to go ahead, as Johnson slips back into her seat, having made her point.

"Allen and his wife went through hell when their kid went missing," Val explains to Johnson and the others who've been brought into the precinct since then. She sits at a desk thumping her pen against the notebook she's set there. "Allen patently denied any current relationship with Cass, claiming they hadn't seen each other since high school before he and Sadie moved into their current home."

Claremont arches an eyebrow at Val. "Let's see if Allen's changed his tune. I'd like you and O'Reilly to question him and Sadie about what they know. Their house is right behind Cass's so they might have heard something last night. We'll need to canvass the other neighbors too. Talk to people at Cass's school and any other friends or associates. I got a short list from the parents when I spoke with them this morning. I'd like a volunteer to go through it." She glances at Gomez, the other former Marine. "Can you head that up, and put a few people on it?"

He nods efficiently. "Sure thing, boss. Will do."

Claremont pulls a small notebook from her pocket and reads before looking up. "Cass's parents were distraught to hear the news as any parents would be. Said their daughter was well liked and they can't imagine who might have been inclined to hurt her." The chief went to see the Curtises right after leaving Cass's house and before releasing news of Cass's death to the media. Out of respect, she wanted them to hear about their daughter's death in person, and from her, the chief of police, first.

"The Curtises weren't as aware of Cass's current friends or connections as they had been when Cass was a kid and still living at home," Claremont says. "They gave me a few names, but suggested we speak with Cass's sister, Robin Marconi, see if there's anything she can add, and possibly Sister Mary Catherine Ward, a nun at Cass's school and with whom Cass was close."

"Gomez?"

"Yes ma'am, consider it done," he says, jotting this down since he's heading the team going to the school.

Claremont stares at me and Val. "Can you two speak to the sister?"

"Of course." It's not even nine in the morning, less than three hours since we found her body, and there's been a hell of a lot going on.

Officer Patel flags down Gomez. "Brady and I can help you out at Our Lady of Our Savior. I know people there, since I've been there before."

Gomez concurs. "Sounds good."

Claremont addresses me and Val. "When you two visit the Wilsons, let's see if we can't delve a bit more into Allen's past affiliation with Cass. We had questions about that during Emma's kidnapping. Now that it might be relevant again, let's shine a much brighter spotlight on it to see if we can come up with anything useful that might help our case."

Her eyes lock on mine and I get her drift. She's wondering if Allen's guilty but won't speculate about that out loud. She'll want something more before bringing him in for questioning or officially naming him a person of interest. Christ. Could it be true? Could Allen have murdered Cass?

Claremont claps her hands together when people don't stir.

"Okay, folks! Let's get moving! Daylight's burning out there."

As people scramble to their feet, Claremont holds up her phone and points it around the room, commanding our attention. "I want everyone to keep me posted up to the minute, do you hear? You find something out, I'm going to need to know it next. And I'm not talking about the next day or next hour. I mean the very next second. Got that?"

We all do.

SADIE
THE WIFE

Now

The doorbell rings and I see through the sidelight it's Captain Rodriguez and Deputy Chief O'Reilly. They're the pair that brought Emma home, and our entire nightmare to an end. That's what I believed back then.

I open the door but nobody flashes a badge. They don't have to. It's like old home week.

"Sorry to bother you," O'Reilly says. There was a time when I called him Shane, but that feels odd now. I haven't seen the man in months. Maybe we're back to formalities? "May we come in?" He's got nearly coal-black eyes and is in his thirties. His buff frame and buzz cut say ex-Marine.

I confirmed this by looking him up last year. I looked everyone up who worked Emma's case, including Val Rodriguez. I inferred they'd gotten together by the time that Emma was found. Hard to think about O'Reilly actually dating Kate Davis, Emma's former kindergarten teacher. She totally pulled the wool over his eyes. Some men are so naive.

Shame swamps through me.

Women too.

How could I have trusted Allen? Believed all his lies?

"Of course," I say, and hold open the door like my heart's not beating a million times per minute, like it's not about to pound out of my chest.

"Is Allen home?" O'Reilly asks. He tries to say it lightly but it sounds like an accusation, or maybe I'm just imagining. Becoming paranoid. *With good cause.*

"No, he's . . ." I pause and lick my lips. Why are they so damn dry? "He's gone to work." I instinctively cover for him, although I probably shouldn't. I can't bring myself to reveal he's run. Can't make myself say those words out loud and admit them to the police. Set up my husband as a suspect in a woman's murder, when I don't even know the truth myself.

"No worries. We'll catch up with him later." Tension knots my gut when they step inside and when I shut the front door behind them a weird silence floods the hall. Spills into the dining and living rooms, laps at the base of the stairs. Washes over the three of us as if we're frozen in time. I swear I hear the clock ticking in the kitchen. It's the large-faced kind and is mounted over the door that leads to the garage. If they check it, they'll find Allen's SUV parked in its customary spot. They'll ask how he got into work then, since my SUV's parked beside his, and they'll know they've caught me in a bald-faced lie.

"Good to see you, Sadie," Rodriguez says. "How are you?" Her first name's Val but I've never called her that. I didn't know her all that well during Emma's investigated kidnapping, not like I knew Shane. He tried to warn me about Allen, but I didn't want to listen, couldn't believe hard truths about my husband until circumstances forced my hand. Are there harder truths concealed in the darkness and waiting to spring into the light?

I swallow past the raw burn in my throat and try not to let them see me glance at the driveway through the dining room window where a dogwood flutters in the breeze. Their squad car's there waiting at the ready to haul someone away. Will that someone be Allen? Only if they find him. "Um, good. Really great, thanks." I return the cordial gesture.

"And you?" I'm getting ahead of myself, really I am. Allen's capable of many things, but murder? No. Never.

Rodriguez sets her chin. There's a dimple in its center. "Been doing all right."

O'Reilly crosses his arms. They're obviously not here for chitchat. They're here to question me and Allen. His gaze probes mine and then he steals a look down the hall and past our breakfast nook, out the large windows with a view of our backyard and the fence between our house and Cass's. Blossoming red, white and pink azaleas line the fence and bright-yellow daffodils hedge the wooden gate with pink and purple pansies swaying between them. "You might have heard the commotion this morning," O'Reilly says, "emergency vehicles out back?"

"Yes, I heard sirens around six a.m. and went outside to investigate." Guilt stabs at me. It would be stupid to lie about this too. The officer I spoke with is sure to inform them I'd been at the gate asking questions, if he hasn't done so already. "I spoke with a police officer at the back gate briefly—his name was Brady—but he asked me to leave the scene." I brave the dark question, already knowing the answer. "Cass though? Is she all right?"

O'Reilly sets his lips in a hard line. "I'm afraid not."

"Sadie," Rodriguez says solemnly. "We have some bad news. Cass Thomas is dead."

"Oh my God." My forehead feels hot and sweat trickles down the back of my neck. I slide my hands across my rib cage and tuck them under my arms, trying to act casual about it. I realize I must look defensive so try to loosen up, ease my stance. Still. My brown cardigan sweater feels sweltering over my light cotton T-shirt. I have to ask, have it confirmed. "How did Cass die?"

Rodriguez answers. "I'm afraid we can't reveal that."

O'Reilly narrows his eyes like he's trying to peer into my head. "How about yesterday evening? Did you and Allen hear anything then? This would have been around dinnertime," he says. "Or possibly later into the night?"

"No, no," I lie again. "Everything was quiet here." I embellish further even though I know I shouldn't. Everyone says that augmenting lies only makes them more transparent. "It was quiet before dinner and we all slept soundly through the night."

Rodriguez and O'Reilly exchange a look, standing in my foyer. "Well, if you think of anything else," Rodriguez says. "Remember any little detail."

O'Reilly digs into his uniform shirt pocket and hands me his card. There was a time I had his number on speed dial. His and his boss's, Chief Claremont's, as well. I deleted those contacts in an effort to put my past behind me, and yet now—it's grabbing me by the throat.

"Thanks," I say bravely. "I'll let you know."

When they leave, I sneak into the dining room and peek out the window at the driveway. I take care to keep my body hidden, craning my neck to the view above the flowering boxwood beyond the glass. Rodriguez buckles her seat belt on the passenger side as O'Reilly settles in behind the steering wheel. He lifts a cell phone to his ear and waits, their police cruiser idling.

Allen's phone starts ringing upstairs.

SADIE
THE WIFE

Now

O'Reilly and Rodriguez back into the street and slowly drive away. I sensed O'Reilly's reluctance to leave. The way he peered around my house and peeked up the stairs gave me the willies. It's like he guessed that something was up when we spoke, like he could tell I knew more than I was letting on. He's a good cop and skilled at reading people. Shit. Did he see right through me?

I'm sweating, and my T-shirt feels damp, warmer under my armpits. Crap, I'm hot. The weight of my cardigan sweater's not helping. I remove it, and shake it out, drape it from the back of the desk chair in my office that sits on rolling casters.

I have to devise a strategy for dealing with this. But how? I don't even know where Allen is, or what the fuck he was doing last night. When I told the police we'd slept soundly, that wasn't exactly the truth.

SADIE
THE WIFE

Before

I awake at two a.m. and Allen's gone. I sit there in the dark, insecurities gnawing at me. Did he sneak out to see her again? That would be so awful, to have him break my trust again. I'm not sure how many more times I can go through that. Allen's standing on such thin ice and it's cracking, spreading out in all directions. It won't be long until our marriage is underwater again at this rate, and the next time we falter, the next time we fall—that will be the last time for me. I can't keep going through this with Allen. It's too damn hard.

The lights are out when he returns so he doesn't see me at first, propped up against the headboard with a pillow behind my back.

"Where were you?"

Allen startles in the doorway. Stares around the room. "Sadie, you scared me. What are you doing up?" He's in sweatpants and his hair's a mess, like he's been running his fingers through it. Or maybe somebody else has. A lover. My stomach sours like curdled milk.

"Where'd you go, Allen?"

"I couldn't sleep." He blows out a breath. "I went for a walk." I wish I could read his eyes but his face is swamped with shadows. His gait is easy, relaxed, like he has nothing to hide, which only makes me distrust him more. He lied to me about working late, lied to me about his relationship with Cass, and God knows what else.

Doubt claws at my soul and ravages my heart, drives my anxiety higher, so high I fear it might hit the ceiling and break through the roof. Vault over the moon and into the stars. "In the middle of the night?" I ask.

He shrugs and kicks off his shoes, entering our walk-in closet. "It's a safe neighborhood."

"Right. No place is *that safe*. Didn't we learn that with Emma?"

He returns wearing nothing but his briefs and sits down on the bed, gently taking my hand. I want to resist, pull away, but a larger part of me needs him, now more than ever. It's been a majorly fucked-up day with some very harsh reveals. I want to believe things will get better, that this is yet another uncomfortable era that Allen and I will put behind us, but now I'm not so sure. "Listen," he says. "I know this past year and a half have been tough. And when Emma went missing, oh my God, that was absolutely terrifying."

"What about what happened with Cass?"

"That was a long time ago, Sadie. You were distraught over Emma's disappearance. I don't blame you for losing your temper."

"I'm not talking about Emma's kidnapping, Allen. I'm talking about more recently." My breath shudders when I add, "I'm talking about what happened with Cass tonight."

He frowns. "That was very unfortunate, it's true. But Sadie, *accidents happen*. We'll get through this. We'll find a way." How can he call it an accident? Allen knew exactly what he was doing. He's just trying to keep it from me.

He moves a little closer on the bed and the mattress sinks under his weight. I slide involuntarily closer. I want so badly to believe the awful times are over. I can't bear to have Allen break my heart again, because—this time, I'm pretty sure—I won't survive it.

Allen wraps his arms around me and holds me close. "Sadie, look. I know you're upset and I understand that, but I don't want you to stress over Cass, okay? I'm really good at cleaning up messes and I'll take care of this, take care of you, take care of Emma. You'll see." He peers into my eyes and asks, "Do you believe me?"

I so pathetically need to trust him, I can't do anything but nod.

"Good." A soft smile, the side of my husband I live for. The good guy, the knight in shining armor I married and made our precious girl with. The man I need to believe with my whole heart is still there. He kisses the top of my head and whispers soothingly, "Now, let's get some sleep, all right?"

SADIE
THE WIFE

Now

Someone's at the front door and for a moment I think it's the police returning for further questioning, or potentially with some news about Allen. O'Reilly's rung Allen's cell phone six times today. He also called me later in the morning, saying he and Rodriguez had gone to Allen's office, where they learned he'd never arrived for work. Now they've come back to grill me about why I lied in the first place and ask me what I really know.

But when I walk through my front hall I spot an unfamiliar vehicle in my driveway, a chunky dark-blue sedan. It looks like a newer model but I'm not great at identifying cars. I see a woman with curly black hair standing on my front stoop through the sidelight and surmise she's a solicitor, or someone passing out leaflets for the Latter-day Saints. I open the door partway and poke my head around it. Raise my eyebrows. "Yes?"

"I'm sorry to barge in on you like this but—"

"I'm sorry, I'm really not interested." I try to shut the door and she stops it with her palm. She's got large hands for such a small woman, and a strong build. Gray eyes and a slightly freckled face.

"I'm not selling anything, if that's what you're thinking."

I push the door toward her firmly and it gives a little. She's not going to fight her way in here. That gives me some relief. "My husband and I already have a church," I say thinking she's some sort of missionary.

She sighs and drops her hand. Runs her fingers through her bouncy hair that lands about chin level. "Not selling religion either."

I close the door farther. "I don't mean to be rude, but I'm in the middle of work."

"Sadie," she says suddenly and my heart jolts against my chest. "We need to talk."

My senses go on high alert. "How do you know my name?" I ask, my neck and shoulders tensing.

"I know about you and Allen."

Oh my God, she's one of those stalkers O'Reilly warned me about. Someone who glommed onto Emma's case and weirdly made it personal. Followed each and every news story and press conference and now believes that we're familiar. Thinks she knows my family and is somehow a part of us. *More than a little creepy.* "I think you'd better go."

"But—"

"Now, please. I don't want to have to phone the police."

"The police will be here soon enough."

"What? Why?"

"I called them."

"You?"

She peeks furtively over her shoulder. "Please let me in. We don't have much time."

"Who *are* you?"

She stares straight in my eyes and says, "Diane."

DIANE
THE OLD GIRLFRIEND

Before

The TV is on in my motel room but I've got the volume muted. I'm taking a smoke break with the window cracked and sitting on a ratty bedspread, hunched forward and nervously watching for news updates while tapping my cigarette ash into a soda can. I saw the emergency vehicles at her house and hope it's not what I think, and that Cass is okay. I've been through three cigarettes so far and the pack is almost empty. I'll have to buy more for—*fuck me*. Cass's face appears on the screen. It looks like a teacher photo, probably one from her work.

A woman in a navy blue jacket and pressed white blouse delivers the story. Large, black-framed glasses cover a third of her face.

> Chapel Roads is reeling after the unexplained death
> of one of our residents, Our Lady of Our Savior gym
> teacher Cass Thomas.

Death? My stomach sinks. I feel guilty, responsible, although I shouldn't. This one's on Allen and not on me. It's true, I set things up in an effort to punish him, but I never thought he'd go that far. Never anticipated this outcome. It's sick and Allen's dangerous. Holy fuck.

I tune back in to the announcement.

> Cass Thomas was found dead in her home this morning in the Briar Rose neighborhood, after a concerned neighbor called nine-one-one. The cause of death has not been released, but police are looking for the person who last saw Cass Thomas alive and would like that person to come in voluntarily for questioning. Authorities urge anyone with relevant information to contact the local police at the following number.

I grab a notepad and a pen from my nightstand and quickly jot it down.

Shit. I didn't think he had it in him after all these years. He's been married twice and has two kids, for God's sake. I never thought he'd take that risk. Didn't peg Allen as a family man who'd commit cold-blooded murder.

SADIE
THE WIFE

Now

My head pounds so hard my skull aches. "Who did you say you are?" She stands on my stoop, not budging an inch.

"Diane Martin. I knew Allen when we were younger. Our families were close and Allen and I dated for a summer." I feel like I've been sucker punched in the gut. Allen said that she'd died in a horrible swimming accident when the two of them were together.

"Please." She searches the street. "Just give me a minute. I don't want the police to find me here."

"Why did you call them then?" I try to make out the plates on her car, but they're hard to read from here. They're not from North Carolina.

"To protect you." She gives me an earnest look then says, "Sadie, this is serious. You're in danger."

My heart hammers harder, and against my better instincts I let her in. She sighs when I shut the door. "Is your daughter home?" She glances at the stairs and toward the kitchen. Surveys the living and dining rooms from our position in the foyer. "Emma?"

I'm unsettled by her being here, uncomfortable that she knows Emma's name, but of course she would. Emma's kidnapping story was major news. Anyone with a passing interest in our family . . . Wait. This woman is very intense and her interest seems more than passing. She's after something very specific and I need to know what.

I view her carefully, taking note of the details: the frayed hemline of her gray stretch pants, the way her denim jacket's missing a silver button. The beige crewneck top underneath shows a coffee stain and her brown leather shoes look worn. "What's your interest in Allen?"

Her expression hardens and she sets her jaw. "My interest in Allen is him getting what he deserves. He tried to kill me, but he didn't. And now, he's killed Cass."

Panic grips me, makes my heart race. "I don't believe you."

"Sadie," she says seriously. "You're in danger and Allen's on the run. He'll stop at nothing once you've turned against him and spoken to the cops. He'll throw you away, or worse, do to you what he tried to do to me."

"You're wrong. Allen loves me. He loves Emma."

"He loved me," Diane says. "He loved Cass."

"No." My heart hardens. "It wasn't love with her."

"How do you know?"

None of your goddamned business.

Diane stares at me long and hard. "Look, I don't know what Allen's told you. But in my case, it was no accident. We were dating in high school and hanging at the beach, had a few beers, mixed in a little pot. We went out for a late-night swim and started making out. Allen wanted to take things farther than I did and when I said no—"

"Lies!" I press my hands to my ears unwilling to hear it. "That's not Allen!"

"Then what about Cass?" she demands heatedly. "What the hell do you think happened to her?"

"I don't know." My face burns hot. "Maybe an accident."

"How many accidents can one man be connected to?" I don't like her insinuation.

"Sadie," she says. "I saw Allen sneaking out of your house this morning. The minute the police showed up at Cass's, he fled. That's got to tell you something. Make you question what his motives are. Innocent people don't run."

"You're wrong, Diane. Allen never would have harmed Cass."

"Oh? Like he didn't harm me, you mean? Or his parents?"

"What do Allen's late parents have to do with anything?"

"Maybe a lot." Little snippets of our conversation start sinking in. She's been *hiding* outside our house, trying to trap Allen in a snare? My temper flares and I charge toward her. "Why are you here, Diane? How could you possibly have known something might happen to Cass? And what the actual fuck were you doing spying on my house?"

She backs up and lifts her hands. "I didn't know something bad was going to happen to Cass, I swear! But when I saw Allen go into her house last—"

"What? You were spying on her too? Spying on both of them? All of us?" I gesture wildly and huff. "Who *the hell* do you think you are?"

"Someone trying to help." She stares out the dining room window and anxiously up the street. "Look," she says suddenly. "I've got to go."

"If you know so much," I say bearing down on her, "why won't you stay and talk to the police yourself?"

"There's too much at stake. I've got too much to lose." There's more she isn't telling me. I can see it in her eyes. "Allen tried to kill me once," she says. "If he learns I'm alive, he'll want to finish the job."

O'REILLY
THE COP

Now

Val and I wrap up our talk with the neighbor who called nine-one-one. We sit in her living room on old stuffed furniture with floral patterns that reminds me of the decor in my grandma's house. She lives to the right of Cass when viewing their homes from the street. Gwen Trilby is a retired nurse who lives alone. Last night she had trouble sleeping because she was fretting about Cass. She heard the altercation and is now upset with herself for not calling the police earlier when she first heard the breaking glass.

"She's been a really good neighbor. The sort that bakes you cookies at Christmas and checks in on you when you're ill. Tragic about what happened to her husband and son. Doubly so now that she's gone." Her face wrinkles up when she frowns. "I can't imagine who'd want to harm her. Can you?"

That's my question too. I'm hoping for leads from the forensics reports. Allen's going AWOL is looking more suspicious all the time. Officers Patel and Brady went to his workplace and confirmed that he never came in. When you put two and two together, you get four.

"We're looking into that," Val says. "Did you know Cass well?"

"Well enough for a casual acquaintance. We weren't best friends or anything like that, but she was always friendly and outgoing, and close to her family it appeared. She was a very popular teacher at that Catholic school. I heard that from my daughter, Louisa. Louisa has friends who send their children there."

"Did you notice anything different yesterday?" Val asks her. "Maybe a visitor? Someone coming and going?"

Gwen shakes her head. "I didn't see the other person. I was in my den watching the evening news. The shouting was loud though and I think it was Cass and someone else. I peeked out the window, but her driveway was empty. I suppose she could have brought someone home after work, or maybe it was one of the neighbors, someone who lives nearby."

Val and I look at each other. We're both thinking of the Wilsons. And, once more, I'm wondering about Allen and where he is. But why would Allen hurt Cass? What could his motive be? The only connection between them had to do with Cass knowing Allen in high school. That hardly seems enough of a reason for someone to commit murder. Unless. There's more to the relationship between Allen and Cass than the police are aware of.

We thank Gwen for her time and stand to go.

As she shuts her front door, my cell phone rings. "Yeah. What ya got?" I glance at Val. "It's the chief."

"We're still waiting on data from the fibers retrieved from the broken window, but we rushed the prints on the wine bottle. One set came from Cass and the other was an easy match since the individual was already in our system."

Fuck. Both Allen and Sadie were fingerprinted during Emma's disappearance, as protocol to eliminate them during an evidence sweep. "Allen?" I ask.

"Yes." So Allen was definitely with Cass last night.

"O'Reilly," Claremont says. "That's not all. We had an anonymous tip called in from an untraceable number, a burner phone we suspect, and get this. Allen was spotted this morning fleeing his neighborhood on foot. Three guesses as to what he was carrying."

My mind does a mental review of the crime scene. I sensed something was off when I saw that kid's baseball mitt. Apart from the fact that there is no kid, Jesus.

DIANE
THE OLD GIRLFRIEND

Before

Allen creeps out of his house and slowly closes the front door. He slings a backpack over his shoulder and strides through the rain. I'm parked in a cul-de-sac near the Wilsons' house, but not the one directly in front of it. This cul-de-sac forms an L shape with theirs. Suburbia. Sigh. It's a nice neighborhood and way fancier than anything I could afford for Nellie. We live in an apartment building in a run-down part of town, but at least the area's safe.

The windshield fogs and I crank up the defroster, turn the windshield wipers on for a few quick flicks. Lean forward to peer out the window over the passenger's seat. Allen skulks down his steep driveway and takes a left toward the main street leading deeper into the neighborhood and away from a rural highway. Wait.

He's heading up the hill toward a playground. I follow him at a snail's pace, taking care to hang back in case he sees my vehicle, but he's too intent on his mission to notice my rental sedan. Not that Allen would recognize me anyway. He's not expecting me to be alive.

Allen reaches a section with swings and a slide. A merry-go-round-type contraption for kids to hang on to and make themselves dizzy.

Nellie enjoys playing on those because they make her giggle. Nellie's spending her spring break at her uncle Mark's house, getting to know him and her aunt, Elena. I dropped her off a few days early because I had things to do here.

Mark's a pharmacist in Miami, and his wife Elena's a successful muralist. They've got two kids and a nice house with a large fenced yard. Obviously doing well enough to take on another kid in an emergency.

Dot encouraged me to make the connection, saying I should make arrangements for Nellie, just in case. Everyone needs a will, she said, even a thirty-nine-year-old woman like me, especially since I've got sole custody. I'm actually surprised Mark turned out so well. He used to be really messed up, basically a junkie. Looks like he got his act together and went from using drugs to prescribing them. Good for him.

Allen slinks around the playground like a gangster on the lam, steps past a giant sandbox and darts his eyes this way and then that. Then he walks up to the slide and squats beside it. Pulls something out that's been buried in the mulch.

My automatic windshield wipers slow to an occasional swipe across the glass as I idle at a safe distance. He still hasn't seen me. His gaze is on a path through the trees.

Allen glances around one more time, securing the hood on his hoodie.

Then he slips into the woods with the backpack on his shoulder, the grip end of a baseball bat poking out of it.

KATE
THE EX-CON

I got in touch with Diane. It was all I could do to wait until I got out of prison, and then she ignored my calls and texts, and kept changing her number. Finally, she agreed to a phone chat but it was stilted and cold. We didn't have much to say to each other after so much time, especially with me now knowing the things she's done.

Dotti was supposed to keep it a secret, but she couldn't help bragging about her so-called accomplishments at the lunch table. When it was just the two of us one time, she let the whole sordid thing spill. It was so Dotti-esque for her to take pride in her own wrongdoings. Not one ounce of remorse. That will serve her well with the parole board—*not*. She'll stay locked away for the duration of her forty-four-month sentence.

I was charged with concealing and tampering with evidence during the course of a kidnapping, and if it had only been that, with no prior record in North Carolina I might have gotten out in as little as three to four months. But the court wanted to set an example to discourage other bad actors in child abduction cases, so the state prosecutor additionally levied accessory-to-kidnapping charges against me, which if proven, could have sent me up the river for nearly as long as Dotti.

So my defense counsel plea-bargained for a sentence of twenty months in prison, which was not in my eyes ideal. Once eighty-five percent of my sentence was served, and assuming I'd been a decent prisoner, my attorney told me I'd be eligible for parole and could likely serve the remaining balance of my sentence by doing community service. I could either risk going to prison for longer or take the deal. I took the deal.

After seventeen months in the same joint as Dotti, I finally got sprung in February and am completing the rest of my debt to society. Oh yeah, I'm also mandated to check in with my parole officer once a week and keep seeing a shrink. Nobody ever said it was going to be easy, but at least the worst of it's behind me.

I'm at the soup kitchen now, tying on my apron and preparing for my afternoon shift. I open the pantry door and walk inside the cavernous space. It's about six feet deep and three feet wide with enough food stocked here to feed an army, which is a good thing in these times.

I feel for those poor souls who are so down on their luck they have to come here for sustenance, but at least they can get a square meal and some comfort. Growing up, I had a small taste of what it was like to be hungry, and that wasn't a pleasant experience. My mom would withhold food and threaten to feed me dead flies when she suspected I'd misbehaved. She'd scoop flies off the windowsills to save as ammunition, their petrified bodies and brittle wings pressed up against the glass of mason jars. If any of us kids talked back to her—which included protesting our actual innocence—we'd get a mouthful.

My dad was more direct. He used his fists and a belt. Slugs for the boy, whips for the girls. Mark got his jaw broken once and his arm dislocated a few times. When she was fourteen, Diane had welts on the backs of her legs that lasted three weeks. Since I was a lot younger than both of them, I spent a lot of time hiding. It was better to forgo dinner than to try and speak up. When my twisted mom saw my empty spot at the table, she was probably glad.

My folks were remarkably different individuals in front of their friends: the life of the party, doling out drinks and rollicking good times. Both working professionals, if you can believe it. Dad an insurance agent and mom an engineer. In private, their dark veil lifted, and they scared the crap out of me. They weren't exactly exceptional parents, which is why all three of us kids got the hell out as soon as we could. In that way, I understand Diane's choices, but not all of them. I shake off those negative thoughts because dwelling on my childhood's a flip switch I'm trying to disconnect.

It's my turn to heat and serve the green beans today. That part's easy and mainly involves opening cans. Nick walks into the pantry and instantly starts helping out. Pulling cans from the shelves and setting them on the counter in the industrial-style kitchen. Nick's an ex-con like me. He's beefily built and shaves his head, I suspect because he's balding. Or maybe he just likes looking badass. If you didn't know he had a heart of gold, you'd be scared to death if you saw him coming at you down a dark alley.

"Green beans," Nick says with a jokey scowl. "Yummy." Nick looks like he's fifty, but he's really about ten years older than I am, so somewhere close to forty, and rough around the edges. Divorced, and a recovering drug user—and dealer. Life's left its marks on his craggy features, but when I look at him, I see his true spirit. He's one of the purest people I know, because the top thing I admire about Nick is he doesn't lie.

Even if he guesses I won't like the answer, he'll always tell me the truth. Like when I asked him about the murder charge that landed him in prison and he mentioned smashing some guy's head against a curb, on purpose. The other man started it and had a knife. Nick had shortchanged him in a drug deal to pocket some extra cash. Nick's not ashamed of his former behavior, because he's striving to be different now. The best way to improve, he says, is by not hiding from your past, but learning from it.

I told him about Emma's kidnapping and he didn't judge me. Said he probably would have done the same thing in my shoes. Though he'd think twice about that now that he's reformed. When I grow up, I want to be Nick.

He reaches for the cornbread mix and takes an assortment of muffin baking tins out from a lower cabinet, laying them down in front of him. "How're things going with your lady doctor?" He's a little gender specific that way, but I give him a pass. Nick's old school but he doesn't mean it badly. He respects the hell out of women. Present company included, and it feels good to have earned the respect of a guy like him.

Katherine hisses in my ear, taunting. *He's a pussy.*

But I know she's wrong. Nick's incredibly strong. It's not easy staying on the straight and narrow. So I tell Katherine to *shut the fuck up*, before remembering I'm not supposed to engage her and add fuel to the fire. So instead, I draw in and hold one deep breath and imagine a big orange tabby cat purring on Nick's lap. Nick's stroking its head and smiling. The kitchen gets noisy as more volunteers arrive. Some are here to set up or clean up afterward, others to cook and serve. More hands are available to help where they're needed.

Nick has more than a few visible scars on his face and neck, and bulging arms. He once showed me a bullet wound on the right side of his chest, but he may have been wanting me to see his tight six-pack. Despite our age difference, I think he might like me. The Kate me, anyway. And I'm working hard to stay her most days, since she's the one with a future in society.

Sometimes I think I might like a future like regular people have.

My therapist Adelaide says it's good to have goals.

Still. I wouldn't marry Nick. I'm not in the market for a romance, and I've got personal work to do besides. "Okay," I answer about my doc. "She scolded me last time for going off my meds."

"Was it intentional?" he asks.

"Not on my part, no." *Score one for the team!* Katherine shouts in my ear and I sigh. While I haven't vanquished her completely, Adelaide keeps promising me that day will come. We're trying a new type of behavioral therapy, and I've been through an arsenal of prescription drugs. They started me on some pills in prison that got me so hyped up I wanted to climb the walls. Others made me feel like I'd taken a dozen Dramamine. We've finally got the balance right.

Fucking chemistry.

I was never any good at it.

"Teamwork's important," Nick says almost like he's read my mind. "As long as you believe Doc A is on your side, that's a good thing."

"I do believe that, thank you." I remove a crank can opener from a drawer and get to work opening cans. We've got two electric can openers here, but both are broken. Other people have come into the room. Betsy's working on chicken and dumplings. Melissa's doing dessert. Looks like banana pudding. I can't imagine who'd want to eat that, but tastes vary, I guess.

"Hey, Kate?"

"Yeah, Nick?" His neck has gone a little red.

"I was wondering if you're doing anything later?" My heart thumps. This is so unexpected. Is he asking me out?

"What?"

He shrugs. "After dishing out all this food, I figure the two of us might be hungry. Go somewhere low key and grab a bite to eat?"

He *is* asking. Holy fuck.

Don't get too excited, Katherine says. *He probably just wants a piece.*

I shut her down with a mental peace sign in rainbow colors.

Interfering bitch.

"Aww, Nick, that's really sweet, but I—"

He looks suddenly embarrassed. "It doesn't have to be a date. Just a friendly outing."

"Of course." I feel myself blush. Wow. That's a new one for me. "I know that. I, erm, just made plans for this evening already."

Nick fills up his corn muffin pan by scooping batter into each section. "It's all good. Another time."

"For sure! I'd like that," I say, oddly understanding that I would. I don't have many friends anymore, as in zero. When I was a teacher, there was a small group of us who sometimes hung out after school, or socially on weekends. None of them wants anything to do with me now. "It's just that today," I explain to Nick, "I'm meeting up with my sister."

"Didn't know you had one of those."

"I didn't know either, until recently."

"You've been estranged?" Nick asks about Diane.

I start stirring my enormous pot of canned green beans with a wooden spoon. "Something like that."

KATE
THE EX-CON

Before

I've just finished my shift at Café Latte and am on my way to the soup kitchen when I stop at the Fast Mart to gas up and use the facilities. When I come out of the restroom, I'm pretty sure I'm hallucinating. Diane stands there at the register, bulky dark curls and all, buying a pack of cigarettes, and my jaw hits the floor. I haven't seen my sister since I was a kid. Back then, I worshipped her. Now, I'm madder than hell at what she put me through. She looks almost the same but older, and with different-colored hair. She used to be blond like me.

"Diane?" I call her name and she turns after making her purchase.

Her face goes white like she's seen a ghost, but, sorry, I'm claiming that one.

Her voice wafts in a whisper. "Katherine?"

I inhale deeply and hold my ground. "It's Kate now."

"Oh right. I heard that." From Dotti she means. Or maybe she read it in the news.

"What are you doing in Chapel Roads?" I ask her.

"I had some business to settle."

I think of Cass's suspicious death this morning and the breaking news story that popped up on my phone while I was at the coffee shop. "Oh my God."

"Don't go jumping to conclusions, Kit-Kat."

"Please don't call me that."

A laugh and a tilt of her head. "We probably both want the same things, don't we?"

"I'm not so sure about that." If she's resurfaced after playing dead for twenty years it can't be for good purposes. "Who else knows you're here?"

"No one," she says. Her expression darkens. "And I'd like to keep it that way. Kate, please listen to me. My life depends on it."

I can see why she'd want to hide, but I'm not thrilled about what she's culpable for. It doesn't matter who got caught. If you're aware that something horrible is about to happen—and you don't stop it—you own some of the guilt. "What does that mean?" I challenge her.

Diane purses her lips, thinking. "Why don't we meet up later? I can fill you in."

"All right."

"I haven't lived here in a while," she says. "Maybe you can pick a place?" She glances over her shoulder. "That's, you know, out of the way?" She means off the grid.

"Where are you staying?"

She names a motel off a local highway, and I suggest a nearby diner and a time, after my duties at the soup kitchen end. When she leaves, she climbs into a blue sedan with New Jersey tags, but I'm not so sure she lives in the Garden State. Last we talked, she said Arizona. Probably a rental.

CASS
THE MISTRESS

Before

I invited Allen over to talk about it, because honestly? It's not like I've got much choice. The truth has a way of haunting you, of stealing back in like a ghost: once vaporized, now visible in the mist. Coming closer. Watching. Waiting. For that inevitable moment to appear. I didn't used to believe in ghosts, but now? I'm not so sure.

I think I hear them playing sometimes, Richard and our boy in the bedroom upstairs—Richard's big roaring laughter, a child's giggly joy—and my heart shatters. But then I remember what I still have and am thankful for the things I've got.

I set two wineglasses on the counter and pause to peer out the window over the sink. Through the intentional green screen of planted pines, I spy a sliver of their house beyond the fence, the gate between us solidly closed. I saw Allen in his yard tinkering with it again last Sunday, his dark blond hair covering his eyebrows as he leaned forward, fiddling with the latch on either side. It's like he thinks he can keep me out, stop me from intruding. But no, he can't.

Secrets have a way of unraveling like threads tugged from a sweater. You can't pick at one without creating more damage, without expecting to leave an inevitable hole. Without risk of exposing what lies beneath.

I know Allen lied to Sadie about me. Maybe he thought it was for good reasons. I considered telling her myself, but decided against it. I understand the trauma of losing a child firsthand. I wasn't about to heap disillusionment on her anguish, not when she was suffering so badly. I'll leave that task to Allen, if he chooses, and I hope he will. I check the time on my cell phone charging on the built-in desk. Six twenty-three. Allen should be here shortly. He'll likely judge my house the way Sadie did. Deputy Chief O'Reilly, the cop that came around when Emma disappeared, was the same.

I could see it in their eyes, the sad surveyal of a not-quite-done house with minimal furnishings and no artwork on the walls. When Richard and I moved in, I was all about making our nest a home. But then things happened and I never had the energy, not between my job and other obligations. Apart from my sister Robin and her husband Leon, almost no one knows the truth about what happened back then. I confessed it once to Sister Mary Catherine. She's the pastoral minister at Our Lady of Our Savior, the Catholic school where I teach. I'm the gym teacher there and staying active suits me.

I try to keep myself fit and rarely drink. Tonight though, I pull my best bottle of pinot noir from my wine rack, remembering it was Allen's favorite. I remember a lot about Allen and couldn't have been more shocked when he and Sadie moved into the house right behind mine. I'd be lying if I said I wasn't curious about seeing him again.

Turns out I wasn't the only curious one.

CASS
THE MISTRESS

Before

Allen arrives on my doorstep the very night after I dropped off my welcome bottle of wine with Sadie. He doesn't tell her he's stopping by. I never mention it later either. My life has gone on and so has his. Let bygones be bygones, they say.

"Cass Curtis." He smiles when I answer the door. His expression's open, friendly, but I suspect he's not as at ease as he acts. "What are the odds?"

I lay my hand against the doorframe and assume a carefree stance. "It's Cass Thomas now." I don't mean to say it flirtatiously but the words lilt toward him just the same. "Allen Wilson, how *are* you?"

"I'm doing o-*kay*." He rakes his hand through his hair and studies me, and I can't take my eyes off him. He's as gorgeous as ever, maybe more so than the last time I saw him and that says a lot. "How about you?"

"I'm good, thanks." I aim to stay pleasant and not lay my whole depressing history on him. So much has transpired since we last spoke. So much more than he knows. A pang of guilt stabs at my heart but I brush it aside, focus on his grin and his sparkling blue eyes.

Everything I've done has been for the best.

The right motives for the right people.

"I can't believe we moved in behind you," he says shaking his head. "Small world."

"Super small, yeah." I want to ask him in but feel like I shouldn't. Like he'd read that the wrong way, like I'm making a pass. I toy with the idea in my head then dismiss it. He chose Sadie over me before. He'd do it again in a heartbeat. I don't need to reopen old wounds or sit around wondering *what if.* So when he asks me to never tell Sadie about how things were. When he begs me to keep our secret. I acquiesce.

DIANE
THE OLD GIRLFRIEND

Before

There's a vacant house for sale two doors down from Cass's and closer to the intersection. It's easy to park in the driveway behind a tall hedge and have a clear view of Cass's driveway and house. Tonight's the night I helped orchestrate: Cass and Allen's big showdown. I can't wait for the proverbial shit to hit the fan, and for Allen's life to fall apart.

Cass is a bit late coming home from work, and then I see her easing down the street in her Jeep Cherokee, while drinking from a tall paper cup with a lid. She parks at her house and gets out, purse hanging from her shoulder, paper cup in hand.

Cass shakes the paper cup and takes one last sip, tossing it in an outdoor rolling trash can positioned near her garage. From my peripheral vision, I note another vehicle trolling by my location. I take my attention off of Cass entering her house and closing her door and scan the area. *Maybe there?*

I spot a newer SUV parked closer to the cul-de-sac behind some other vehicles. The driver appears to be a woman, but from this far away it's impossible to be sure. They stay sequestered behind the steering wheel and cloaked in the shadows. Maybe they're caught up on a call or busy texting? Possibly waiting on someone they're picking up to come out of that house? The funny thing is, they wait as long as I do, and when I go—they're still there.

Finally, Allen's SUV arrives on the street and he parks beside Cass's Jeep, before she welcomes him into her house. After what seems like forever—but is rationally more like twenty minutes—Allen leaves. He appears distraught, storming toward his SUV and yanking open the driver's side door, before climbing inside and slamming it shut.

Good. Let the repercussions come.

Allen couldn't hide his dirty secrets forever.

CASS
THE MISTRESS

Before

I'm twenty-eight and enjoying life tending bar at a divey college place downtown. Not yet serious about anything but I feel the press of time. Six years out of college, and I've basically done nothing. No, not fair. Truth is, I've had fun and traveled a lot. Seen national parks and camped across the country. My first boyfriend had an RV. The second guy a motorcycle. We had good times, but neither guy was what I'd call daddy material.

I recognize Allen in a flash. That sexy build, those drive-me-wild blue eyes. He looks somehow beleaguered, and he's wearing a frown. I wonder if he's tired or has had bad news. Slightly hopeful he's had a fight with his girlfriend, or that maybe he hasn't got one at all.

He takes a seat on a tall stool and studies the bar menu written on the chalkboard at my back. I wipe down the counter in front of him, wondering if he'll recognize me.

"What'll it be?" I ask leaning toward him.

He takes in the draft choices on the pull handles, selects a pale ale, sixteen-ounce pour. I fix it for him my heart pounding. I had such a thing for him in high school, but he probably saw me as a kid. I'm not a kid anymore. I hand him the glass a little clumsily, in a way that makes our fingers brush. "Ooh, sorry."

"No worries."

Shit. He's wearing a wedding band.

Of course. My luck.

Allen sips from his beer then suddenly looks up. "Hey, wait one minute." He shakes his finger at me. "I know you."

"Yeah," I say and smile. "I'm Cass."

"Cass Curtis from high school?" He laughs and shakes his head. "Man oh man, talk about a blast from the past."

I laugh along with him, but my face grows warm.

A woman at the end of the bar gets my attention and I go to fix her party another round. She's here with two others on a girls' night out. They all drink chocolate martinis. From the snippets of conversation I've overheard they're new moms and basically exhausted, here to blow off steam about sleepless nights and colic. I should be so lucky. The baby hunger in me grows. My sister Robin must be rubbing off on me with all her incessant baby talk. She and her husband Leon have been trying for months and it's all she ever talks about.

When I approach Allen's spot near the center of the bar, he holds out his glass. I'm surprised to see he's drained it. "Make it one more?"

My eyebrows arch as I take the glass. "Rough day?"

He sighs. "The roughest. I'm on jury duty this week." His shoulders sink. "Unfortunately, the case is tough."

"Want to talk about it?"

He shakes his head. "I'm afraid I can't."

To me, he means. A basic stranger at this point. "I'm sure you can tell your wife?"

I pry my gaze from his wedding band, but it's too late, he's caught me peeking. He twists it around his finger and then in a stunning move, he takes it off. Drops it on the bar and it clanks, doing a reverberating dance before lying silent. He looks up. A tight grin. "Separated."

"Oof." I feign chagrin. "I'm really sorry to hear it." I hold his glass and pull the lever on the tap. IPA rushes out, flooding the glass. I tilt it just right, so it crowns with golden bubbles.

"Don't be," he says when I set his beer down in front of him. He takes his wedding band and shoves it in his pocket. "Should have taken this thing off months ago." He glugs down half his pour and I worry he's going too fast, even for a guy of his size. "Wasn't meant to be."

"Want to order something to eat? The burgers are great here. The loaded nachos too."

"Maybe in a bit." His gaze washes over me, as if he's remembering all that embarrassing high school stuff. The revelations about my crush. He takes a slower sip of beer. "But enough about me. What've you been up to?"

I hold up my hand in a *wait* signal when I'm summoned to the other end of the bar. Food's been delivered and I carry the plates over to the mom group. Loaded nachos and chocolate. I can't even. Maybe it's their hormones gone haywire or trying to reset.

I return to Allen, eager to continue our conversation. "I've been traveling a bit," I say and tell him about New Mexico and Wyoming. My jaunt to Montreal.

"Sounds cool." He telegraphs respect. "Always wanted to go to those places."

"So why don't you?"

"Maybe I will." He rubs the back of his neck. "Someday."

"Something stopping you?"

A grimace but pride shines in his eyes. "I've got a kid."

"Go you! Boy or girl?"

"A son, Forrest. He's almost two years old."

"Aww."

"I'll still be a good dad," he assures me. I know he's talking about his divorce.

"Never had any doubt."

He takes another swig of beer and chuckles. "Remember that thing you wrote in my yearbook?"

"I didn't write it," I retort a bit too defensively, but there's play in my tone. I roll my eyes—I hope cutely and not in a way that looks dumb. "It was one of my girlfriends."

He sets his elbows on the bar and grins broadly. "Kind of had a thing for me, huh?"

"Kind of?" I huff but then I chuckle. "Okay." Make a motion with my thumb and forefinger. "Maybe a tiny one."

"Tiny?" He lays a hand on his chest. "I'm crushed."

I swat his shoulder with my bar rag. "You had a girlfriend! What was her name? Jennifer? Jessica?"

He shrugs coyly. "I'm single now."

I scoff like I'm offended, but I'm not. I'm very turned on. "Just what are you suggesting?"

He sets down his glass. "What time do you get off?" His voice is low, sexy. If he thinks I'm easy, he's right. Just not for everybody. I'm particular. I've also been particularly attracted to him. Forever. If he'd been interested in me in high school, I would have slept with him I'm sure. Cherished him as my first instead of waiting until prom night of my senior year with Duncan, a kid from a neighboring private school I didn't care much about.

The man three stools down from Allen holds up his hand. He's here on his own. An older guy who looks like a traveling salesman, but in these parts he's more likely a professor. I'm printing out his check at the register right by Allen, when Allen asks, "Would you go out with me?"

I blink but hide my shock. My back is turned, and I carry the tab to the customer who's waiting, laying it on the bar. I return to Allen and say, "I might, if you asked me."

A slow sexy smile. "I'm asking."

My stomach flutters and my chest grows hot. "In that case, yes." He holds out his hand and I slide my phone out from under the bar and pass it to him. He types in his number and gives me his phone so I can add my contact information in his. He grins and electric tingles shoot through me. I can't believe this is happening. It's like a freaking dream. Another customer summons and I start to turn, but Allen takes my hand. "Don't make me wait, Cass," he says all growly. "We've already waited too long." I know what he's saying and I don't care. Don't care if it makes me look needy and horny. Because the whole truth is I'm both. I get Trish to cover for me and take my break.

Ten minutes later we're fucking in the bathroom.

I don't even know how it happens so fast, or where my panties went. Thank God it's a one-stall room and we've locked the door. He's got me up against the wall, my skirt bunched around my waist, and my butt in his strong hands. My arms and legs tangle around him. His mouth is hot and hungry on mine.

I melt into him and over him.

Ooh. Sweet.

Someone bangs on the door. "Busy!" I cry and Allen laughs. Covers my moans with kisses, pounds into me some more.

When it's over, he zips up his fly as I step into my panties. I find them in the sink.

"I'll text you," he says.

I check my phone obsessively hour by hour, day after day.

I know I can reach out to him but I don't want to. I need him to want me for once, for him to make the move. The next week he *finally* contacts me. We have drinks at a swanky restaurant. Wind up back at his place. Have sex in hotel rooms and in his SUV, once on the mats in the weight room at Our Lady of Our Savior very late at night. Another time under the bleachers at our old high school, living out my teenage fantasies. I think we're in love, feel like I've died and gone to heaven, have found my fated one.

Two weeks later, I see him out to dinner with his supposedly soon-to-be ex-wife. She's weeping and they're holding hands, and I know in my heart he's going back to her and forgetting all about me.

Allen comes by my house the next day and says we're over. He still loves Teresa and they're going to try to make it work. I'm too hurt to cry or speak.

Until he and Sadie move into my neighborhood, I never hear from him again.

TERESA
THE EX-WIFE

Now

Allen told me about the Walsh trial and it spooked me. Allen served on a jury in a case where a teacher became a convicted sex offender. Given where we lived, Forrest was zoned for the same school. Of course it would be three more years before he entered kindergarten at Stonefield Elementary, possibly four if we held him back that extra year as is sometimes done with boys. Later, when Emma went missing, I never suspected a connection at all. The police did though, and so did Allen. It all makes sense to me now.

What I never made sense of was Allen's brief affair with Cass. He told me about it and it broke my heart. I knew our divorce was pending but I wasn't prepared to believe it, kept hoping against hope that Allen would change his mind.

I shuffle some files on my desk and set them aside. I've been trying to focus on my research to keep my mind off the news. But it's hard to forget the impact Cass had on our marriage. If she'd never gotten in the way to begin with maybe Allen and I would have been okay. Maybe he never would have left me that second time and found Sadie.

I scroll through the data on my computer, surveying the various equations and charts. Henry's done a lot of work on this study, and his input's been invaluable. We make such great partners on the job, and I want to advance his career in astrophysics. Not because I'm sleeping with him but because he's talented. When this paper publishes, he'll get the lead credit. He's brilliant and has earned it every step of the way.

Henry raps at my open door and I look up at his roundish face with horn-rimmed glasses. He's dark complected with dark-brown hair, and not a bad-looking guy. Five foot ten with a solid build and a squarish chin. But he's not what you'd call drop-dead gorgeous either. No, sadly, that's Allen.

"How's it going in here?" he asks with a frown. "I guess you've heard the news?"

"About Cass Thomas?" I ask him and push back in my chair. "Yeah. Poor woman. That's really such a shame."

He leans a shoulder against the doorframe and crosses his arms, wearing jeans and a plaid button-down shirt. Brown loafers. "Who do you think could have done it?"

I shrug, thinking of Allen. "Sounds pretty open-ended to me. Maybe an accident?"

Henry strokes his chin. "That's what I'm hoping." He nods. "No foul play."

"Well." I click my tongue and Henry knows to take that as a dismissal, because my gaze is back on my work, laser focused. "Guess we'll find out soon enough."

"Right you are!" Henry hesitates before leaving. "Coffee later?"

"Sure." I look up and force a smile. "Why not?"

My office is near the center of the building so has no windows, apart from an opaque pane of glass beside the open door. There were times when I locked that door after Allen came to visit. I've never had sex with Henry at work. It somehow doesn't seem right. With Allen, though, everything always did. Any place. Any time. I couldn't hold back. I'd rip my heart out of my chest and sew it back in if I knew we could have what we had again. But we can't. I get that.

After being with Cass, Allen came back to me for a while. I believed we were starting to be a family again. I always wanted a second child with Allen, and he knew that absolutely. Given how tentative our relationship was, I never should have brought it up. Our marriage was dying and that last conversation was the final nail in its coffin. If I could take it all back now, I would.

TERESA
THE EX-WIFE

Before

We're at the breakfast table and Forrest is sleeping in his crib upstairs. A baby monitor sits on the kitchen counter. The wide opening to the living area provides a stunning view of the high-ceilinged room with exposed wood beams and its enormous windows facing the woods. It's daybreak and sunlight weaves through the trees, birds chirp on their branches. Their song gives me courage. Hope.

"Allen," I say and take a sip of coffee. He's reading on his laptop and looks up.

"Yeah?"

"I was thinking about the future."

He shuts his computer, and gazes at me in a heartfelt way. "Let's just take things one day at a time, hmm?" He claims he's giving us a second chance, but I want some reassurances. Another baby would mean he'd stay. He tore himself inside out at the thought of leaving Forrest. He'd never walk if we also had a daughter. Two precious kids.

"I hear what you're saying," I assure him, "but with you moving back in here, the time clock on our separation is resetting."

"Doesn't have to reset." A dagger to my heart. "Only if we tell the judge."

"You don't mean that."

"Teri, yes." He cocks his head. "Look, I said we could give this a try, one last chance for the two of us for Forrest's sake."

"And it's been working out," I contest a little too shrilly. I don't like his partial frown.

"I've been trying," he says. "But."

My heart stutters. "But?"

Allen blows out a breath. "It's not the same, Teri. Not like it was in the beginning."

"Of course not," I say on a breath. "We've been through a rough patch. I'm working harder now to be present. You have to admit that's true."

"Are you? Really?" His eyes penetrate mine and I feel so jumbled inside. I am trying harder, I am. "You swore you wouldn't bring work home."

"That's unfair. I'm a professor. My work follows me where I go."

"Not until after midnight."

"Only sometimes."

"Not when we've got plans then have to cancel. Jesus, Teri. Why can't you ever think ahead and prioritize? Prioritize us, prioritize me?"

"Are you talking about the concert?"

"It wasn't just for any old thing, Teri. It was for my birthday, you said you were excited to go."

"Yes, but then my grant deadline got bumped up—"

"It was one night. One freaking night." His neck is red above his shirt collar. He tugs at his tie. "You could have done a work-around, made the sacrifice."

"I set up the sitter!" I cry in my defense.

"No." He sets his chin. "That was me. You canceled her."

This discussion is not going how I wanted it to at all. "Allen, I know I've been in the wrong and I agree I've not always been great at juggling my schedule. But I promise I'll do better, as things settle down and we adjust to our new normal—"

"What new normal is that?"

I swallow hard then brave it. While the timing's not ideal maybe my planting the seed in his head will help it grow and blossom into something wonderful. An idea he's excited about as well. "I was thinking—as part of our starting over—maybe we could talk about expanding our fam—"

"Another baby?" His gobsmacked look crushes me. Makes me ill with fear. "For God's sake, Teri." He abruptly pushes back in his chair. "You don't even have time for me, how will you fit another kid in?" That stings like a slap across my face.

"Allen, please." My words tremble weakly. "Let's discuss this."

He stands and hangs his head. "This was a mistake."

My insides weep and my heart burns. He's taken a torch to my soul. "You don't mean it."

"Yeah." He purses his lips. "I'm afraid I do." He's clearly disappointed in himself, and in me. In us. In the fractured thing we are that he believes can never be mended. Hurt wells in my heart and builds in my eyes. But I don't want to cry. I want to scream. Beg. Anything to make him stay.

"I'll move my things out tonight after work. I didn't bring that much with me anyway." He still has his small apartment near the campus. He's held on to it for these past few months. I should have taken that as a bad sign, like he was hedging his bets in case we didn't work out, but I couldn't face facts. Didn't want to.

"Please don't be rash," I plead desperately. "I'm sorry I brought another child up. You're right, that's premature."

"That's more than premature." He turns before he goes and says cruelly, "That's never happening."

SADIE
THE WIFE

Now

Diane's not gone long when O'Reilly and Rodriguez arrive. Their expressions are dire.

"Sadie," O'Reilly says when I answer the door, "I'm sorry to have to do this, but I've got news to share about Allen."

"May we come in?" Rodriguez asks.

I'm too numb to do anything but nod. *What kind of news,* I wonder. Must be something pretty damning for them both to look so grim. "Can we sit?" O'Reilly asks.

I'm not sure I could stay still. My nerves make me jumpy. I cross my arms and hug my elbows. "I'd rather stand. Emma will be home soon. I'll need to go meet her bus."

Rodriguez's eyes fill with compassion. "Of course. This won't take long."

A pang of fear seizes me. What if something's happened to Allen. Something horrible? "Allen though? He's all right?"

"We believe so," Rodriguez answers.

O'Reilly sets his lips in a hard line. "I'm sorry, Sadie, we've now named Allen as a suspect in Cass's murder. We have forensic evidence that places him at the scene and we need to bring him in for questioning."

My stomach sinks. "What? Why?"

Rodriguez reaches into her shirt pocket and removes a small notebook. "We got a tip about him fleeing the area on foot around the time Cass's body was discovered."

From Diane. I can't believe that what she said is true. Allen's not like that. He's no cold-blooded killer. He's sweet and caring, and a great husband and dad. Sure, he's made some mistakes and has his weaknesses. But commit murder?

Rodriguez continues, "We also have reason to believe he might have been carrying the potential murder weapon."

Her statement slams into me like a sledgehammer. "What was it?" I ask looking from one of them to the other.

O'Reilly shakes his head. "Sorry. For the time being that's confidential." He meets my eyes and it feels like he's unwrapping my lies, peeling back the layers of my deception, as if he already knows the answer to what he's about to ask. "You lied to us, Sadie, didn't you? To me and Rodriguez earlier. You knew Allen hadn't gone in to his office."

I anxiously fiddle with a button on my sweater. "I . . . wasn't sure where he'd gone." My mouth goes cottony dry and I lick my lips. "I thought maybe he'd taken an Uber." Even to me that sounds absurd. Like I'm getting really desperate, grasping at straws.

"Has he been in touch?" O'Reilly asks. "Tried to contact you?"

My face heats at the truth. "No, he left his cell phone here. Also his wallet and keys." Which is so unlike him. Allen is deliberate, careful. Yet he obviously left in a hurry. Maybe he didn't want to be traced via card purchases or have the police on the lookout for his vehicle. "But he's got to come back! We're leaving on our trip . . ." I abruptly stop. Of course there will be no second honeymoon trip. Our flight leaves in less than twenty-four hours. Who am I kidding?

Rodriguez flips open her notebook and starts writing stuff down. "Where were the two of you going?"

"Aruba." My throat burns hot. I try to swallow and it hurts. "It was supposed to be our second honeymoon, a chance to celebrate our new beginning, with Emma being home safe and our marriage back on track. It was Allen's birthday gift to me."

"Where does Allen keep his passport?" Rodriguez wants to know.

I shift on my feet, hug myself tighter. "In our fire safe upstairs. It's still there. I checked."

"We'll need to keep that, please," O'Reilly says. "His wallet and phone too. Also his computer, if he's got one here."

Rodriguez responds to my questioning look. "We'll need to go through his purchases and phone messages, online communications. See if there's any connection." To Cass, she means. There's bound to be information on Allen's computer or phone. They're sure to find something.

"Is there anything missing from the house?" O'Reilly prods. "Valuables? Cash?"

My heart thuds when I say, "We keep some spare cash in our safe for emergencies, and it's gone."

Rodriguez writes this in her notebook. "How much?"

"Not much." I name a sum that could purchase a few weeks' groceries.

The two share a look. "That won't get him far," Rodriguez tells O'Reilly.

O'Reilly turns to me and says, "Our source said they saw Allen at your neighborhood playground. He slipped onto a path leading into the woods. Where does that go?"

"The trail connects to a greenway that's accessible by several neighborhoods."

A muscle in O'Reilly's cheek flinches. "Including Teresa's?"

I feel sick. I hope to God she's not involved. Complicit in this somehow with Allen. Is she helping him hide? Are the two of them planning some kind of cover-up together? Or worse, are they trying to concoct a way to pin Cass's murder on me?

"Mind giving her a call to see if she knows anything?" O'Reilly asks, watching me like a hawk. I know the police could phone her themselves, but this is some kind of test. They're watching my reactions, my every move. Maybe even thinking I have something to do with what happened to Cass and am collaborating in some horrid way with Allen and Teresa. I need to make them believe I have nothing to hide.

"Sure." I retrieve my cell phone from my home office on the other side of the pocket doors from the living room and stand in the foyer with them and dial her number. "Teresa, hi."

"Sadie. Oh my God. I'm so sorry. I heard about Cass. There was a report on the news."

"Yeah, I know. It's terrible." I glance at the police officers in the hall. "Look, I was wondering if you've heard from Allen?"

"Allen? No. Why?" She gasps audibly then whispers. "Oh my God. What's happened?"

"He's—gone missing, Teresa. He's not at home, and I can't reach him."

"Have you tried calling?"

"He left his phone here."

"That sounds bad."

"Yeah."

"Ask her if she's at her house," O'Reilly prompts. "We'd like to stop by."

I temporarily cover the mouthpiece and nod, then continue speaking to Teresa. "Are you at home?"

"No, work. But I'm headed there shortly. Forrest is home though. Why?"

"The police want to stop by your place."

"What on earth for?"

"Allen was last seen heading in that direction."

"Shit." She pauses a beat and then says, "Listen. I'm happy to talk to the police but can you please ask them not to show up until I get there? I don't want Forrest having to deal with this alone."

I stare at O'Reilly and he bows his head. "Of course."

"Give me twenty minutes," Teresa says, and Rodriguez tucks her notebook away.

O'Reilly lays his hand on the doorknob, preparing to leave. "Allen could return later this evening," he says seriously. "And, if he does, we'll want to be ready. We'll send a squad car over to keep an eye on your house." A sudden chill runs through me and I wrap my cardigan sweater around myself tighter, tucking one side of it under the other concealing its row of buttons. O'Reilly picks up on my body language but doesn't comment on it. He likely figures me for a nervous wife, and I am nervous. Worried sick over Allen and what he might have done.

My voice trembles a little when I ask, "Can you wait until Emma's left on her trip? I'd hate for her to come home and find the police here."

"What time does she leave?" O'Reilly asks.

"Her aunt Pat's picking her up at five."

O'Reilly nods. "We'll still want to watch your house but I can instruct the team to keep a low profile until around six or so. Maybe stay on patrol."

I release a grateful breath. "Thank you."

O'Reilly's eyebrows arch. "Where's Emma off to?"

"Her aunts Pat and Gayle are taking her on a kiddie cruise to the Caribbean. Next week is Emma's spring break. She'll be gone the whole week."

Rodriguez exchanges a glance with O'Reilly then says, "Maybe that's a blessing in disguise."

"Right about that," O'Reilly answers.

There aren't too many blessings in this scenario, I get that. But yeah, having Emma safely away from Chapel Roads while all this nastiness gets sorted out is all to the good.

Rodriguez passes me a card, and I take it and hold it in an unsteady hand. "This is Officer Patel's direct number. She and Officer Brady will be here a little after six then and stay all night. If you see something, say something, Sadie. You might think you know your husband, but given the current situation, an ounce of prevention is worth a pound of cure. You do have your child to think of."

My heart twists painfully as I choke out in a whisper, "Yes."

O'Reilly walks onto the front stoop then seems to have another thought and turns back around. "You still keep that spare house key out back?" He remembers this from Emma's investigation.

I nod. Although we moved it to a different spot, Allen and I still keep a hide-a-key near our patio door. The only people who know about that key are Teresa, Forrest, me—and Allen. O'Reilly can't possibly think I need protection from him? But, after the way he left and under such damning circumstances, do I really know what to believe anymore?

"All things considered," he says darkly, "you might want to bring it in."

DIANE
THE OLD GIRLFRIEND

Now

I knew I could get dirt on Allen if I just dug a little deeper. I asked Dot to help me, and Dot would have done anything I requested. She was eating right out of my hand. Believing everything I'd told her, down to the details about my past. For a long time I worried we'd had a witness, someone there hiding in the shadows, maybe Kit-Kat, who was eight. Who else would have been up that late at night following me? If it had been one of my parents or Mark, they would have spoken up.

My parents were desperate for Allen to be punished for my death. I'm sure they were equally grateful I was gone. Of the three of us kids they worried the most about me reaching out to the authorities. Namely, because I threatened to contact child protective services numerous times. That always resulted in a mouthful of flies and a few strong lashes from Dad's belt.

While they claimed their parenting techniques were within their custodial prerogative, my mom and dad weren't stupid enough to want to have our family's dirty laundry aired in public. Mark was never going to go to the police, or to anyone else. He self-medicated instead, and Kit-Kat was way too young to do anything but hide in the back of her closet. She even wet herself a couple of times because she was too scared to come out. Then, she got punished for that. I almost feel sorry for her being left alone with those monsters after I went missing and Mark ran away.

My parents evidently cut off all communication with Allen's folks after my death was ruled an accident. Dot told me this from the scraps of information she'd gleaned while she was under investigation. Beforehand, the two couples had been as thick as thieves, bragging on their portfolio investments and doing lines of coke on the kitchen island, while knocking back shots of expensive tequila.

Oh yeah, I saw them partying late at night when they thought us kids had gone to sleep. Where do you think Mark got his first taste of cocaine? They didn't give it to him. He stole it. You almost needed to stay stoned to survive the upbringing we had. It's no wonder Kate, as she calls herself now, developed issues. Though, in her defense, she's trying to pull herself back up.

I'm alone in my ratty motel room preparing for my sisterly conversation with Kate. She'll probably be displeased with my actions, but it's okay if she doesn't understand. Kit-Kat's my baby sister. She doesn't need to know everything. I'm older and more savvy to the world than she is. I've been around the block a time or two and know what I know.

There are different kinds of people in this world, some of them worse than others. You've got your average scum, and then your lower-than-low bottom-feeders. My parents fall into that latter category. Sadly, so does Allen.

There's no greater pain on earth than being rejected by someone who holds all the cards. The individual who can fill your heart with hope, then rip it to shreds completely. When I was little, I used to pray my parents would outgrow their terribleness and actually come to love me.

They took us to church, if you can believe it, even behaving the way they behaved. Maybe they silently asked for forgiveness during the personal prayer time, but somehow I doubt it. Once, I almost told my Sunday school teacher the truth when she saw the bruises on my small arms, but then I grew afraid of even worse repercussions at home, so I kept my mouth shut. I lied to my teachers at school, made up stories around my friends.

Allen was the first person I ever told what was going on. He didn't understand how bad things were in the beginning and said yeah, his folks were shitty too. Lots of teenagers say that. Few mean it as sincerely as I did. When I started recounting the stories, Allen was appalled. I told him we could run away maybe, make a fresh start. He said no, we were too young, fifteen and sixteen, we'd never make it. I had an idea then to make him change his mind.

The room smells musty and I'm pretty sure these brown-and-gold quilted bedspreads haven't been washed in months—if ever. I'd really rather not think on whether or not the sheets are routinely laundered. I sleep on top of them wearing my clothing, just to be safe.

I lean back on one of the twin beds smoking a cigarette with the window cracked open and the bathroom fan on. I started smoking in high school but got clean when I lived at the teen shelter. It was a requirement of living there and I was thankful for the roof over my head. Not about to fuck that up.

That's where I met Caleb and things were good between us for a while, until Allen served as Caleb's jury foreman in a trial that never should have happened. Caleb lost his job and our marriage fell apart. I had to take our daughter and move to another state to protect her from the fallout. I couldn't have my kid growing up under that dark cloud. I also was afraid the increased scrutiny by the press would somehow alert my shithead parents to the fact that I was not dead, but very much alive and living under a new name in the same town.

I stayed off alcohol and cigarettes for years but gave in to those old vices after my prison visit with Dot. I couldn't get her face out of my head or erase the sound of her voice. It made me feel guilty for being involved, and I don't like feeling guilty. I like being vindicated. Proven right. And if there's one thing I want proven before I die, it's that Allen's a despicable person. Someone who doesn't care in the worst kind of way.

A man who leaves people behind.

Buries secrets.

But buried secrets can be unearthed.

All you need is a shovel.

My shovel was Dot.

TERESA
THE EX-WIFE

Now

When I get home, I deal with Forrest as calmly as I can. "Hey. How was your day?" I leave my purse and car keys on the kitchen table. Find him in the great room with its panoramic view of the woods.

He doesn't look at me from the sofa where he sits watching TV, his socked feet on the coffee table. "All right." It's some sci-fi film about the end of the earth. I don't know how to tell him our apocalypse is coming, but I must. It's my job to prepare him for any ugliness that might lie ahead.

I sit down beside Forrest and lift the remote from the coffee table. Turn off the TV. "Hey!" He gawks at me, drops his feet to the floor. "What'd you do that for? It's Friday and the start of spring break."

"I know, son." I frown and release a breath. "But I've got some news."

His face is suddenly serious, a mirror image of his father's, and that breaks my heart. "What's happened?" His voice cracks awkwardly. "Mom?" I want to assuage his panic but I can't. Mine's racing out there ahead of his. Leaping and bounding toward a new sort of future. If Allen's locked away, will we survive it? Of course, I know we will. Forrest and I can survive anything. I'm less sure about Sadie. I should reach out to her later. She may not want to hear from me, but—in light of the police being after Allen—that would be the decent thing to do. If there's anyone who knows about losing Allen, and how to move past that, it's me. Ironically.

"I'm so sorry to have to tell you this, but the police are on their way here."

"What? Why?" His mouth hangs open and then he shuts it. "Does this have something to do with what happened to that woman? Dad's neighbor, Cass Thomas?"

I steady my nerves because lying's not going to help here. "I'm afraid your dad is now a suspect in her death. The police have found some evi—"

"No!" Forrest jumps to his feet knocking forward the coffee table. It keels like a sailboat in a storm, before slamming back down on wobbling legs. Coasters and the remote crash to the floor, piling on the carpet. His hands clutch his head, fingers rake through his hair. He glares at me sideways. "I don't believe it. It's a lie!" A small twist of the knife. I should be bolstered by Forrest's faith in his dad; instead, I feel the jab to my gut. When it was me on the line, my son was all too quick to judge, instantly believe me culpable for a horrendous act. Now that his dad's integrity is in question, he vehemently denies the possibility.

Poor Forrest.

So much to learn.

"If you don't want to speak to them when they get here," I say, "you can stay up in your room."

Forrest crosses his arms and hangs his head. Blows out a breath. "No," he says staring at me. "I'll stay." His Adam's apple rises and falls. "In case you need me."

My eyes burn hot and I hold back a sniff. My barely twelve-year-old son is trying to be here for his mom. I almost can't bear his dedication. It's so far and beyond and above what I expected. Probably more than I deserve.

"Thanks," I say softly. I scrub back my tears with my fist as the doorbell rings. Fucking already? I check my watch. I asked for twenty minutes. They gave me thirty. Maybe I should be grateful for the extra ten.

"Want me to get it?" Forrest asks, looking beleaguered, and this is only the start. Things are sure to become even more difficult from here. *Damn you, Allen. If only you'd thought of your family, of all of us.* But no, clearly he didn't.

"No, hon. I'll go." I stand and my legs are unsteady, but I make my way to the door. Lay my hand on Forrest's shoulder as I pass him.

I'm equal parts devastated for Forrest and angry at Allen.

I wonder how much Sadie knows about what happened to Allen's parents? About Diane? You'd have to be completely obtuse to ignore the pattern of Allen doing away with inconveniences. I hate to think that Forrest and I became inconvenient to him, but in my heart I know we did. I did, certainly. And the *half time* he gives our son might be better than no time, but it's obviously not as good as if Allen had been here *full-time* all along.

I answer the front door with Forrest standing near me, yet a few paces back. I recognize the pair: Shane O'Reilly and Val Rodriguez. Rodriguez is okay. Deputy Chief O'Reilly always rubbed me the wrong way. I didn't like his interrogation style during Emma's kidnapping. Fortunately, I'm not on the hook here. He's got bigger fish to fry.

O'Reilly bows his head in greeting. "Ms. Wilson."

"Teresa's fine."

"We're sorry to barge in on such short notice." Rodriguez darts a glance at Forrest. "Maybe we should speak in private."

I look over at my boy, who is soon to be a man. A man who I hope is different from his father in certain ways. "It's all right. Anything you have to say to me you can say in front of him. Forrest can stay."

"If you insist." O'Reilly narrows his eyes like he disagrees with my parenting style. Well, fuck that. I disagree with O'Reilly on lots of things. If he'd been smarter, he never would have named me as a person of interest in Emma's disappearance, wouldn't have caused that tremendous upheaval in my life. The police were one hundred percent wrong about everything, and there was hell to pay.

"We're here investigating Cass Thomas's death," O'Reilly says, "which we now view as suspicious."

"Why do you blame my dad?" Forrest blurts out and I worry this was a bad idea, having him here.

Rodriguez sighs and addresses me rather than my boy. "Allen's prints were found at her house. He was obviously there recently, we believe as recently as last night, which was when Cass died."

O'Reilly sets his hand on his duty belt. He wears a long-sleeved shirt and uniform slacks. He's fully decked out as a cop and weaponized accordingly. Rodriguez's outfit matches his. "Allen was also seen fleeing in this direction this morning. Did he stop by here?"

"What?" I blink and answer. "No. Forrest left for school and I left for work soon after."

"When was the last time you spoke with your ex-husband?" O'Reilly asks.

"Yesterday afternoon."

"In person?" Rodriguez starts writing stuff down.

I shake my head. "By text. Forrest had left his soccer things at Allen and Sadie's and we needed them for his soccer practice last night. Allen couldn't bring them by because he was busy, so Sadie volunteered to bring them over."

Rodriguez adjusts the tight bun at the nape of her neck. "Did Allen say what he was doing?"

I shrug. "I assumed wrapping things up at work. He and Sadie had their trip coming up. They were supposed to leave tomorrow."

I can't mention my meeting afterward, because then the police will drag me into their investigation, and I need to stay as far away as possible from their probing questions. I have Forrest to look after, and our well-being to protect. Especially in the worst-case scenario. If Allen gets convicted, I'll be all Forrest has got left. I don't imagine his bond lasting with Sadie, without his dad being around. Much less with his little sister, whom he despised for years and years. Maybe he'd secretly find it a relief not to have to deal with them?

O'Reilly scratches the side of his head, setting his hat askew. He rights it and then asks, "Any thoughts on why Allen might have been heading in this direction?"

"Sadie said the greenway?"

Rodriguez nods. "He probably couldn't have covered too much ground on foot."

Forrest's eyes water and his cheekbones turn bright pink. "How about by bike?" His voice is high and frail, suddenly a child's again.

The three of us turn to him. "Forrest?" I ask gently. "What do you mean?"

"When I got home from school earlier, I went out for a ride on my new bike." Forrest trembles slightly, looks like he might cry, like he's grasping the seriousness of the situation. His dad's suspected of murder and could go to jail, or worse. Still, it's clear my kid is one of the good guys. He won't be complicit in covering things up. "My old ten-speed," he says miserably. "It's gone."

Rodriguez and O'Reilly stare at each other.

"Where do you keep your bikes?" O'Reilly asks.

"In the shed out back, at the end of the driveway." We exit the house and head to the shed. Forrest works the dial on the lock securing the door.

O'Reilly sends me a glance. "Who else has the combination?"

"Only Forrest, me—and Allen."

Forrest opens the shed door, and sure enough . . .

One of the bikes is gone.

ALLEN
THE HUSBAND

Now

I pedal and pedal until my thighs burn and sweat runs down my back and neck, Cass's baseball bat digging in between my shoulder blades as it's buoyed in the canvas backpack. I've only covered half the distance I need to but the rain has stopped, thank God. I know these country roads and woodsy trails like the back of my hand, because I used them a lot as a kid. I had a dirt bike and an ATV and went all over the place with my friends. We even did this trek a time or two to sneak off for some weekend parties.

When I heard the sirens this morning I knew I had to act quickly. There was no time for second-guessing. I had to protect my family. And, no matter what else happens, my family will always come first. Look, I know I screwed up in a big way. I slept with Teri after I was married to Sadie and I'm not proud of it.

Both times were before Emma's kidnapping, and on that super dark day when Emma went missing everything changed. My entire world whipped into very sharp focus, and I had a crystal-clear understanding of what mattered most: Sadie and my kids, Forrest and Emma. I prayed to God so many times for Emma to come home and cut all sorts of heavenly deals. I'd have made a deal with the devil, I mean it. I was so freaking desperate I would have done anything to ensure my little girl's safety.

I turn down a quiet road lined by towering trees, their verdant branches dripping with purple wisteria. The sun is high in the sky and beaming down on me and the bike casting our shadow on the pavement ahead. Then I find the dirt path partly covered in underbrush and creeping ivy sending tentacles across a pebbly landscape of red Carolina clay. I hop off the bike and enter the wooded trail that will lead me to more back roads, grateful I remember this course. By nighttime, I hope to be there.

The police are sure to know by now I've run, and Sadie too. I have no idea what she's thinking and I wish I could have told her, but I wanted to shield her from getting in too deep. So, no. There are certain things that it's better I've kept to myself. The backpack's on my shoulders holding Cass's heavy baseball bat, a water bottle I bought from a rest stop machine, some cash and two house keys. Sadie knows about the first key, but not the second.

My eyes heat and I'm overcome with grief about my last exchange with Cass. I wish I'd known earlier and that she'd said something before. I didn't take the news well. In fact, I took it badly. Could have—*should have*—handled things in a different way.

Now Cass is dead, taking our secret to the grave.

SADIE
THE WIFE

Now

Emma and I are upstairs placing the things we've laid out on her bed in her suitcase. Enough outfits for all six days, two sets of pj's, her bathing suit and flip-flops, toothbrush and toothpaste in a travel kit, hairbrush, barrettes and bows. Before I close the suitcase, I pick up Night Doggie from his perch by her pillows. "How about this guy, want to take him?"

She screws up her little face, thinking, and crosses her arms. I sense her inner struggle: big enough to be away but not without her lovey. "Why don't you take him?" I suggest gently. "He'll probably have fun."

"No," she says shaking her head. "He can save my spot."

Heat prickles my eyes and I set the stuffed toy down, settling it in on Emma's quilt. Night Doggie saved Emma's spot very bravely when Emma was away the last time. "Are you sure?" I force myself to remain cheerful with a happy smile. I can't let Emma know how terrified I am by what's happening, and the uncertainty that looms ahead.

"I'm sure," she says decidedly and pats his head between his two floppy ears. "Be a good boy." Then she whispers to him, "Don't let Forrest take you." She says it sneakily like she's attempting a joke, and winks. Her newfound sense of humor pulls me out of my gloom and I laugh. I'm sure she knows Forrest won't steal Night Doggie. He's twelve now, and way past the point of playing pranks on his younger half sister. He's also gone to Northern Virginia to be with his grandma. I'm glad both kids will be away for the next couple of days. I don't want either of them exposed to what's going on with their father.

In the best-case scenario, I'll have this all figured out by the time Emma returns from her cruise, and Allen will be back here safely after explaining the huge misunderstanding to the police. Though, even as I try to convince myself, I don't buy it. Can't believe Allen running off involves a colossal mistake.

He took our cash with him. He didn't leave without thinking about it. His disappearance was intentional and he didn't trust me enough to tell me what was going on. It's hard to think of him as anything but guilty given the circumstances, but I'm trying to keep an open heart and mind. It's not easy.

Emma stares up at me with hopeful eyes. "Is Daddy coming home to say goodbye?"

"He wishes he could, sweetie, but he's still at work. He asked me to give you a big hug and a kiss and sends his love for a great trip." I hug her small shoulders to my chest and hold her, my heart beating wildly. Kiss her precious forehead. Emma nestles against me, her embrace tight and firm.

"Okay," she says with such sweetness I want to scream—at Allen for leaving, and for everything he's done to land us in this mess. How could he do this to me? Why would he do this to his daughter? Is Allen truly as self-focused as Diane says? Do none of the rest of us matter?

The doorbell chimes.

"Aunt Pat!" Emma cries, racing out of her room and down the front stairs. I zip up her pink backpack containing books and games for the plane ride and carry that and her rollaboard suitcase down after her.

By the time I reach the foyer, Emma has already let Pat in and they're standing in the hall facing the living room.

My ten-years-older-than-me friend wears her hair in a pageboy and heavy dark bangs skim her eyebrows. I met her when I was still working in the office as an actuary. Pat was my supervisor but has since moved on to a different firm. She and Allen were in business school together and became friends there. That's how Allen and I met, at Pat and Gayle's wedding; she was our mutual connection.

"Hey, munchkin!" she says reaching forward and pulling Emma into a hug. "Are you ready for our trip?"

Emma wraps her arms around Pat's neck and her small ponytail bobs from side to side, as Pat squats low to hold her. "Uh-huh!" She's in jeans and a kid-size sweatshirt from Stonefield Elementary. It's dark blue with stenciled white lettering on it.

After our ordeal last year, I wasn't sure about Emma continuing kindergarten, thinking we should coddle her by providing a recuperative year at home. Our family counselor advised us that establishing a more normal routine for kids her age would be the best thing for her.

Emma's presence at Stonefield Elementary might have been awkward for some of the parents who'd been following the news stories, but the other children accepted Emma instantly and her new teacher was phenomenal. Someone just out of school who'd only been substitute teaching until that point, while hoping to land a regular job.

After subtle pressure from the school board, Principal Rand resigned. She was close to retirement age anyway and had two black marks against her in many people's eyes for tragedies that had occurred during her tenure. Allen and I were, frankly, glad to see her leave.

"Can we go swimming on the boat?" Emma asks Pat with a hopeful gaze. She knows that's the plan since we packed her bathing suit and asks out of eager excitement.

"You bet we can," Pat says. "There are five swimming pools and one has a waterfall, and another a waterslide!"

Emma grins over at me, while still hanging on to Pat, but then there's a pout. "I wish you and Daddy could come, Mommy."

"I know, sweetie," I answer, "but you'll have the best time."

"Yes, we will!" Pat promises, hugging Emma tighter until she giggles. "Aunt Gayle and I can't wait."

My heart warms at the sunny portrait, then I recall the dark clouds hovering overhead. I need to fill Pat in but not in front of Emma. "Emma," I say as they break out of their hug. "Why don't you run outside and play while I have some coffee with Aunt Pat?"

Her small eyebrows knit together but then she brightens. "Okay!" It's a gorgeous springtime day, mild and sunny, with this morning's rain and fog completely lifted. Flowers flank the patio and hem the fence line beyond the play set. Bright red azaleas shield pretty pink and purple pansies and the dogwood near the slide is in full bloom. Emma traipses down the front hall and exits by the door to the patio to the left of the breakfast table and runs out into the yard.

SADIE
THE WIFE

Now

Through the wide windows facing the backyard, Pat and I see Emma skipping toward the wooden play set Allen constructed shortly after we moved in. It's got black swings and monkey bars across the top, and a bright-yellow slide bordered by monkey grass and daffodils. A blue sandbox shaped like a tugboat sits on one side and a flowering camellia bush towers over it lending shade and providing magenta bursts of color from its blossoms. The lid is off the sandbox, and toys burrow in mounds of sand: an upturned green bucket, a red plastic shovel, a sifting pan for play.

Pat and I walk into the kitchen and approach the coffeepot.

"Still nothing from Allen?" she asks darting a gaze out the window over the sink. Emma's swinging happily on her play set, singing some kind of tune. I fill two coffee mugs and hand one to her. We both drink our coffee black.

I frown and answer Pat, "I'm afraid not. And things are worse than I thought. Allen was spotted leaving our neighborhood with what the police believe is the murder weapon."

"Gracious. A gun?" Pat appears aghast as I motion toward the kitchen table. She sits on the bench facing the backyard and I take a chair at one end, with my back to the den. We both have a clear view of Emma, her youthful innocence on full display. Despite everything she's gone through, she's still a happy, upbeat child.

I'm so grateful for that aspect every day. "They wouldn't say."

Pat's face is drawn. "I'm so sorry about this, Sadie." She lays a hand on my arm. "Are you sure we should still take Emma? Maybe she should stay—"

"To become embroiled in this?"

"You're right," Pat agrees. "The kid doesn't need more drama, especially in light of what she's already been through. She'll never catch wind of what's going on back here, Gayle and I will make sure of it. We'll keep things fun and upbeat, but will you keep us posted, please?"

"Of course." I smile softly. "I can't think of anywhere else I'd want her to be, other than with you and Gayle." As nervous as Allen's disappearance makes me, I'd be twice as concerned if Emma were around, accidentally discovering somehow that her dad is a suspect in our neighbor's murder. That might be hard to hide with the police poking around, and the neighborhood's a little gossipy so I can't count on things not to spread.

"Well hopefully this is all a big misunderstanding and Allen will be home soon to clear things up."

"Yeah, hope so too."

"What are you going to do about your trip to Aruba?"

I shrug. "Even if Allen comes back, he won't be allowed to travel. The police have got his passport and will probably hold it until he's cleared."

"Oh, Sadie. How heartbreaking. I know how much you were looking forward to that trip."

My eyes mist over. "I don't much feel like going on it now."

"Of course not." She takes both my hands in hers. "Maybe you can arrange a travel credit with the booking company, so that when all this settles down—"

"Oh, Pat," I ask desperately. My voice cracks. "Do you think it will?"

"Gayle and I will be sending up so many strong prayers, trust me."

"Thank you."

She tightens her hold on my hands. "What about you, Sadie? Are you okay?" She hesitates then says very directly, "I mean, I know you and Allen had some troubles when Emma went missing. Do you think what's happening now has anything to do with that?"

"I'm not sure," I say honestly. "I had my doubts about some things Allen told me then. I know now he lied about his relationship with Teresa, and also"—my breath shudders before I can finish—"about Cass."

Pat blinks. "The dead woman?"

"I didn't want to tell you on the phone," I say.

She holds her coffee mug tighter and leans toward me. "Sadie? What is it?"

I purse my lips and share the hard news. "Allen slept with Cass too."

"Oh my God, no."

"Not while we were married," I add quickly. "Not that I know of. It happened before Allen and I met and while he was separated from Teresa."

"How do you know this? Who told you? Allen?"

I stare out the window at her house. "She did."

"I see." Pat frowns, staring out the window at Cass's house too. She turns back toward me to ask, "So you confronted her?"

I'm not proud of my behavior, but I was beside myself, distraught. I had so many lies raining down on me from all directions like jagged icicles from the ever-changing winds and sky. "Yes, and she admitted as much, said it happened years ago and was over."

"And you believed her?"

"Strikingly I did, but that didn't lessen the pain of Allen's betrayal. He may not have cheated on me with Cass, but he might have told me the truth when we moved in right behind her. He could have confessed the truth when Emma went missing, and Cass was suspected of being involved. And all this time with me not knowing. It makes me feel like a fool, Pat. Like the two of them played me. Maybe I shouldn't be telling you all this. I know that you're Allen's friend too."

"Honey, I'm both your friends, but you've got to know one thing: If Allen's been a shit, I'm your friend first, and Gayle is right behind me."

"Thanks for your support." I smile sadly. "Gayle's too. It means a lot."

I take a few sips of coffee then say, "It still burns me that Teresa knew about Cass and Allen. That he'd told her but never me. I can't help but feel like this is a pattern, Pat. Allen shielding me from inconvenient truths."

"Well, I'm hoping he has a way to explain that and everything else, a way to exonerate himself in Cass's murder too. Although I'm going to be honest with you, Sadie, Allen going into hiding right now is not helping his case."

"I know."

I don't tell Pat about Diane because she's already on information overload, and Diane's appearance out of the blue is just one more thing that implicates Allen. Could Diane be right? Could Allen be a dangerous person? Did he really attempt her murder? Was he successful in getting rid of his parents, as well? Allen's admitted to me over the years that he viewed his folks as an embarrassment. They represented self-important new money in the worst possible ways, and they befriended those with similar values, like Diane's mom and dad.

I wonder now if either couple had seen the dark underside of the other if they sensed a kinship in their mutual despicable parenting. Though Allen's parents were more absent than abusive to hear him tell it, he still didn't want them around his friends, particularly after he had ambitions of attending a nameplate university and charting his own path.

Allen once hinted his folks sabotaged his potential acceptance to his number-one-choice school, because his dad showed up drunk during the student interview day, but it's hard to believe that's true. Surely, the college admissions officer couldn't have held a son accountable for his father's transgressions. In any case, Allen blamed his dad for the fiasco and hated him for it. His mom wasn't much better. Allen claims he basically raised himself.

Allen's tales of his childhood used to make me so sad when I compared his upbringing to mine. Though I lost my parents young to different circumstances, my parents were never anything but loving and kind. When Allen talks about his late mom and dad, there is a cold distance there. Like he's remembering someone else's family entirely, as opposed to his own. This used to break my heart and make me feel sorry for Allen.

Now his cold disregard for his parents makes me suspicious.

Compassion lines Pat's face. "I'm worried about us going on our trip now and leaving you here alone to deal with this." She stares out the window again, watching Emma, who's jumped off a swing and is now taking repeated trips down the slide. "Maybe we should stay in town and nearby. Gayle and I can take care of Emma at our house. We can shield her from the media, be extra careful."

"No, I think it's better for Emma to be off having fun and totally oblivious. Besides that, I'll be okay. Deputy Chief O'Reilly's sending a patrol car over later to keep watch on our house."

Pat takes my hands again and squeezes them. "Are you sure?"

I smile glumly. "I think it's good for Emma to be away from this mess."

"What does she know about the situation?"

"Nothing. She heard sirens this morning but I told her it was a false alarm."

"And her dad?"

"She thinks he's at work."

"Sadie," Pat asks softly, "are you worried about Allen? Afraid that he might come back here and do you some harm?"

"Of course not," I say, although my heart is racing. I don't know what to believe about what Allen's capable of, or—more frighteningly—where his true allegiances lie. When Emma went missing, I couldn't help but bristle at his unwavering support for Teresa. There were also times when he appeared overly defensive of Cass.

Now the pieces are falling into place. He shared a bond with both women as former lovers. I get sick to my stomach every time I think of Allen with another woman. The very notion of him being that intimate with someone else literally makes me ill.

To believe something is in the past is one thing, but when that past invades your present, the gloves come off. I mean, they have to, am I right? What woman in my circumstances wouldn't have felt—and reacted—the same?

"Where do you think Allen's hiding?" Pat asks.

"I wish I knew."

ALLEN
THE HUSBAND

Now

I made it to the cabin—at last. After taking a bit of a breather here, I'll enact my plan for tonight. I'm on the screened porch staring out at the dock from my position on a metal rocker, the sort that glides back and forth. The cove is quiet, low waves rolling across its glassy surface, left by a trolling motorboat. Its skipper wears a captain's hat. A tall curly-coated black dog leans into the wind by his side as he stands at the helm.

It's early evening and sunlight gleams behind towering trees, sending out long glistening ribbons across the darkening water. While the cabin's rustic from outward appearances, my parents paid big money for this place, mostly because they bought up all the land surrounding the cove. My folks weren't ones for nosy neighbors, but they did like to entertain. Back at our main house, not here. This place was their refuge.

Fitting that it killed them.

I raise the Cuban cigar to my lips and take a long draw. Savor the tang in my throat, and taste on my tongue. Feel my lungs expand and hold it, before tilting back my head and blowing out smoke. My dad gave me my first cigar when I turned fourteen. At fifteen, he handed me a beer. Other kids might have found that cool, but not me. I kept thinking, what kind of dad does that to his kid? I consider Emma and my heart constricts. I'd never do anything other than protect our little girl. And yet, now, there's this: a larger worry I have to contend with.

Cass said some things last night but I wasn't the only one she spoke with. That's my problem to deal with now, and I will. Once I figure out how.

I stub the cigar out on the ashtray on the table beside my chair. The old hammock in the corner's been beaten to shreds, its colorful pattern faded by wind and rain pelting through the tattered screen over the years. It's anchored on either end by heavy chains secured by gigantic screws into structural beam posts. The inside of this cabin's been more or less preserved as it was when my parents died. Except it's gotten dusty and there are cobwebs in the corners. Evidence of mice that have decided this is a nice place to stay.

There's no electricity because I haven't paid the utility bills in years. Sadie doesn't even know I own this place. Mentioning that part of my life leaves such a bad taste in my mouth, I didn't want to tell her. She's aware of my parents' accident but not the details.

I couldn't bear to tell her I'd been investigated by the authorities because they thought I might have had something to do with my parents' accident, or that at the very least I'd been negligent in letting them die when I might have called the coast guard or gotten help. Even Teri disappointingly judged me, when I told her the story. Christ. And she was in love with me then. Maybe she still is. Sometimes I wonder.

SADIE
THE WIFE

Before

The music swells and I tug Allen onto the dance floor amid five hundred wedding guests. "Slow down!" he yelps as I pull him along. "You're going to kill me before we get there, and I promised not to step on your feet!"

I laugh at his flustered look. For an otherwise seemingly confident guy, Allen appears very out of his element in a tuxedo and on the dance floor. "Won't be much chance of that if we don't start dancing!" He's a very nice-looking guy and seems smart and witty. I think I've hit his weak spot with the dancing and he doesn't appear to have many of those.

"Okay now," I say and drop his hand. "We're here!" I start moving to the music and he stands there like a deer caught in somebody's headlights. "Allen?" I ask and chuckle, shuffling from side to side. It's a fast piece, really jazzy and fun. "What are you doing?" He tries to mimic my steps but is abysmal at it.

"I told you I don't dance!" he shouts above the DJ who announces the cake will be cut soon. I can't help but feel sorry for him—and think he's adorable. I can tell he's concentrating on his feet too much. Looking down then up making sure he's got it right. The music crescendos in a pulsing beat and we have to shout to be heard.

"Everybody dances!" I say.

"Nope. Not everyone!" He takes a few more stabs at moving awkwardly. "What do you do for a job?"

"I'm an actuary." I do a little twirl to show off in front of him. I've got on my sexy blue dress. It's strapless with a very short hemline. "How about you?"

"I'm a wealth manager."

"A what?"

"I help millionaires make money!" he yells as the music winds down. His whole face reddens when people stare his way.

"I wouldn't be ashamed of that," I banter.

The DJ makes a different selection. "And now to slow things down. After this one, folks, it's cake time!"

We're treated to a much slower tune with sultry strains of jazz. "Now, this," Allen says assuredly, "I can do."

"Oh yeah?"

His eyes twinkle devilishly. "Yeah." He holds out his arms and I walk toward him. This is a different Allen on the dance floor, one much more in command. He holds me securely with one hand on my shoulder and another at the small of my back.

I go a little breathy. "I thought you said you couldn't dance."

His lopsided grin makes my pulse flutter. "Fast learner."

We're both friends with Pat Meyers and she's just married her dreamboat Gayle Harnett. They're chatting with a small circle of friends beside their towering wedding cake, which is beautifully done and decorated with actual flowers. They started out wanting a more intimate wedding but then their guest list exploded. Allen and I were happy to benefit from that. Pat's a work friend but we've been getting closer and Allen and she were in the same tight-knit group from graduate school.

"Where'd you grow up?" I ask him.

"Here. You?" He keeps moving to the music, guiding me along. It feels like we're skating on ice, so seamless.

"Charlotte."

"Ah, let me guess." I fall into his deep-blue eyes. "At least one of your parents is a banker, you went to private school, and when you get married it will be at the country club."

I smirk at him. "Wrong on all counts. I went to public school and my mom was a physician who couldn't heal herself."

"I'm sorry." His face takes on a serious cast. "Cancer?"

I frown, suddenly melancholy. "Yeah."

"And your dad?"

"Cancer, too, only a different kind. He was a teacher."

Allen holds me closer. "Both gone?" he asks softly. When I nod, he says, "Oh, Sadie. I'm sorry. I lost my folks too."

I raise my eyebrows at him. "Maybe we should start a club?"

"What kind of club is that?" He twirls me out into the room and back toward him.

"The Little Orphan Allen and Sadie Club."

His deep rumbling laughter makes my skin tingle. "Now that's what I call making lemonade out of lemons."

I can't help smiling. "I like lemonade," I quip. "Don't you?"

"Yes." He leans toward me and whispers. "But I like champagne better."

The music stops and the DJ announces it's cake-cutting time, but we don't move. I'm trapped in a bubble with Allen under the spinning dance floor lights.

"I like champagne," I murmur like my heart isn't beating wildly.

"And I like you." He strokes my cheek with his thumb and my face warms.

Then he leans forward and kisses me and the magic begins.

Later that night, Allen swoops me into his arms and carries me from the hallway into his swanky hotel room with a panoramic view of downtown's twinkling lights.

"Allen, what are you doing?" I kick my feet in my sexy heels when I laugh. One of them slides off and plops down on the floor.

"Carting you over the threshold, of course!"

"That's for the wedding couple, silly." He sets me on the king-size bed and goes to retrieve my shoe. Presents it to me grandly.

"Cinderella," he says, handing it toward me with a bow.

"Oh!" I can't help but joke. "Why don't we see if it fits?"

He laughs and complies getting down on one knee, and I stretch out my shoeless foot, wiggle my toes in a demonstration. His hand gently supports my instep and my breath catches. Then he very tenderly slides my foot into my high-heeled sandal. His voice grows gravelly when he says, "It's the perfect fit."

He looks up and I fall into his endless blue eyes. They remind me of the ocean on a sunny day and I suddenly want to be at the seashore with Allen, and at the lake, and in the mountains, or on a boat, train or plane. Anywhere and everywhere. I'm so pulled in. "You know what this means, don't you?" His grin makes my heart pound faster.

"No?" I ask breathlessly. "What?"

"We're bound for our happily ever after."

"Oh yeah? And you're a prince?"

"Some say," he teases warmly.

"Some who?"

"Doesn't matter. I've already forgotten every other woman but you." He sets his hands on my hips and leans forward to kiss me on the lips. "Would you like that, Sadie? Would you like to ride into the sunset with me?"

His kiss is warm and tender and so swoony it makes my head light. "I think I might." I catch a small breath. "If you play your cards right and have a brave steed."

He climbs up on the bed beside me and takes me in his arms. I don't know how to explain what I'm feeling. All that I know is it's right, that Allen is right—for me. "Sadie?" he asks as he gently lays me down on the pillows. "Is this all right?"

"My kingdom is yours," I say, and he sweeps me away.

SADIE
THE WIFE

A tear splashes across the page of our wedding album and I wipe it back with my sweatshirt sleeve. Such a sweet trip down memory lane, and now so much has changed. Allen's and my wedding wasn't anywhere near as grand as Pat and Gayle's. We had a simple ceremony at the courthouse and Pat and Gayle stood up for us as witnesses. I didn't wear a wedding dress but a pretty, pale-pink jumpsuit and held a bouquet of silk flowers. Allen dressed in a charcoal suit with a crimson tie and a dusty-rose boutonniere.

Later that afternoon, we had a cookout in our backyard including about thirty of our friends. Our friend Amy is a professional photographer. As a wedding gift to us, she offered to come along to the courthouse and take photos there as well as during our reception. Looking back on those memories has always made me smile, but now they break my heart. Allen and I look so young and hopeful in the pics; our new life together was just beginning.

It was far from the country-club wedding Allen predicted I might have, but it was the kind of wedding I wanted. Low fuss and being together with the ones I loved. I've kept my inner circle tight since losing my parents. While there are plenty of people I might hang out with, and Allen and I have our couple friends, there are very few with whom I share my most intimate secrets. It's hard for me to build trust, and rebuilding it was even tougher work after I learned about Allen's affair with Teresa.

Shadowy movement outside captures my attention through the gloom. It's late evening and a heavy fog cloaks Emma's play set in its thickness. Wait.

I stand and close my wedding album, set it down on the coffee table. Walk to the patio door and flip the floodlights on. Bright beams permeate the fog revealing an occluded image darting across the lawn at breakneck speed. It's a person—running away. My heart slams against my chest as more fog lifts. The back gate to Cass's house stands open. Someone was here.

I grab my phone from the kitchen table and call Officer Patel. She arrives in an instant with Brady at her side. "Stay put," she instructs when I tell her what I've seen. "We'll check things out." Within minutes, she and Officer Brady are sweeping their flashlights across my backyard.

Officer Patel sees me standing at my back door and approaches. "Area's clear," she informs me, when I pull open the door. She tugs on the brim of her hat. "But it's good that you called. Someone was definitely out here. Some of the underbrush looks trampled near the gate."

My heart pounds. "You think it was the killer? Whoever murdered Cass?" I'm not going to say "Allen" and incriminate my husband. Why would Allen sneak around like that spying on our house? It has to be someone else.

"We can't be sure, but that's a possibility." She glances at the gate leading to Cass's house, and the garage door that's opposite Emma's play set. "We should probably take a look around. Has the house been locked up tight?"

"Yes," I say and my heart thumps harder. She thinks that person wasn't only spying, they might have been attempting to break in.

Officer Patel trains her flashlight across the yard as Brady walks up behind her. "Mind if we come in and take a look around," she asks, "just to be safe?"

"Of course."

The police survey the downstairs, checking in closets, behind the pocket doors to my office, in the pantry . . . then head upstairs using the front staircase. I hear them prowling around through rooms and doors creaking open and shut. Brady and Patel descend into the kitchen using the back staircase and peek in the garage.

"Everything looks okay," Patel reports and I heave a sigh of relief. She peers around the kitchen and walks into the den where I'm standing, with Brady close on her heels. "We've been watching the front of your house but should have thought of that angle," she says, her gaze on the rear gate. "I'll call for another car to get positioned in front of Ms. Thomas's house, in case someone tries to sneak in that way again."

I steal a look at my formerly darkened backyard, which is now illuminated by floodlights. Their sheen causes the sandbox shaped like a tugboat to gleam unnaturally blue. Could the person prowling around my backyard really have been Allen? Diane said he's a danger to me, but—try as I might—I can't wrap my mind around the idea of Allen being a physical threat to me. That's so hard to believe. Yet still, the tiniest sliver of doubt creeps in. After what I learned about him yesterday, I'm honestly not sure what Allen's capable of doing any longer.

Diane claims murder.

Could she be right?

SADIE
THE WIFE

Deputy Chief O'Reilly and Captain Rodriguez arrive within ten minutes. They perform another sweep of the house and Patel leads them on a tour of my backyard, pointing out the area of trampled underbrush by the gate, while I look on from inside.

When they reenter my house, O'Reilly and Rodriguez suggest I should move to a hotel, but being isolated in a strange environment almost feels creepier to me. I've never liked staying in hotel rooms alone. This is my home. I'd rather stay here in my familiar surroundings. A second patrol car is on its way to get stationed in front of Cass's house and Officers Patel and Brady came in a flash when I called them.

O'Reilly's shoulders sag and he sighs. "Doesn't sound like she's budging," he says glancing at Rodriguez.

"Well, if you change your mind at any point," Rodriguez says, "just let us know. We can arrange it."

"Thanks." It is somewhat freaky that someone was watching me from my own backyard. I experience an uncomfortable déjà vu from the days of Emma's kidnapping. Someone was also spying on us then, me and Allen. We never discovered who it was. Although in the end, we suspected it might have been Dotti, we never had that fact confirmed, not even by her. And Dotti was a woman who liked to brag on her sins.

When the police leave, I return to the den to put away my wedding album. Part of me wants to hear from Allen so he can explain what he's done, and why he felt the need to run away. But another part of me fears learning the truth and then having to live with that knowledge forever.

Could I really set aside such damning information? If I learned Allen's murdered Cass, I don't see how I could let that go. It's a bridge too far for me. I don't know how I could cross it and still be here for Emma, understanding that her dad's a killer. But if I turn against him and tell the police everything I know, will Allen turn his rage on me like Diane warned?

I don't see Allen as a violent man but that doesn't mean he hasn't behaved differently with other people. You hear about hardened criminals who are able to switch personas at the drop of a hat. Serial killers who are menaces to society but who are just regular husbands or fathers at home. Concerned neighbors. Presidents of their HOAs. Is Allen like that? Has he hidden his true nature from me?

I never thought he could do anything like that until the period of Emma's kidnapping, but then I started learning more things about him. How he'd hidden his affair with Teresa, and now I know he'd also concealed his past with Cass. Can a man who's lied about so much really be counted on to be honest? I just don't know.

I slide our wedding book back onto the bookshelf and another volume catches my eye. It's Allen's yearbook from his senior year of high school, the one from which I first discovered his long-ago connection to Cass.

I can't help torturing myself by pulling it from the shelf and carrying it over to the sofa, where I sit settling it on my lap. I flip through glossy pages and stop at the ninth-grade year, staring at Cass's cute smiley face framed by blond ringlets.

Then I flip through some more. There's Cass again. On the field hockey team. I hadn't noticed her sports photos before. There's another girl on the team who looks a lot like her. Could that be her sister? I thumb back through the pages, then there! I've found her, another Curtis, which was Cass's maiden name. This girl's in the tenth-grade group and her name's Robin.

She and Cass could pass for twins if you weren't looking closely. I never knew about Robin and Allen didn't mention her, but why would anyone bring Cass's sister up? Apart from the police. I'm sure they know. They've always got to notify the family when there's a suspicious death, or as they're calling it now—my blood chills—a murder.

I scan through some more images, appreciating Allen's teenage good looks, then frown when I see him standing in a photo with the cheerleader who was obviously his girlfriend. I never liked those kinds of girls in school because I never was one of them. I didn't blossom myself until college. I developed more confidence then and started dating, but I always kept my heart guarded. At a distance. The first man who really broke through was Allen.

Finally, I take the dark drive down memory lane to read the inscription in the back of Allen's yearbook. The inscription that got me so upset eighteen months ago when I discovered it, but which Allen dismissed as a high school prank. Cass Curtis had had a crush on him, he said. She didn't even write the note herself. A friend of Cass's probably did to razz her.

I know Cass was just a kid and she was likely joking. But still it makes my blood boil when I read what she wrote in her big loopy letters and signed with hugs and kisses.

I want to have your baby!
XOXO
CC

I scowl at Allen's yearbook and slam it shut.

My one consolation in this whole twisted scenario is that she'll never get the chance.

ALLEN
THE HUSBAND

I paddle our old canoe out of the boathouse, the ebony surface of the water glistening in the moonlight. Small ripples emerge each time I dip my paddle in, alternating left and right. It's been ages since I've paddled a canoe but some things are easy enough to remember. Like the day I first met Sadie, and the day our infant daughter came home from the hospital. Those are the details you hang on to in your memory, hold them close to your heart like cherished photos in an album. It breaks me apart to think I might never see them again, my girls.

I have to talk to Sadie about getting this sorted. Need to find a way. I have so much to tell her, confessions to make. Will she believe me? Forgive me? God only knows, but I can pray. She may not trust my reasoning, but she'll surely understand once I explain. Everything that I've done has been to protect her.

A light breeze blows riffling my old windbreaker. I found it here in the hall closet. The cabin is like a freaking mausoleum, fossilizing our former belongings. We kept things here to allow for easy weekend getaways. Spare clothing for all of us, nonperishables in the cupboard, though everything is so far past its date now I wouldn't dare to chance it. Although if I get hungry and desperate enough, I could change my mind.

For the time being, I purchased groceries from the local market. Fruit and canned goods. Things that don't require refrigeration. I took care to disguise my appearance during my brief shopping adventure. I wore Dad's ratty fishing hat and wading boots and kept my head downturned, purchasing live bait and a few lures for good measure. If anyone starts asking around about a stranger in these parts, I blended in with the dozens upon dozens of fisherfolk frequenting that store during spring fishing season and didn't exactly stand out.

I promised Sadie I was good at cleaning up messes and I intend to make good on my word. The moment Cass's death is declared an accident, we'll all breathe a little easier, and I'll be cleared to come home. In the meantime, I know exactly what I must do.

My muscles burn as I dig into the water, pulling back against the resistance, and the canoe glides forward. An array of lights dots the shore. Condos, new houses, a smattering of high-end docks and boathouses. I'm surprised by how built up this part of the lake has become. If my parents hadn't bought out our cove, that little section of the lake would have suffered the same fate.

I reach the spot I've targeted which is somewhere dead center of the lake where the water is the deepest and lift Cass's baseball bat from the floor of the canoe. It's a heavy hitter made of ash, porous yet dense. I dangle it over the edge of the canoe, and drop it in.

As it sinks to the bottom, I recall another moonlit night.

ALLEN
THE HUSBAND

Before

A full moon glows through the window as Sadie sits up howling and clutching her middle. "Sadie? Sadie? What's wrong?"

Fear washes over me when I feel the seeping warm liquid spread across the mattress. "My water . . . I think it's broken." I switch on the light and throw back the sheets. She's panting, with terror in her eyes. Shit. A puddle wells out around her and she winces, moans, hugs her stomach tighter and cries. "It's too early! Too, too—" Sadie's voice shudders and she sobs.

I bring my arms around her, pour warmth and determination into my reply. "Sadie, it's going to be okay. I'm taking you to the hospital."

She nods but she's weeping and her shoulders shake. She rubs the mound of her stomach and wails, "My *baby*."

"We're going to save her," I say. Shit. Shit. Shit. I'm scrambling for my stuff. Wallet, keys. Dressing quickly. We haven't even packed Sadie a hospital bag. This is two months early, for fuck's sake. I grab her robe from the closet and gently position it around her shoulders, help her into her slippers trying very hard not to fall apart myself. That won't help her, won't help me, won't help our baby. I steady my hands on her knees. "We could call an ambulance, but I could probably get us there faster if we leave now. Your call."

"I don't want to wait." She bursts into more tears and covers her face.

"Okay." I heave a breath. "You stay here. I'll get the car ready and come back and get you. Don't move, all right?" I have a prescient moment and hand her the phone. "Do you think you can phone your doctor? Let her know we're on our way?"

Her chin trembles. "Yes." She takes the phone and dials, my heart pounding all the while. I get the car warmed up and come back for her. The next few hours are a blur.

As they whisk Sadie away from me on a gurney, she grabs my hand. "If it's me or the baby," she says with labored breaths. "Please?" She pleads with weepy eyes and I know what she's saying, if it comes to a choice, she wants me to save our daughter, but how could I ever do that? Forsake Sadie?

I anxiously pace in the waiting room, not knowing how I'll face it if the baby doesn't make it. If Sadie doesn't make it. Christ. After being admitted through the ER, Sadie was immediately taken in for an emergency C-section. Luckily, her obstetrician made it here in time. After examining Sadie and getting monitors hooked up for the baby, she approached me with a drawn face. "I'm going to be really honest with you, Allen. We're going to do everything we can but things look bad. This is a very touch-and-go situation."

"For the baby?"

"For both of them." She pats my arm. "I'll let you know when we have news."

The wait is interminable and then the doctor finally appears.

She tugs down her face mask and she's smiling softly.

My heart breaks with joy.

TERESA
THE EX-WIFE

Now

I sit here staring in the dark holding my morning coffee and thinking about what's transpired in the past twenty-four hours. Cass is dead and Allen's on the run, wanted in connection with her murder. I hate that it had to come to this, but this is where things are.

I'm on the sofa in our great room enthralled by the rain-soaked woods. This used to be our place, mine and Allen's. We built this house with love and it was here we conceived Forrest. Our life could have gone so many different ways, but it's disappointingly landed here. I experience these moments of deep depression where I feel I'm treading water and barely keeping my head above the surface. Gulping in choking sobs as I thrash and gasp.

It's springtime in Chapel Roads but it feels like everything's dying. My hopes, my dreams, my heart. Instead of driving them apart, Emma's kidnapping merely brought Sadie and Allen closer together. That's why they planned their second honeymoon trip to celebrate the supposedly fantastic marriage they have.

Allen didn't say that in so many words. I could detect his wistful joy as he described their private cabana with its own beachfront hot tub.

Allen tells me these things because he mistakenly views us as equals: two happily matched-up people, him with Sadie and me with Henry.

But Henry can never be Allen. That's an impossible feat. It's been a decade since our divorce, yet my insides still *ache* from the wreckage he left inside me. My heart pummels my rib cage, painfully bursting at the seams. Soon it will explode right out of me, bloodying the plate glass window in front of me. I can see the carnage in my mind's eye, crimson streams running in rivulets down the glass, and it's almost a relief not having to feel anymore.

But no, I have Forrest to be here for and he needs me. I have a job teaching physics at the university as well, one that rightly could have been taken away from me in the wake of my actions during Emma's kidnapping. I could have lost my lab at the observatory too. Lost my grant. Lost my funding. Lost my freedom. Lost this house.

I held on to *all those things* but not the *one thing* I wanted.

And now it's too late.

O'REILLY
THE COP

Now

"Okay, folks!" Chief Claremont gives us our morning briefing. "Cass's autopsy report is in and some new evidence has surfaced. Given the prowler last night at Sadie Wilson's place, we've increased surveillance. Apart from a second squad car positioned outside Cass Thomas's house, we'll have additional squad cars performing regular neighborhood patrols."

"You think it was Allen trying to sneak back in?" Bev Johnson asks.

"It's possible it was him," Claremont answers. "Either him or the person who killed Cass." She pauses and sets her chin. "Unless they're one and the same." She points to Cass's cadaver photo on the board. "We got the analysis back on the wine that remained in the bottle, which was untampered with. So no leads there, although the toxicology report was revealing. Along with a slight amount of alcohol, a hefty dose of zolpidem was found in Cass's system."

"Sleeping pills?" Brady asks.

Claremont nods. "Brand name Ambien."

"There wasn't anything like that in her medicine cabinet," I tell the chief. "I checked."

"Yeah," she agrees. "Me too."

"Could the pills have been crushed and added to Cass's wine once it was already in her glass?" Patel asks.

"Most certainly," Claremont answers. "But, since those wineglasses went through the dishwasher, we may never know."

"Could the zolpidem be what killed her?" Brady asks.

"Likely would have," Claremont says, "if she hadn't suffered a blow to the head first."

SADIE
THE WIFE

Now

My cell phone rings and it's Pat.

"Pat, hi," I say in exhausted tones. She said she'd call with updates and I hope that's what this is, good news. "Is everything okay?" I'm in my home office, trying to get credit for our canceled travel arrangements, although it's hard to imagine finding a time we'll want to use them. The idea of celebrating and taking a vacation is antithetical to everything I'm feeling right now.

"Yes, fine! We set sail this morning and it's going swell." I hear laughter and happy shouting in the background. Splashing sounds. Mariachi music. "We're having the time of our lives. Emma just wanted to tell you about it." She passes over the phone.

"Hi, Mommy!" Emma's sweet voice coos.

"Hi, sweetheart. How's the cruise?"

"Amaze-ing!" she says with great joy. "I've made some friends."

"Have you? Oh?"

"Liza and Jemma. They're twins."

"Well, that's fun."

"I can tell them apart though," she says proudly. "Jemma's got pierced ears."

I laugh at her good detecting. "I'm glad you've found some playmates your age."

"We're in the kids' club together," she says. "We learned hula dancing!"

"Okay." I'm not sure how that connects to the Caribbean but I don't want to rain on her parade.

"It's from that Hawaiian movie," she explains. "I met some of the characters! It was cool!"

Ahh, got it. "Fun!"

"We're going to a special island too!"

"Yeah?"

"Yeah. I get to snorkel with the dolphins."

"Wow! Go you!"

She giggles. "Aunt Pat's taking lots of pictures."

Good. "I can't wait to see every one." I'm so happy she's having fun and relieved she's away from the turmoil of what's going on here.

"I have to go now!" she says. "Liza and Jemma and I are practicing our snorkeling in the pool." She's so caught up in her fun she doesn't even ask about Allen, which is a relief in many ways.

"Okay, honey. Great talking to you. Love you!"

"Love you too, Mommy!"

"Can you give the phone back to your auntie Pat?"

"Hello?" Pat says. It sounds like she's walking away from the commotion as the background noises fade. "Gayle's watching Emma and her friends," she whispers. "I've stepped around the corner. Sadie, what's going on back there?"

"Nothing new yet. The police are still looking, trying to find Allen." I don't tell her about the person prowling around my house last night, because I worry she might overreact and pack them all up and bring them home. That would be the worst thing in the world for Emma. Clearly what's best for her is staying there.

"Well, will you please keep us in the know?" Pat asks.

"For sure. I'll reach out if anything changes."

"In the meantime I'll send you some pics."

"That would be fantastic, Pat. Thanks so much, and truly thank you for what you and Gayle are doing. It really means the world to me and—" I'm about to say "Allen" and instantly stop, my throat going raw.

"It's all right, Sadie," Pat replies kindly. "We know."

O'REILLY
THE COP

Now

Val and I go to see Cass's sister, Robin Marconi. She lives in a simple ranch-style house in an older neighborhood. It's brick and is painted white with black shutters. A nice array of flowers adorns the front of it: blue hydrangeas flanked by golden forsythia blooms and butterfly bushes with conical lilac blossoms.

I stand up taller, straighten my uniform collar. Ring the bell. I note it's the sort with a camera and a recording device. If you told me the woman who answered the door was Cass's sibling at first I wouldn't have believed it. She's a heavier-set person with fine gray streaks coiling through her dark hair.

We introduce ourselves and she says, "Thanks for coming by." When she speaks, I spot the similarity of mannerisms between her and Cass, the high, rounded cheekbones, a certain way her eyes crinkle at the corner when she smiles, although her smile looks sad. She says her husband is at work. She's taken the day off herself to process the horrible news. Her daughter's home playing upstairs.

Robin invites us into the kitchen and we sit at a round country table in cushioned chairs with wide arms and curved, spindled backs. "Can I get you anything to drink? Water? Coffee?"

Val and I decline politely.

Val takes the lead. She's better at this in delicate situations, has the right soft touch—although she's as tough as nails in her questioning, she emits compassion, understanding. "We're so sorry about your loss. Your parents say that you and Cass were close."

"Yes, we were." Her eyes water and she sniffs, putting on a brave front. "Very."

"What's your difference in age?"

"Only a year, really thirteen months. I'm . . . *was*"—her chin trembles—"older."

As they talk I survey our surroundings, a load of kid artwork on the fridge, a school photo of a little girl, maybe in the first or second grade, held on by a magnet shaped like a watermelon, framed photos on the walls. One is older, from when the two sisters were younger. Holy cow. They looked almost identical then. "That you and Cass?"

Robin nods. "In high school." Both wear sports uniforms and hold field hockey sticks. Their jerseys say "Chapel Roads Bulls." "I was the captain of the team. Cass was a goalkeeper."

My senses alert. "So you also went to school with Allen Wilson?"

"That's right." She nods but starts fidgeting with her hands, clasping them tightly together, but her thumb pads pulse against one another. Tap-tap, tap-tap, tap-tap. I don't think she's aware she's doing it. I see Val notice and then she averts her gaze.

"Was he in your class?" Val asks.

"No, older. Cass was a freshman and I was a sophomore in the photo. Allen was a senior then. He graduated after that year."

Val writes these details down. "And all of you were friends?"

"Hardly." There's a snap to her tone, then she adds more mildly, "I mean, everyone knew Allen. He was popular there. Class president, athletic."

I insert what I know and the police learned during the other investigation. "We understand Cass had a pretty big crush."

Robin shoots me an offended look. "How is that relevant?" Her hands pull apart and she lays them on the table palms down, combative, shoulders angled forward.

Val lightly touches Robin's sleeve. "We need to know who might have had a motive to harm her."

She gasps, going pale. "Do you think Allen could have done this? Murdered my sister?" She appears equal parts incensed and ill.

"We know he was at your sister's house on Thursday night," Val says. "Did Cass talk to you about her relationship with Allen Wilson? Mention he was coming over, or why?"

Robin sits so still we can hear her ragged breathing. After too long a pause she says, "No."

Val subtly shakes her head at me because Robin's in a trance, staring at her refrigerator door, as if remembering. But what?

"Is there anyone else you can think of who might have had problems with Cass?" I ask. Although Allen's in the frame, we can't rule out other suspects. It would be irresponsible to only zero in on him without making the broadest possible sweep for information. "Maybe an old boyfriend?"

She shakes her head.

"Someone at work?"

Robin shakes her head more vehemently. "Cass was well liked at Our Lady of Our Savior." I note the school uniform on the kid in the picture on the fridge.

"Does your daughter go there?"

"She does, and we're very happy with the place. Cass was happy too. The faculty and students loved her. She was bright and funny, made the kids laugh. Put people at ease. She had that way about her."

Yet now she's dead.

Val starts to close her notebook but thinks twice. "She never mentioned anybody she didn't get along with? Maybe some run-in she'd had?"

"My sister didn't have run-ins with people, Captain Rodriguez. That's not who she was. Cass was a peacemaker. Getting along with others was important to her. She never had a bad word to say about anybody until . . ." The blood drains from her face and she stops talking.

Val leans forward and quietly asks, "Until?"

"That horrible exchange during Emma's kidnapping."

"What?" Val asks and Robin hardens her stance.

"My sister was violently attacked for no reason. Lunged at and throttled. She had to phone the police. Ask him." She stares at me. "He was there."

CASS
THE MISTRESS

Before

To say I was surprised to hear from Allen's ex-wife, Teresa, is putting it mildly. She wants to meet for coffee, as soon as I get off work. She says it's urgent which is strange, since she's essentially a stranger to me.

We meet at a coffee shop in town. The one that used to be an old gas station. Teresa has a table outside and she flags me down with a wave.

"I'll just go and grab my coffee," I tell her. "I'll be right back."

"Let me treat," she says standing. "I asked you here after all."

I peek inside the café at the folks tending the coffee bar. Good God, Kate Davis is one of them. She darts a glance my way and her eyebrows shoot up. She lowers them suddenly and looks away, acting like she hasn't noticed me standing here with Teresa, but I know she has. Those of us connected to Emma's case are tightly tied together in this very gnarly web, whether we want to be or not. "Uh, okay, sure," I answer, not super interested in venturing inside. "I'll take a double-shot latte. Low-fat milk."

Teresa nods and I settle myself in at the short metal table with a colorfully painted tabletop resembling a mosaic and Ceylon-blue legs. The matching chair's uncomfortable. Stiff and unyielding. Chilly at my back. Daylight's fading and the sun's begun its quick descent behind the longleaf pines. I zip up my jacket and wait.

Teresa returns with our coffees about ten minutes later.

"What's this about?" I ask as she scrapes back her chair. We're on a section of the paved patio below an awning and bordered by springtime flowers. More tables surround us and picnic tables pepper the grass. Teresa sits and sips from her cup. It's a tall order of something with a lid like mine, but a tea bag tag dangles down one side of her cup.

"I know this is a little unusual and I hope I'm not overstepping . . ." Which is exactly what people say when they're about to overstep.

I hold up a hand. "If you're here to talk about Allen, then no. Off limits." It's nobody's business but my own, and his.

She leans closer and lowers her voice. "I know you're seeing him this evening."

I blanch, caught off guard. That doesn't sound like Allen. He's better at keeping confidences than that. She reads my expression then adds, "He didn't tell me. I saw your text on his phone. It popped up when he was over and I couldn't help noticing." She shrugs like she's sorry, but I'm certain she's not. I get the idea she spies on Allen often.

"Yeah? So?" I set my chin, unwilling to share any information with her. I also don't see the point in denying what she already obviously knows.

Teresa ominously lowers her eyebrows. "So does Sadie."

"I don't have anything to hide," I say, but my pulse pounds furiously, beating relentlessly in my ears. Making my face hot. I pick up my latte, take one minuscule sip which I find very hard to swallow.

"Look," Teresa says. "Allen says that you two are over, and I for one believe him. Sadie, though? She's cut from a different cloth. Not as understanding as I once was. She's . . ." A dramatic pause and then she finishes, ". . . unpredictable."

My heart slams into my chest and I'm suddenly back in Sadie's foyer. She's choking the living daylights out of me, like a woman who's completely lost control. That was during Emma's kidnapping so I let that excuse it. But I can't deny that Sadie's got that side to her, when provoked.

Teresa sets down her cup, twirls it around in her slim fingers. "I just wanted you to be prepared," she says. "On guard." She purses her lips. "In case."

"Sadie doesn't know anything about the past," I say.

"I'm afraid she does."

"What makes you say that?"

Teresa sinks back in her chair. "I told her." There's no regret in her tone, only a grim finality, like this is an outcome she not only predicted but wanted.

She's hoping to put the fear of God in me about Sadie. I take my latte with me and go. Don't bother to thank her. I know when a woman's being catty. She's loving this moment. Probably thinking unkind things about me, her gaze glued to my back as I round the corner and—crap—nearly run smack into Kate!

She acts like she's retying her apron, looking down at her hands rather than staring in front of her and at me. What was she doing so close to our table? Eavesdropping? I shudder.

Teresa knowing about Allen and me is one thing and Sadie's going to have to face the music sooner or later. But I still don't want my business getting all over town. Besides that, Kate's got problems and I've got enough problems of my own.

SADIE
THE WIFE

Now

It's the second night with Allen away, and I have trouble sleeping, tossing and turning in my empty bed. Each time I drift off to sleep I reach out instinctively for Allen, try to snuggle up against his back, spoon in. I wake up with a start and stare at our empty room, my mind churning. My soul cries out in the shadows. I'm so desperately afraid of what will happen next.

If Allen is innocent, why hasn't he turned himself in? And, if he's guilty, you'd think he'd want to bring things mercifully to an end. Grant us some closure, me and Emma, because I couldn't abide Allen living here if he's guilty of murder. I've decided that. Even if he's never charged or becomes acquitted, I would still know.

It's so quiet in this house without Allen and Emma here. Though, yes, I'm grateful Emma is gone. Pat and Gayle will dote on her endlessly and spoil her rotten on that cruise, possibly even make her impossible to live with when she comes home. I sit up in bed and hold the duvet to my chest, knowing, no, that's not Emma. She's not one of those diva little girls. She's a sweetheart through and through.

A noise startles me out of my skin.

Glass breaking downstairs.

And then footsteps, someone moving in the den, crossing through the kitchen, climbing the back stairs. If it's Allen he doesn't call out, doesn't try to calm me. So maybe it's someone else, like Diane, or I don't know who, maybe the person who really killed Cass, if it wasn't Allen. Someone who's come for me. Or maybe it's Allen himself and Diane was right.

My heart leaps into my throat and I spring out of bed, race down the front steps and grapple with the front door, its dead bolt and chain. Someone runs down the upstairs hall. A shadow standing at the top of the very steep staircase.

I scream and wrench open the front door.

Run out of the house, barrel down the driveway and toward the police cruiser.

Officer Patel steps out immediately from behind the steering wheel, her hand laid on her pistol. "Sadie?" she asks alarmed, staring up at the house, at the open front door. Her partner, Brady, is out on the pavement through his door in a flash.

"Someone's in there!" I wheeze. "They broke in!"

"Could it have been Allen?" Patel asks quickly. "Did you recognize the person or their shape, anything at all?"

I shake my head. "It was too dark. I was frightened. Didn't want to stick around to look closely."

"Stay here," Patel commands, making her way toward the house. She motions to Brady who follows her. First, he opens the back door to their cruiser. "You wait in here. I'll call for backup. We have other patrols in the area, who should get here quickly."

I huddle in the back seat of the cop car, watch their flashlight beams pan the downstairs of my house, train through the upstairs rooms. The police officers who were stationed in front of Cass's house pull around to meet them. When that car arrives I climb out of the cruiser.

"See anything?" Patel asks the other team, as she comes down the driveway toward them.

"That's a negative and we were watching closely," one of the other cops answers. I see his name is Gomez. He addresses me directly next. "But the gate between your house and Ms. Thomas's was left ajar."

Patel instructs Gomez and his partner to return to their post in front of Cass's house, as a third police car arrives. Patel explains the situation to the officers and the first one says, "We'll check around out back." Her name is Johnson. "See what we can see."

Patel stares at me when they leave. "A pane in the patio door was broken, and someone turned the dead bolt from the outside to come in. We've called in our forensics unit to dust for prints. I'm not sure if they'll get anything, but it's worth a shot." She glances at Brady. "Can you hunt around for something to patch things up temporarily once they're done?" She turns to me. "Maybe some duct tape? Cardboard?"

I nod. "We've got both things in the garage." I speak to Brady next. "I can show you where they are."

The third set of officers returns within minutes after we're all back in the house, and Officer Johnson fills us in. "Looks like the individual in question might have slipped behind the shed in Cass's neighbor's yard and that tall row of camellias in the backyard abutting yours to the right, thereby avoiding detection from the street." She points out the window beyond the breakfast room table. "There were footprints trailing from behind the shed to the next yard over, where a house is for sale. A dirt footpath directly across the street from the vacant house leads into the woods."

Patel absorbs this information then turns to ask me, "Where does that footpath go?"

I release a shaky breath. "To the playground." The playground that connects to the greenway trail. That's the same way Allen was seen going by Diane. Allen knows this neighborhood well, but it still seems so unlike him to have broken in.

"I'll let the chief know our surveillance missed this," Patel assures me. "No doubt she'll want to step things up even further."

A short time later, the police patch up the broken glass in the back door, as the forensics team leaves.

Patel addresses me in the kitchen area while Brady finishes covering the broken pane in the door with heavy cardboard and duct tape. She's just gotten off the phone after having a private conversation with Chief Claremont while standing in my dining room. "Given that incident"—she nods toward the patio door—"I think you'd be safer with one of us staying inside tonight until we can get that broken door pane repaired tomorrow. Chief Claremont agrees."

"I don't want to be a bother," I tell her.

"It's no bother," she assures me professionally. "It's our job." She glances at Brady. "I'll stay." I offer her blankets for the sofa but she says she intends to sit up and keep an eye on the house. Once Brady goes and Patel has situated herself in the den, I consider my intruder, wondering if it was Allen. It's hard to imagine him breaking into his own house, unless he felt a desperate need to because he had no key.

Wait.

O'Reilly's admonition comes back to me about bringing in the spare key we typically keep outside. We used to keep one under the flowerpot on the patio but changed its location after Emma's kidnapping because too many people knew about it after that. We now hide a key in a fake rock near Emma's sandbox, and I did bring that inside after O'Reilly's warning. But there's an additional key we keep in the house.

It's the key ring we use when we don't need our whole sets holding car keys and such, only the single key to this house. For instance, when we're going on a run or a walk, or elsewhere in the neighborhood like the pool or playground. We keep that single key in a drawer in the hall table in the foyer. I look for it now, and it's gone.

One of us could have misplaced it, but I don't think so. What's more likely is that Allen took it when he left, thinking he'd use it to get back in, but why and when? My forehead warms when I consider telling the police. Though I don't know for sure Allen has it, it's only a heavy hunch. I'm also incredibly conflicted about whether I want to see Allen or not. Maybe if we talk things out and he explains his actions, I'll feel so much better about everything.

Or, maybe I won't. My darker fear is that he won't be coming here to talk, he'll be coming here to silence me like Diane said, because I now know too much.

I know that Allen was with Cass the night she died and I know she told him something upsetting. I also heavily suspect he snuck back over to her house at two a.m. and the very next morning the woman was dead.

I peek down the hall and out the breakfast nook window at my floodlit yard and the gate to Cass's house. I can see a police cruiser parked at the end of her driveway and through the sidelight by my front door I see Brady in his cop car on our street. Another patrol car eases by and does a slow turnaround in the cul-de-sac. The police presence is strong, and Officer Patel is staying in the house, so I'm safe for the night.

But where is Allen hiding?

ALLEN
THE HUSBAND

Now

I get up Sunday morning and go for a run thinking of Sadie. Being cut off from communications without my phone and electricity puts me at a disadvantage. I need to find a way to talk to her, but heavily suspect the police are watching our house, and on the lookout for me. I wear a baseball hat and aviator-style sunglasses as a precaution. The sunglasses belonged to my dad and are a relic from the nineteen seventies. They literally cover half my face.

I stop into a convenience store on my route. It's the small lakeside shop with a dock that sells petrol for boats and where I've been buying my modest groceries. I check the local newspapers stacked by the door on my way in. My face is splashed across the front page. I'm wanted for questioning as a suspect in Cass's murder.

I steal a look at the cashier laughing and chatting on his cell phone. He's not the kind of dude who reads the papers or listens to the news, so at least—here—I'll have no worries. I can live with being named in the inquiry and will find a way to explain things to the police. A court can't really convict me without a murder weapon, can they? Any evidence they've got must be circumstantial, like my fingerprints at Cass's house.

Those only prove I was there, not that I'm guilty of Cass's murder. I don't have the full story about what really happened that night. All I have is what Sadie told me.

After I bring Emma home from Gayle and Pat's, I'm watering our plants outdoors when I hear a window shatter behind me. I spin around to stare at Cass's house then glance indoors, where Emma sits cross-legged on the love seat in our den watching television. Sadie hasn't come home yet. Where is she?

I wait and watch Cass's house. Then I try contacting Cass on the message app we use. No answer. I get a real prickly feeling that something has gone seriously wrong. I try to busy myself in the yard. Do some hedge clipping along the back fence and keep my eye on Cass's house. All seems quiet inside. Too quiet maybe.

I try texting Cass one more time but get nothing.

I'm suddenly gripped by fear. Did Sadie go over there? Maybe to confront Cass? How would she have known to do that to begin with? Who could have told her I'd be there, because that's the only explanation for her going herself. And then, it hits me. Only one person was aware of Cass's and my plans to meet up, apart from the two of us.

I heave a frustrated sigh.

Teresa.

ALLEN
THE HUSBAND

Before

I drop Forrest off at Teri's on Wednesday evening. She's taking him back early on account of Sadie's and my trip, and wants a few days with him before sending him to stay with his grandma over spring break.

"I'm so happy for y'all, Allen," she says sweetly. "You two deserve it."

When she's like this I understand why it was so easy for me to love her. Teresa has so many strong suits. She was just never the right person for me. I'm glad we're all settled with that now and she's with Henry. He seems like a really great guy.

"Thanks, Teri. It will be great to get away. We can't wait. Did I show you the website for our resort? It's amazing."

"No, you didn't."

I can't help wanting to share. I pull out my phone and bring up the link and click it. The page loads, the glamorous resort on display with a ritzy main building and expansive cabanas hugging the shore. Palm trees dot the white-sand beach and the ocean's teal blue. Palapas shielding lounge chairs line the beach. "Each cabana has its own private hot tub."

"Oh, nice!" She takes my phone and holds it, flipping through the resort's galley.

"If it's as great as I think, I'll share the info. Maybe you and Henry would like to go sometime?"

"Henry? Sure." Suddenly she stops and frowns, staring at my phone. "You just had a message alert pop up." She stares at me cockeyed and wrinkles her nose. "From Cass? Something about seeing you tomorrow at her house, six thirty?"

Oh shit. I take back my phone. "Yeah, sorry. She's been wanting to meet up."

"About what?"

"No idea."

"Allen," she says in singsongy tones. "Careful there. The woman might still be after you." Teri's always thought that about Cass, ever since back in the day.

I laugh at her teasing. "Don't think so. She knows I'm tight with Sadie."

"O-kay." She pauses then asks, "How did Cass get your number?"

I shrug. "It's in the neighborhood directory, I guess."

"Your cell?"

"Yeah, sure. Sadie and I don't have a landline." I attempt to put her suspicions at ease, because Teri is a suspicious woman. "Look, I'm sure that it's nothing major, but she's started texting a lot, so I decided it would be better to meet up with her in person and clear the air."

Teresa gasps. "Oh my God, Allen. Tell me it's not true. You never told Sadie about you and Cass?"

"Come on, Teri. What was the point? That was years ago."

"Well." She bites her lip. "The point might have been transparency. She is your neighbor. She was a person of interest in Emma's kidnapping."

"Yeah, so were you!"

"Touché. But the police were looking at you too, Allen. Don't tell me that they weren't."

"Hey, all of that is over, thank God. Emma is safe and Sadie and I have been trying to move on. Now that things are going so much better,

I'm not about to rock the boat. Cass and I were over way before Sadie and I met. Sadie might not understand. She can get a tad—jealous."

"You don't say," Teresa comments sassily.

I hold up my thumb and forefinger and she laughs.

"That just proves what a catch you are, Allen Wilson."

"Yeah, right." I shake my head, ready to end this conversation, which is really none of Teri's business. "In any case, I'm off! I hope Forrest has a great time with his grandma."

Her eyes sparkle brightly. "Have the best time on your trip!"

O'REILLY
THE COP

Now

Val and I go see Sadie early Sunday morning, before heading in to the station. We got a call from Officer Patel shortly after midnight last night, saying Sadie had experienced a break-in even on top of the added security at Cass Thomas's, but that everything was under control. They called in an extra team to help them and Patel consulted by phone with the chief. Val and I wave to Brady parked on the street and he waves in return. Another pair will take over shortly for Brady and Patel. They've been here all night.

"You're not convinced that Allen killed Cass Thomas, are you?" Val asks as we approach Sadie's front door. Val's always so astute when it comes to me. I might keep things from other folks, but not her.

"No."

"Why not?"

"I've never liked him, it's true, and I hate how he treated Sadie."

"But?" Val asks leadingly.

"But then, there's Emma. He does authentically love his kid. I do believe that much is true. I felt it, *saw it*, during our investigation into Emma's kidnapping. Would Allen really kill someone in cold blood, knowing what that could mean for his family? For his wife? His little girl?"

"Maybe it wasn't in cold blood?" Val shrugs. "Maybe it was in the heat of the moment?"

"Yeah," I say, conceding, though doubts niggle at me. "Maybe."

I wait as she rings the bell and Patel greets us, then steps outside with her things to give us a moment with Sadie who's in her office. Sadie comes and joins us in the living room. "Please, have a seat." She tells us what she knows, which isn't much. "Someone broke in, but I couldn't see who it was, just a looming figure in the shadows."

"Man? Woman?" I ask. Val and I are on the sofa and Sadie's in a chair.

"It's hard to say," Sadie answers. "It was dark, my eyes were still adjusting after having been woken up. I gave a full report to the police last night and they entered everything."

"Sadie," I say, "I've got to ask, and I hope you'll be truthful with me because I know you want to help Allen."

"Allen didn't do this." She firmly shakes her head. "Couldn't have broken in and I know my husband. He couldn't have killed Cass."

"If not him, then who?" I ask.

"Isn't that the police's job to find out?" she banters boldly.

Rodriguez raises her eyebrows at that retort. "Fair."

"We learned what Allen was doing at Teresa's," Val volunteers.

The color drains from Sadie's face. "Oh?"

"We believe he took Forrest's old ten-speed bike from their shed, which is how he got away so quickly," Val says. "Any thoughts on where he's gone?"

Sadie's shoulders sink under the weight of our questions. "I told you before and I'll say it again, I have no clue where Allen's disappeared to. Have you checked area hotels and the like?"

Val nods. "We're looking."

I meet Sadie's eyes with a serious stare. "Sadie, you're going to need to face the fact that Allen's in this deep. He's wanted as a suspect in a woman's murder. We have evidence that places him at the scene and a witness who saw him fleeing the area. The best thing you can do for Allen is to encourage him to turn himself in and come down to the station for questioning. If he's as innocent as you believe he is, coming clean is the best way for him to clear his name."

"What about Allen's computer and phone?" she asks. "Did you find anything on them?"

"His computer search history was unremarkable," I answer. "Nothing unusual in his emails. His phone showed mostly text communications with you, along with routine messages to Teresa about Forrest's visitation arrangements."

"Nothing to or from Cass?"

Val darts a look at me before responding and I nod for her to go ahead. "We think they might have been communicating over an app that delivers end-to-end encryption," Val explains to Sadie. "You can set it to delete messages instantly after they've been read."

"What makes you think Allen was using this app?"

"He had it downloaded on his phone," I tell her, "but he had only one contact."

Sadie frowns before stating what all of us know. "Cass."

SADIE
THE WIFE

Before

I drive to Teresa's house to drop off Forrest's soccer gear on Thursday afternoon. Forrest left it at our house by mistake yesterday, and he'll need it for his soccer practice later. I've just left Emma at Pat and Gayle's house, and they live close by.

Teresa's been working from home today so she's around. Said she was preparing a research grant proposal, or something like that, and could work better without the distractions at the observatory.

Teresa's rustic A-frame house resembles a charming chalet like you might find in the Swiss Alps. I hate that she and Allen built it together, envisioning it as their dream house. Allen and I never designed our own home or picked out all the particulars—from state-of-the-art appliances to high exposed wood beams. Even though Teresa's house is fourteen years old, everything gleams like new here. Outside, the house is understated elegance. Inside, it's classy chic with stunning views and the guaranteed privacy that living on two acres affords.

She opens the door and I hand over Forrest's soccer cleats, and the sports bag holding his uniform and kneepads next. "Thanks for bringing these by." She smiles politely but I never fully trust Teresa's smile. I've seen her use this same subtle grin with Henry. The only time she smiles warmly is when she's looking at Allen. I'm aware I should pity her, and in some ways I do. In others, it disgusts me to believe she's still not over him, but I hide it, and act like everything's cool between the three of us: Teresa, Allen and me. Because it's me he's chosen after all.

"It's no problem," I tell her. "You were on my way."

Teresa nods and sets Forrest's things on a bench by the door. It's an outdoor bench under a covered front porch with wide wooden floorboards. An assortment of hiking boots and shoes is tucked beneath it. "Thanks! I know how busy you are with you and Allen leaving on your trip Saturday and Emma getting ready for her trip too."

"Yes, I've got a lot of last-minute running around to do these next couple of days. Pat and Gayle are having Emma over for a while so they can get her prepped for their travels with the fun photos and videos they've received from the cruise line. They need to select certain adventures and register for those in advance, so they're wanting Emma's opinion." I laugh. "Hula lessons or swim with dolphins, things like that."

"That sounds *amazing*," Teresa says. "How fantastic for Emma. I would have killed to take a trip like that at her age." She chuckles and shakes her head at the excess. "In fact, I wouldn't mind taking one like that now. Swim with dolphins. Really? That's so cool."

I get that the cruise is a bit extravagant for an almost seven-year-old girl, but I also know how much fun she's going to have, so I'm happy to let her aunties spoil her.

"Yeah," I agree with Teresa. "Pat and Gayle are pretty special. They're helping Emma make a packing list for her big adventure as well. I'll pack for her of course, but since she's growing older she wants to feel involved."

"Of course. Sounds like a very busy evening for y'all." Teresa gets an odd twist to her lips then pulls a face. "And on top of everything already on your plate, poor Allen's got his after-work chat with Cass tonight." I feel like I've been hit by a Mack truck. Teresa rolls her eyes. "I'm sure you'll both be glad when that's over. Guess he really wants to get things settled before your romantic vacation."

"I'm sorry. What?" I don't mean to sound stunned but her statement knocks the wind out of me. My eyebrows knit together. "Allen's meeting up with Cass? Our neighbor, Cass Thomas?" This truly came from out of the blue. Allen barely knows Cass. I mean, they were acquainted in high school but just barely, and she was unfortunately named a person of interest in Emma's kidnapping case. Allen and I have tried to put that behind us and have been cordial to Cass of course. We've waved or said hello when we've seen her outside, commented politely on the weather. All harmless stuff. Or so I thought.

Teresa bites her bottom lip and grimaces. "Shoot. Maybe I shouldn't have said anything." She moves back a step and holds open her hands. "Listen, Sadie. I don't want to get between you and Allen. So if he hasn't told you . . ." She shrugs.

"What do you mean Allen's having a little chat with Cass? How would you know that?" I ask that pointed question because I expect a direct answer. Anger boils up inside me. *You have got to fucking be kidding me!* Allen told Teresa about this, and not me. And why the hell is he meeting up with Cass, of all people?

Teresa hangs her head and heat prickles my eyes.

Fuck me. He's put his Teri first once again.

I set my jaw so I don't cry. Still, my cheeks burn hot.

"Look," Teresa says trying to placate me, like she's the grown-up and I'm the child, which only pisses me off further. "I'm sure it's nothing." And yet, her eyes gleam with doubt. "Allen's just trying to put old ghosts to rest. He's doing it for you, Sadie."

"Why does it matter what happened in high school?" I ask in disbelief.

She lowers her voice and looks around as if others might hear, though we're basically in the middle of nowhere. "I wouldn't be so sure that's *all* there was between them." Her eyes glint tellingly. "High school."

I keep trying to catch up and repeatedly missing steps. But this step is impossible to ignore. Allen's been involved with Cass Thomas? Fucking unbelievable! No, I won't buy it. Teresa's trying to make trouble between us. She's smart and likes to play head games.

"Anyway." Again that fake smile and those guileless brown eyes. "I wouldn't worry too much about it, if I were you. It's you that Allen loves. I'm sure he'll set Cass straight." What does that mean? Is Cass still hanging on? Angling to reunite with Allen? Is there something more? A hidden truth I'm not aware of? I'm sure as hell not asking Teresa to fill me in, just to watch her gloat. She's always been jealous of what Allen and I have.

Uncertainty tugs at me and I feel sick to my stomach at the thought of Cass living so nearby. Reexamine every time I've seen and spoken to her through a new lens. The friendly way she looks at Allen is obviously more than friendly. Shit. How could I have been so clueless? And, if it's true that Allen and Cass have something going on, then how can Teresa be so callous? Dropping this on me now, two days before our trip?

I'm almost speechless but I force out the words. "I'd better get going. I've got tons to do."

"Of course!" She stages a sunny wave. "Have the *best* time in Aruba! Text pics!"

Like hell we will.

"Thanks, Teresa." My stomach sours and my heart aches.

As I climb into my SUV, Teresa ducks back into her house, leaving Forrest's soccer things outside. I can't help but question her motives in telling me about Allen seeing Cass. Has she embellished some truth to cast Allen in a bad light? Maybe she's intentionally trying to drive a wedge between us. Teresa covets my happiness with Allen and always has. If that's what she's doing, intentionally trying to cause trouble, it's not only mean spirited but also uncharitable—and devious. And there's no doubt about it, Teresa's got a sneaky side.

SADIE
THE WIFE

Now

I'm doing our laundry, attempting to keep my mind on normal things. I washed our bed linens because I couldn't stand the scent of Allen on his pillow. Though I have a feeling tonight I'll miss it badly. I'm so mixed up. Hating him and needing him. Not knowing what he's done, or why. He's left such a mess for me to deal with, I don't even begin to know how to sort it out. I pull the tangle of damp sheets from the washer and heap them in the dryer, add a dryer sheet and turn the machine on.

It's late morning on Sunday, two days after Cass's body was found, and the police still haven't found Allen. It's probably only a matter of time before they turn their interrogation spotlight on me, when they learn I was also at Cass's house on Thursday night and that I spoke with her. If they somehow discover we argued that will appear even more damning. I shouldn't have lost my cool with Cass, should never have let things get out of hand. What the hell was I thinking? How did I let myself lose control? Allen and I should have been in Aruba today enjoying a carefree vacation, but now Aruba's fucked. That's unfortunately the least of my worries.

I hear a text alert in the kitchen and leave the laundry room to check my phone.

It's Pat checking in and asking how I'm doing. Gayle and Emma are off on their swim-with-dolphins adventure, and she's hanging back on the ship.

Same, I answer. No news.

She sends a bunch of prayer emojis and then a slew of pics. Emma stands with Pat and Gayle on the ship's upper deck and various flags whip in the wind behind them. They're near the railing and all wear cute captain's hats.

There are others of them at a fancy dinner table with linen tablecloths and floral centerpieces. The tables are long and they're seated by another family with two young girls, and aww—look at that!—the ship's captain with his arm around Gayle. Gayle's such a charmer she probably finagled a spot at his table. I'm so happy for them all, so glad for my little girl. I'm relieved that Emma is having fun and not embroiled in a manhunt that involves her father. O'Reilly's been keeping me posted, even if it's only to say there's nothing yet.

I hope I'll hear something more from him today.

O'REILLY
THE COP

Now

Claremont calls an emergency meeting at noon. She starts her briefing with a bang. "Still no news on Allen and his whereabouts, but we're doggedly pursuing every avenue in locating him. Checking CCTV, local hotels, asking in convenience stores and supermarkets, out-of-the-way eateries, and we've distributed a plea with his photo for public information through all our media sources and online."

She takes a sip of coffee and sets her tumbler on the table in front of her. "We dusted for prints after Sadie Wilson's break-in but the perpetrator must have taken precautions because forensics got nothing on that end. We do have some new evidence relating to the crime scene which could potentially implicate another person of interest—or a suspect, because we now have it confirmed that a second individual was at Cass's house the night she died, and this is the individual who we believe argued with Cass or, possibly worse, might have killed her."

Claremont indicates the crime scene photos. There are shots of the living room and kitchen pinned to the board. The living room photos show the body as it was found by the coffee table, and a kitchen shot is of the smashed window facing Cass's deck.

The chief folds her arms behind her back to inform us, "The analysis came back on the clothing fibers found in the broken window. They're a match with a dark-brown wool knit sweater." Her eyes twinkle intriguingly. "It's a very particular type of wool from sheep in the Shetland Islands. There's only one boutique manufacturer that sells these sweaters online and probably only a small handful of clients in Chapel Roads who've purchased from them. They've shared the list."

Val and I stare at each other.

Sadie.

SADIE
THE WIFE

Now

The police are here for the second time today, interrupting my lunch. Not that I've felt much like eating lately anyway. I leave my half-eaten sandwich on a plate on the kitchen table and go to answer the door. It's O'Reilly and Rodriguez. I can tell from their frowns it's more bad news. "I'm sorry, Sadie," O'Reilly says as he enters the foyer. "We're going to need to take you down to the station for questioning in connection with Cass Thomas's suspicious death. We now have forensic evidence that places you at the scene the night Cass died." Oh my God. I wonder which evidence that is, but I don't dare ask them. I'm not stupid enough to incriminate myself.

My pulse pounds in my ears when I ask, "Am I under arrest?"

"No," O'Reilly says. "We just want to talk at this point." I'm wondering if I'll need a lawyer but worry that if I ask about that they'll automatically assume the worst. So I sit on that question for now, hoping things don't get worse.

"We're also going to need your brown cardigan sweater," Rodriguez adds.

Crap. They're worse.

The window. That must be it. Some of my sweater threads must have gotten tangled up in it somehow, but how on earth can they know that sweater is mine? I could deny it, I suppose. There are bound to be loads of brown wool knit sweaters worn by people around here. I step in front of the threshold to the living room, blocking their view of my open office. "Which brown sweater is that?"

Rodriguez points behind me. "We'll take that one, if you don't mind."

My stomach sinks as I glance over my shoulder and see my brown cardigan sweater hanging from the back of my computer chair. There can only be one reason they want it. To compare it to the forensic evidence they have. And if the police are clever enough to have already made a match, bringing in my sweater for analysis will only confirm it. Dammit. I'm caught.

I hold up both hands. "Look, this isn't what you think! I didn't do it! I didn't kill Cass." I should shut up. They might not believe me. I had a motive to kill Cass, but they probably don't know that. Or have they learned that too?

O'Reilly sets his hands on his hips. "I think it would be better if we talked down at the station. We want to get a formal statement about your whereabouts two nights ago."

"I was out running errands," I answer too quickly.

Rodriguez opens her notebook. "Can anyone vouch for that?"

I blanch at her question. "What is this? Am I a suspect now?"

"You might want to grab your purse," O'Reilly says, "and that sweater if you please."

Fuck me.

I retrieve my sweater with shaky hands and pass it to them. Make fists and tighten my fingers to quell their spasms. "Do I need a lawyer?"

O'Reilly tilts his head. "You tell me."

"No, Shane. No." I use his first name to drive the point home. "You know me. I wouldn't, couldn't—"

"Let's do all this officially," Rodriguez says and pulls open the front door. She means in that claustrophobic room with the two-way mirror and cameras.

Fuck.

O'Reilly nods for me to go first. "After you."

SADIE
THE WIFE

Now

I'm down at the station in one of those sterile, white-painted cinder block rooms with a two-way mirror. The sort I'd hoped I'd never have to enter again. Rodriguez leaves me alone with O'Reilly, then Claremont enters. Shit. This can't be good. The deputy chief and chief of police both here together. They're bringing in their top guns. Their sharp shooters. If I'm not a suspect yet, I'm very close to being one.

"Sadie," Chief Claremont says and nods. "It's been a while." She pulls out a chair and sits and O'Reilly sits beside her. I'm seated across from them, my hands resting on the table. I'm not handcuffed or anything like that. God, no. The very idea makes me ill. The very thought of going to prison. Being locked away. The lights in the room seem to brighten then dim. Maybe I'm going to faint. "Still no word from Allen?" she asks with probing blue eyes.

I swallow hard past the lump in my throat. "No."

"I'm sure Deputy Chief O'Reilly filled you in about our finding forensic evidence on the scene that's a very probable match to your brown cardigan sweater. Sadie," she says, "we need to know where you were the night Cass died."

"Is that an official or unofficial question?"

She stops the recording on her phone. "You wanted to say something off the record?"

I feel tripped up, like I don't know the A answer. Will my asking for counsel make me seem more guilty or not? "I'm just wondering if I need an attorney present before we proceed."

She sends O'Reilly a look then answers, "You're entitled to a phone call, if you'd like one. We have no problem with that."

Yes, but who should I contact? Apart from Allen, damn him, my most trusted people are Pat and Gayle, and they're out of the country—with Emma. I would never alarm them over this. Not yet. Not now. Besides, what could they do from there? They're on a cruise.

We don't have a regular attorney either. Who does? There was the woman who wrote up our wills, but Allen hired her after Emma was born and I can't even remember her name. We had a real estate attorney do our settlement when we purchased our house, but that's the wrong kind of law too. The state could appoint a lawyer for me, but I'm not sure I should ask for one now. That will only make me look more guilty. No.

What I need to do is phone a friend. I should let someone else know I've been brought down to the precinct. In case they decide to hold me, in case things get worse. But I've got no one to reach out to. I have a few casual mom friends, the mothers of Emma's playmates, and women I chat with at the gym, a group of yoga buddies that I occasionally lunch with. I am not phoning any of them.

There's only one person left.

"I would like to make a phone call, if that's okay?"

"You can use your own phone," O'Reilly says. "That's fine." He pushes back in his chair. "We'll wait."

And listen.

Great.

I punch in her number and she picks up right away. "Sadie? Hey, what's going on?"

"I'm down at the police station, Teresa."

"Oh, Sadie." She sounds distressed. "Is it Allen? Have they found him?"

"No," I say in warbly tones. "It's me. They've brought me in for questioning."

"What? You? You've got to be kidding me. Why?"

"They just want to ask me some questions. I'm sure everything will be okay."

"Don't worry," she says with the fierceness of a lioness protecting her cub, "I'll be right there." I've never been a fan of Teresa's, but at the moment I couldn't value her more.

"Thanks."

Claremont sets her phone to record. "Let's resume our questioning. Where were you the evening Cass Thomas died?" She gives the date.

I think of my sweater and how Rodriguez and O'Reilly had me bring it in. They turned it over to someone in the evidence room. I'm quite sure it will be analyzed. They must have gotten fibers from the window somehow. Maybe some of them snagged in the glass when it shattered. After they analyze fibers from the sweater itself, they'll know that for sure it's a match and that I was there. So, if I say I didn't see Cass that night, they'll know I'm lying.

I heave a breath to calm myself and then I begin, carefully devising my story. "I had some errands to run on Thursday afternoon. Emma was at Pat and Gayle's and then . . ."

Claremont's forehead wrinkles. "And then?"

"I went to Cass's house to confront her." I avoid O'Reilly's eyes. He was my ally once and I feel strangely like I'm disappointing him, letting him down. That's silly. Maybe he doesn't really believe that it's me who's done it, the one who killed Cass. Maybe he's secretly pulling for me. That would be nice.

"What time was this?" Claremont writes something in her notebook even though she's got a voice recording. I dart a look at the video cameras suspended from two corners of the room. There's likely a video feed too, and someone on the other side of that mirror is watching. Who? Officers Patel and Brady? Captain Rodriguez? Are they betting on outcomes, eating popcorn? What? I really hate this.

I spin my cell phone around in my hands, turn it over, face down on the table. If I were truly in custody they wouldn't let me have this or my purse, but I'm not. "Around six thirty." I push my hair back behind my ear and continue. "I'd received some information about Cass and Allen, and I wanted to speak with her about it."

Claremont looks up from her note-taking. "What kind of information was that?"

"I learned that the two of them were meeting up on Thursday after Allen's work."

"Who told you that, Sadie?" O'Reilly asks.

"Teresa Wilson, but I'm not sure she meant to. It might have been inadvertent, or maybe it was intentional. I don't know. It's sometimes hard to say with Teresa."

"And yet, you just phoned her for support?" Claremont asks skeptically.

"Come on, Chief," O'Reilly says. "Who else is Sadie going to call? Her best friends are away with her kid, and Allen's gone AWOL."

Claremont shrugs. "I'm sure Teresa has her strengths." She pins her attention back on me. "So what was it that Teresa let slip exactly?"

I sigh and gather my wits, at least feeling like Shane is on my side. Not so sure about Claremont, but then that's her job as chief of police. Shane likes me because it's personal. We developed a connection during Emma's kidnapping and I appreciate his compassion.

"Teresa hinted that Cass and Allen needed to settle something, made some insinuations about them either being currently involved, or having been romantically involved in the past, and beyond their high school years."

"Oh yeah?" Claremont looks me straight in the eye. "So what did you do?"

"I wanted to learn what was really going on between them. So I decided I needed to talk to Cass myself."

"Cass but not to Allen?" Claremont asks.

"Yes, her initially. I thought I'd get more from her one-on-one, you know. Woman to woman." I roll back my shoulders and say, "But first, I wanted to make sure that Teresa had been telling the truth about Allen and Cass meeting up. I needed to see for myself if Allen was *lying* when he said he was staying late at work."

"And was he?" O'Reilly asks.

SADIE
THE WIFE

Before

I'm parked at the curb behind some other cars a few houses down from where Cass lives. She steers her Jeep Cherokee into her driveway and parks, getting out, but she doesn't see me from her vantage point because I'm farther down the street. She carries her purse and a paper coffee cup to an outdoor dumpster and drops the coffee cup in before rolling the trash can to the curb. Tomorrow is trash pickup day in our neighborhood, same thing on my street. She goes inside and turns on some lights at the back of her house.

That's Cass's kitchen. I know this from the one time I went inside, when we arranged that failed playdate between Emma and Cass's imaginary kid, Bobby. I mean, the woman is clearly fucked in the head. What on earth can Allen want with her? How can he be attracted? Is it her looks? Her curvy figure? What the hell *what*? I realize I'm working myself up but I can't help it. I can't believe that I'm actually sitting here stalking my neighbor.

I hope it's all for naught, and that Teresa's lying. I'd hate her for that, but at least I'd know that's her way. That she's done it just to make waves between me and Allen. She wants to sink our ship so she can dive into deep water with him. Well, guess what, Teresa? You're out of luck.

I'm not taking your stupid bait. I huff when I realize I already am. She's got me in a state and that's probably what she wanted. I draw in some deep breaths and release them, close my eyes and count to ten. Maybe Allen won't show?

That hope grows feeble as night starts to fall. Cass's house is yellow with black shutters and smaller than ours, but the exterior of it is neatly kept with boxwoods hedging the front porch railing and a flagstone path leading to the driveway. Her outdoor porch light turns on. She's preparing for his arrival. Expecting someone, like I am. A pair of headlights creeps down the street and a blinker flickers on, indicating a left turn. My stomach sinks.

That's Allen's SUV turning into Cass's driveway.

I can't believe Teresa was telling the truth. That Allen's meeting up with Cass. That there's something going on between Cass and my husband or *was* at the very least. A silent rage builds inside me, so furious and fierce I can't contain it. Can't bottle it up and hold it in. I feel like such a fool. So taken advantage of. They've both been lying to me, but for how long? Teresa acted like it was over. That whatever had happened between Allen and Cass was in the past. But we're not talking about high school now, are we? We're talking about the here and now, and the evidence stands before me as plain as day. Allen's on Cass's front porch. *Fuck.*

I stare at Cass's house considering my options. Will Allen catch me here, sequestered in the shadows like a low-rent private detective from some cheap noir film? No, he doesn't see me in my SUV. He's got his hands in his pants pockets and is hanging his head. Cass's door pops open and he looks up, as she asks him in then shuts the door.

Should I confront them both? Storm in and ask what the hell's going on? No. I need to handle this carefully. If I ambush them together, it will be two against one. They'll back each other up some-how. Side against me and gaslight me about the entire thing. Act like I've heightened the situation in my head, making it out to be more than it really is. That's just like Allen, isn't it? To make it all about me and my paranoia, the frailty of my feelings. Well, I'm about a hundred times stronger than he knows.

I wait and watch for Allen to leave but he doesn't. Five minutes turns to ten, and ten to fifteen. Twenty. They could be screwing in there for all I know. Ripping each other's clothes off. Making love on her kitchen counter, on the couch or the floor, for God's sake. And right before our romantic getaway.

There's a metallic taste on my tongue like bitter copper pennies and for an instant I can't breathe. I'm hot all over and lightheaded too. In a cold sweat, as my imagination spirals into worst-case scenarios: Allen and Cass being in love, him leaving me for her. But then I heave a deep breath, my pulse humming. Try to calm down and decide what to do.

Panic won't help me here. What I need is a plan. One thing I know: I've got to put a stop to whatever the hell is going on in there and demand some answers. A calm realization washes over me. But I can't demand answers from Allen. I don't trust him to tell me the truth. I need to speak with Cass alone, because—if she's pushed—I bet she'll tell me.

I mean, it's not like she can deny their involvement *now*. I've basically caught them red-handed meeting up on the sly. But before I can confer with Cass, I need to get my duplicitous husband out of there. I just need to think up a good enough excuse to make him leave.

CASS
THE MISTRESS

Before

Sadie doesn't wait for an invitation, she steamrolls her way right past me. "What was Allen doing here?" She shuts the front door furiously and wheels on me. "Are you two having an affair?" He's only just left moments ago, because Sadie called him about picking up Emma, claiming to be caught up running some errands. What the fuck? Her "errands" were coming here?

I blanch when she comes at me. "An affair? What? No! What on earth are you talking about?" She's wild eyed in a way that scares me, like she was that other time. I back up into the hall and trip over something, the baseball bat Allen dropped on the floor.

"Then why did you ask him over?" she demands.

"For the love of God, were you spying on me?"

"Answer me, Cass." She's incensed, the bridge of her nose and temples pink.

"We had to talk. There was something important I needed to discuss with Allen. Why aren't you asking him yourself?"

"Because I'm asking you." She advances toward me and I bend down, set my hand on the baseball bat's grip. My stomach roils and the lights go out before blinking back on. What the hell? I'm dizzy. The wine? Maybe that allergy tablet I took after sitting outdoors at the coffee shop? I forgot about that when I opened the wine. I probably shouldn't have mixed them. My head feels so light but my body is lead. All sludgy. I stand and grab the wall steadying my palm against it. The baseball bat is in my other hand.

She darts a glance at the bat, and squints suspiciously. "What are you doing with that?"

Sadie moves forward and I retreat, intuiting I'm in danger. Sadie's lost it somehow. She's worked herself into a state. I don't know why she's so fired up, but I've got to keep her at bay—and away from me. "Sadie, stay where you are."

She doesn't. She strides closer, casts a dismissive eye at the baseball bat. "You think you're going to scare me with that? Fat chance, Cass! I want answers!" She's shouting now, Jesus. The neighbors will hear.

I raise a palm in her direction.

I'm *not* letting go of this baseball bat.

My life could depend on it.

"Fine," I say calmly. "I'll tell you anything you want to know." I keep her looking me in the eye so she doesn't notice my subtle movements, how I'm inching closer to the kitchen island where I've left my cell phone.

"Then tell me about you and Allen."

"We dated, yes, it's true, but that was years ago." She tries to see what I'm looking at but I redirect her, staring at the refrigerator instead. She glances that way and scowls, turns back toward me. She insists on knowing more.

"When, Cass? When did you and Allen date?"

"Before you were in the picture, Sadie," I tell her reasonably. I don't want my voice to tremble but it does. "When he was separated from Teresa."

"Oh my God." She looks sick. "And you both kept this from me? All this time, Cass? We've been living here for a year and a half! Neighbors! And—fuck." Her tone converts to a growl. "So that's why Allen defended you during Emma's kidnapping? Why he refused to believe you could do anything sinister? It was because you were former lovers?"

She appears so stricken I slacken my hold on the bat. Step back and continue, "Allen didn't want you to know. When you first moved in he came to see me."

"How rich." Her eyes flash. "This just keeps getting better and better."

"No, Sadie. It wasn't like that. We discussed it and decided to let bygones be bygones. That was so long ago, water under the bridge." I frown sadly. "Only it wasn't."

"What does that mean?"

She does need to know but not like this, not now, not when she's so on edge. "I can't tell you right now. I need to talk to Allen first. He and I have things to work out, discuss."

"What the hell? What do you need to tell him?"

"Sadie, let me talk to Allen, please, and he can explain everything to you later."

"Fuck you!" she spouts. "Fuck you, Cass! You've always been after Allen, and now you what? Want to get my blessing for the two of you to be alone. Sorry. Not happening!"

I dive for the counter and snatch up my phone but in so doing drop the baseball bat. It clatters to the kitchen floor, and she snatches it up. Fuck.

I lift my cell phone up in front of her. "I think you need to go or I'm calling the police."

"On me? What for?"

"I feel threatened," I tell her honestly. "Sadie, you're scaring me. Please go."

"Not until you tell me the truth, Cass."

She raises the baseball bat and my stomach goes sour. "Sadie!"

"How did you find him? When was this affair?"

"It wasn't me who found him. He walked into my bar." I've started babbling and my head doesn't feel right. It's like someone's placed a wedge of cotton in my brain. I don't get it. What's wrong with me?

"What bar?"

"Smokey Joe's downtown." She starts pressing me for details and I start babbling stuff, trying to buy myself time. I have to think, have to get away from her. But it feels really hard to put my thoughts together. My hands shake so badly it's hard to hold the phone. I place the emergency call: nine-one—

Fuck! Sadie springs at me and I drop my phone. It breaks open on the floor, its guts spilling out. She drops the baseball bat and grabs my shoulders, backs me against the wall, but I'm stronger even though I'm dizzy. I fight back and whip her around toward the window. She digs in with her fingers pinching my upper arms. The lights flash. I lose my balance and I fall, dragging her with me. We smash into the window with a crash.

SADIE
THE WIFE

Now

Claremont's getting all of this down in her neat precision scrawl. She writes so tiny I'm amazed anyone can read her notes, including her. I'm hyperaware of the cameras, sensitive to the recording device on the table. Feeling these barren walls close in on me. I imagine a prison cell would be worse. "So, you rang Cass's bell, then what happened next?"

All hell broke loose.

But that's not what I say.

O'Reilly repeats the version of the story I told them as we sit in the interrogation room. I had to doctor it slightly to keep myself from looking bad. I mean, the woman is dead. I can't admit to attacking her, or that I shouted accusations in her face. That would not sit well with a jury. I had to tamp things down. "So you and Cass argued," he summarizes, "and then she admitted to her and Allen's affair."

"Yes, she said it was years ago and that it was over."

Claremont's eyebrows arch. "And you believed her?"

"Of course."

"In that case, why did she want to meet up with Allen?" O'Reilly asks me.

"I think maybe she had designs on him, hopes of the two of them getting back together."

"After all this time?" Claremont asks disbelievingly.

O'Reilly purses his lips and tells her, "During Emma's investigation, Cass did admit to having quite a crush on Allen back in high school. Maybe she never got over it, especially now that we know there was more to their relationship than some infatuation of hers during their teenage years."

I can't tell if they're playing good cop, bad cop with me or whether O'Reilly really believes this. Either way, I appreciate his help. "Exactly," I answer. "That was my take too."

Claremont considers me a moment. "What about the window?"

"Cass became irate when I said it would never happen. Allen is with me now and I'm the woman he loves. I'm pretty sure he told her the same thing and hearing it twice in one night was more than she could bear. She really lost her temper then. I honestly thought she was going to kill me. She bruised my right shoulder when she threw me up against that window. I was afraid for my life."

"Still have the bruise?" Claremont asks.

I lift the short sleeve of my T-shirt peeling it back to reveal my bra strap and the ugly black bruise beneath it.

"Ouch," O'Reilly says. "Looks like that hurt."

"It did." I tug my shirtsleeve back down.

"How did you end things?" Claremont wants to know.

"I got the hell out of there before Cass could take another swing at me," I say emphatically. "She was holding a baseball bat."

"I see." Claremont closes the notebook and turns off her recording device. "Thanks for coming in."

I'm a little stunned it's over so quickly. I blink and stare around the room. "That's it then? I'm free to go?"

O'Reilly stands and pulls back my chair.

"We'll let you know if we need you again," Claremont says. "Don't go anywhere."

TERESA
THE EX-WIFE

Now

Sadie looks like she's been through a war. She emerges from the interrogation room wearing a long face and a frown. I don't really plan it but suddenly I hug her and she squeezes the life out of me. "Thank you for coming."

"Of course." I pat her back thinking this is awkward but also maybe how things are meant to be, the two of us supporting one another under some very fucked circumstances. "Are you okay?" I gently hold her shoulders and she winces, rubs one shoulder when I let go.

"Ooh, sorry. What?"

"Cass attacked me," she says.

"My God. When?"

She drops her voice in a whisper. "Let's not talk here."

"Okay." I nod. "Did you drive your SUV?" I ask her.

"No, they brought me in their squad car."

"Good God. Like some common criminal?" I scowl in sympathy. "That's horrible, Sadie. I'm sorry." I glance at the exit. "Come on, let me drive you home."

"Thanks, Teresa." She sounds really tired, like they've put her through the wringer. I'm sure that was hard for her, being badgered with questions when she's already feeling so frazzled.

"You don't have to thank me," I whisper as we exit by the metal detectors and security checkpoint. "I'm as concerned about this situation as you are." We walk away from the building with three flags out front: one for the county, one for the state, one for the USA. All three whip about in the breeze beneath a clear blue sky. "What did the police want to talk to you about?"

Sadie swallows hard. "About Allen. They wanted to know more about his location but I didn't have anything to tell them, so they asked me about why I went to see Cass."

"Wait." I stop her. "You went to see Cass? Oh no. You mean on the night she died? Shit." I grimace and slap my forehead. "This is all my fault, isn't it? I never should have told you about the two of them meeting up. I probably should have guessed you'd go over there, and now what? You're an actual suspect?"

She shakes her head. "No, I don't think so. They let me go, so—for now at least—they don't have enough to hold me. They did get my sweater though."

I unlock my SUV and we both climb in.

Now she's lost me. "What sweater?"

Her cheeks color when she says, "I went over to Cass's that night to confront her. To confront them both, initially, but then I decided it would be better if I just spoke to her."

"You didn't trust Allen to tell you the truth."

She sounds heartbroken. "I suppose you know him too."

I buckle my seat belt and start the SUV. "So what happened with the sweater and Cass?"

"I waited until Allen left and then I went to see her. We got into it, I guess." She lifts a shoulder. "Things got ugly."

"The two of you fought," I say repeating what she told me. "Cass attacked you."

"Yes, and unfortunately when things got physical, we fell against a window and it broke. I don't know how they did it because the fibers must have been nearly microscopic, but the police were able to get forensic evidence that matches a sweater I have."

"Oh wow. So wait. They let you go, so they must not believe you did it."

"I didn't, Teresa! Honestly! Why would I kill her?"

"Well, Sadie. Sometimes people lose their tempers."

"I know it's true." She huffs and buckles up, stares out her window. "But I'm not a murderer."

"No, of course not. Of course you aren't."

"Teresa," she says unsteadily as we leave the parking lot and pull onto the road. "I have something to tell you that I haven't told anyone." She's got my rapt attention now. Is she going to confess something about Allen? "Diane came to see me a few days ago. The day Cass's body was discovered, on Friday."

I wrinkle up my nose, not sure I'm understanding. "Diane?"

"Diane Martin, Allen's old girlfriend."

I cough in surprise and grip the steering wheel harder, cast Sadie a glance. "That Diane's dead, Sadie."

Sadie shakes her head. "No, she's not. She's very much alive and she came to see me."

"You've got to be kidding me." My whole world turns upside down. "Allen tortured himself over that girl's death." Although it's true they never found her body, they ultimately ruled it an accidental drowning. "Where has she been?"

"She didn't say, but she was here in Chapel Roads, at least on that day. I don't know why, but she'd been spying on Cass and on Allen. Watching Cass's house and mine. She gave an anonymous tip to the police about Allen running away into the woods carrying some kind of murder weapon."

My heart pounds. "A gun?"

Sadie sets her chin. "She didn't say."

"Oh my God."

"She told me a story about Allen trying to drown her when they were teenagers, saying she got away from him. I didn't want to believe her. That didn't sound like him. I've never known Allen to be violent, have you?" Sadie stares at me and I click my tongue.

"Only when he's backed into a corner."

"Teresa? What? Has . . . oh no. Has Allen ever hurt you?"

"No, but there were a few times I worried he'd try."

"I'm really sorry to hear that. That's terrible."

I turn onto a main road and we continue to drive farther out into the countryside where Sadie lives in her nice little niche of a neighborhood. "I can't believe that Diane is alive. Honestly? I'm stunned. Aren't there laws about that? Faking your own death and such? What if Allen had gotten into trouble for that? What if he'd gone to prison?"

Sadie frowns pitifully. "Then I guess Forrest and Emma wouldn't be here now."

"You're right," I reply. "And hey, Sadie, nobody is all good, or all bad. I think we both know that. Allen has his charming side. He charmed you." I sigh. "And me, I'll admit it's true."

"Cass too," she reminds me. "Also Diane. And here's the scary part, Teresa. Diane didn't show up at my house for a social visit. She came to warn me about Allen being dangerous. Whether he's ever convicted or not, she was quite sure he'd killed Cass because of the timing of when he was there."

"What do you think?" I ask softly.

Sadie hangs her head and peers up at me. "I'm worried he might have done it too, Teresa. There's something else I didn't tell the police. Allen snuck out of our house very late on the night that Cass died. I think he might have killed her then. I woke up and asked where he'd been, and he said he'd gone on a walk. Then he did something really strange. He sat down on our bed telling me I wouldn't have to worry about anything. That accidents happen, and he could fix things for me and Emma."

"'Accidents happen,' Sadie? He said those exact words?"

She grips her hands together. "Yes, and here's the other weird thing. When Diane came to see me she asked a very pointed question about how many accidents did I think one man could be connected to. First she named Allen's parents and then her . . ."

"And now Cass," I finish for her. "Oh, Sadie." I drive down her street and there's a police cruiser parked outside her house. Now I'm glad that it's there. "What are you going to do? Tell all this to the police?"

"I haven't yet, because I'm not sure." Her eyes turn red and her voice cracks. "I still love him, Teresa. What if it's not true? What if Allen's innocent? How can I throw him under the bus? In my head, I know it's logical to think . . . I mean, given all the evidence stacking up against him . . ." She starts crying. "But in my heart, I just can't . . ."

She lays both hands on her chest and sobs some more. She's torn apart by this unfathomable situation, in tatters. Poor Sadie. I want to tell her I know what it's like and what she's going through but I can't, because truthfully it's not the same at all.

I do feel her loss though. It fills my whole vehicle with anguish, so thick it clogs the air, as if it were a tangible thing that you could reach out and grab. I sit and wait until she stops crying, and she wipes her face with a tissue, dabs at her eyes.

I reach out and take her hand. "I'm here for you," I say. "I hope you know that."

"I didn't before, but I do know now." Her eyes gleam sadly. "Thanks."

TERESA
THE EX-WIFE

Now

Allen's been missing for four days and the evidence against him is mounting. His fingerprints were found at Cass's house and he was spotted fleeing the area on foot with a weapon he likely used to bludgeon her to death. Why else would he have taken that baseball bat and run? He's as guilty as the day is long.

My soul aches because of what this means for Forrest. Of course I've known from the beginning that things might end with Allen locked away, but now I view that outcome with near certainty. I feel less sorry for Sadie and Emma than I do for us, but I can never let Sadie know that. Need to show her my solidarity. If I can't be there for her, who will? These are shit times for the women in Allen's life. Shittiest of all for Cass.

She should never have asked Allen to meet up with her. Should never have tried to reconnect. That ship had sailed so long ago there was no hope of it returning to port. I know the feeling all too well. But for now I can't dwell on that. I need to think of Forrest and how I'll help him through this. Things won't be easy with his father in prison, but he'll ultimately adjust. Kids are surprisingly resilient that way, and Forrest has a very strong spirit. We'll get by.

I dial his cell phone number from where I sit on the couch, facing the curtain of trees that surrounds our house. I've always loved this time of day: twilight. The shadowy approach of darkness gives me a thrill. Under the sharp glare of the sun there's nowhere to hide, but under the cloak of night you can be anyone you want, a chameleon. Shape-shifting from one being to another. I've never liked anyone telling me how to be or feel.

Though I do still feel for Allen, and it hurts.

"Hello?"

"Forrest, hey! It's Mom."

"Hey, Mom."

"How's it going up at your grandma's?"

"Okay."

"Have you been into the city?"

"Yeah."

This conversation is like pulling teeth. "Was it fun?"

I can hear his frustrated breathing. "They still haven't found Dad yet, have they?"

"No, Forrest, I'm sorry." Though, what do I need to feel sorry about? Once Allen is caught, he'll only be arrested. Part of me dreads that moment, yet in another way I'd like for it to be over and done with.

"He's going to go to jail, isn't he?" Forrest asks with a painful moan. "He'll stay locked up forever."

"Forrest, we don't know that." I try to calm him. "First, there will likely be a trial."

"Great. Just great," he says sourly.

"Or maybe there won't!" I backpedal. "If your dad is guilty, he could plea-bargain somehow. Keep things from going too public."

"They already *are* public, Mom. After all the shit you pulled last—"

"Forrest!" I say sharply. "Don't talk to me that way!"

"Well, it's true!" he contends. "You ran away and *left me*, Mom."

Oh my God, poor kid. "Forrest, I know that was horrible, unforgivable."

"I will never forgive you," he says, and ends the call.

I sit there staring at the forest for which he was named, and understanding I deserved that. Grasping that certain sins are unforgivable. Guessing I'll probably burn in hell.

Then I pick up my wine and take a slug.

But I don't shed a tear.

SADIE
THE WIFE

Now

I awake with a hand covering my mouth, my head wedged into the pillow so deep the sides of it smash up against my ears. My eyes fly open in a panic and a dark shadow looms over me. A person, no. A man. My mind shouts *scream*, but I can't. I'm paralyzed. But no, I can't lie here, I need to fight.

I squirm and clamp onto a strong forearm, issuing muffled groans against his palm. Gnashing, biting—to no effect. Writhing, while trying to break away. He briefly releases my mouth to wrangle my wrists together. Argh, no. I sit up partway and rasp out, "*Help!*" A hand slams over my mouth, pushing me back down on the bed. My cry was weak, ineffectual, nowhere loud enough for the police to hear from where they're parked on the street.

He's got my wrists clamped together in his grip, my arms bent at the elbows and pressed against my chest. If my heart could beat any faster I'd be in coronary arrest.

"Sadie." A hushed whisper. "Sadie. Shh. Shh. It's me, Allen."

My pulse rate slows and he gradually lets go of my wrists, uncovers my mouth.

"Allen," I gasp sitting up. "You nearly gave me a heart attack. What the hell are you doing here?" I rub my tender wrists, squint up at him in the darkness. "How did you get in?"

"Through the side door in the garage," he whispers hoarsely. "I used our spare key and had to climb over the Harlows' brick wall, sneaking past their swimming pool. The police are crawling everywhere. On our street. On Cass's. Patrolling down by the woods. Sadie," he says and steps closer, causing my pulse to spike. "We need to talk."

"Damn straight we do!" I grate out softly. As outraged and frightened as I am, I'm not sure I want the police to hear. I want to know what Allen has to say first. "What happened with Cass, Allen? Hmm? Why did you run?"

He blanches in the shadows. "I *had to*, Sadie. To protect us."

"Oh my God. Did you—?" I can't force myself to ask it. *Did you kill Cass?*

"I did what I had to do, the only logical thing."

Murder? I feel sick, queasy, like I'm going to throw up right here in my lap.

I think of Officers Patel and Brady on the street, only a few hundred yards away. Staying silent is stupid. Why should I worry about protecting Allen when he could be here to harm me? If I scream louder now, will the cops hear me? Should I yell at the top of my lungs and turn Allen in? My heart's at war with my head now. *He's my husband. How can I betray him? Turn him in?* An inner voice snaps, *Right, Sadie. Like he's betrayed you?*

"Allen," I say in hushed tones, "the police want to bring you into custody. You're their primary suspect in killing Cass."

"I know." He sets his hands on his hips and hangs his head in the darkness. A faint trickle of light seeps in from the night-light in the hall through my open bedroom door. His eerie outline makes my stomach clench, and suddenly he's someone I don't know. Is it true what Diane told me? About what happened with her, and Allen's parents? Has Allen killed or at least tried to kill in the past? Was he successful more recently with Cass? I brace myself and find the courage to confront him because, as much as it pains me to ask, I have to know.

"Did you do it, Allen? Did you kill Cass?"

"Me?" Even through the shadows, I detect the hurt in his voice, but Allen's always been a good actor, capable of covering things up. I've learned that the hard way. "I think you know I didn't."

"I'm not so sure what I know," I say coldly. All the while, I'm snatching glances at my nightstand and my cell phone resting there. I deftly slide one hand out of my lap and onto the duvet, slip it nearer the edge of the bed.

"Sadie," he says solemnly. "I know you're afraid. Terrified, probably. But we can figure our way out of this. I want to help you."

Help me? What the fuck? How stupid does he think I am? How can he believe I'd trust him? My fingers stretch toward the nightstand, my phone's almost in reach. "Diane came to see me," I rasp out.

"What?" He sounds genuinely stunned. "Diane who?"

"Your old girlfriend, Diane, Allen. The one you tried to drown."

"Dammit, Sadie!" He strides toward me and I snatch up my phone, halting him in his tracks. "That's a lie! It was an accident! A riptide! I never—"

"Don't move closer." I wave my phone in the air but far away enough from him so he can't grab it. "I'll call the police."

He rakes his fingers through his hair, huffs out a breath. "Diane Martin's alive?" The utter disbelief seeps through his tone. "Where has she been all these years, hiding?"

"Yeah, from you and her family."

He starts stomping angrily around. I fear he's going to lift something and hurl it at me, maybe knock me unconscious. My eyes have adjusted to the dim light. I'm hyperaware of the brass lamp on his chest of drawers. The standing tie rack by the door. The weighty vase filled with daylilies on my dresser. Will I be next on his list? First Diane, then his parents. Cass after them and then his too-much-in-the-know wife?

"Did you do it, Allen? Did you try to drown Diane?"

He shoots daggers at me with his eyes. "Are you out of your mind, Sadie? Why would I have done that?"

"Diane told me the truth about what happened that night. It was because she wouldn't have sex with you."

"Jesus Christ, she said that?" He stares at me across the room. "And you believed her? Good God Almighty, Sadie! I thought you knew me."

"Allen! It's bound to come out. All of it. Maybe you should turn yourself in."

"Where is she now? Where's Diane?" I don't like his seething tone. "Right here in Chapel Roads?"

"I don't know where she's staying."

"So, she *is* in town? Holy fuck!"

"She saw you, Allen," I say to hurt him. "Saw you running away the morning of Cass's murder."

"How did she know where I was? Where we live?" He stops pacing and crosses his arms. "Shit." His jaw clenches. "She set me up!" A scary darkness creeps over the room, blacker than an onyx shadow. He glances my way. "Diane set both of us up to fall for this, you know that, don't you?"

My grip slackens around my phone and I rest my hand on the bed beside me. "Why would she do that, Allen? Hmm? Why?"

"I don't know."

"What about your parents? How did they die?"

"They were drunks," he says bitterly. "They had a sailing accident."

"Did you have anything to do with that?"

He uncrosses his arms and gestures wildly. "What the hell, Sadie? Who has poisoned your mind with this crap? None of it is true. All I've ever done is love you and Emma."

"What about you and Teresa then?"

"That was a mistake, I told you. I've apologized over and over. We worked through that in counseling."

"And Cass?"

"That was over before you and I met, I swear."

"I don't know what to believe anymore."

"Sadie." He steps toward me and I pick up my phone.

"I think you'd better go, Allen. Leave now or I'm calling nine-one-one."

"But, Sadie," he pleads. "I'm *innocent*. You know that. Jesus. I love you no matter what you've done. I don't care. It doesn't matter. What matters is in here." He thumps his chest with his fist. "You will always come first for me, you and Emma."

Heat burns in my eyes. "Go, Allen. Please." I don't want to see him in prison, can't bear that for Emma. But I'm at a crossroads where I can't do this anymore. I can't defend Allen if he's done so many horrible things. My heart won't let me convict him either. That's got to be up to a jury, and not me. Tears leak from my eyes and stream down my cheeks, trail down my trembling fingers and across the back of my hand holding my phone. Then I turn my phone over and punch three numbers in.

"Nine-one-one," the dispatcher says crisply. "What is your emergency?"

"Fuck, Sadie. Fuck," Allen says, retreating. Jogging, running. His footsteps echo in the hall, reverberate down the back steps. The kitchen door to the garage door opens and slams shut.

"Hello?" the dispatcher asks. "Anybody there?"

I press "End call" and drop my cell phone to my lap.

Sob into my hands, my shoulders heaving.

ALLEN
THE HUSBAND

Before

I'm in college and home for the weekend. My parents wanted to go up to the lake, I didn't. Maybe I should have stayed home, at our regular house, by myself, but my parents didn't trust me not to throw a party. If they only knew how many secret parties I've thrown here.

I'm sitting on the screened porch with my laptop on my knees, wearing shorts and flip-flops, a billowy Hawaiian shirt that's catching the warm breeze. It's midday but already getting dark out with heavy humidity building. What's a nineteen-year-old kid supposed to do in a place with no Wi-Fi, totally off the grid? I'm bored and watching movies on my laptop that I downloaded ahead of time. My dad's given me a six-pack to keep me occupied. That's so like him. He can't talk to me, but he's happy to help mess me up.

Thunder rumbles across the lake and dark clouds gather in the sky. I hear my parents calling to each other by our boat ramp. What the fuck are they doing? They can't go sailing in this. I get up and walk out the creaky screen door. "Mom! Dad! What are you doing?"

They've got their sailboat almost all the way in the water. Mom's sitting on its stern while Dad wades in deep dragging it by its towline.

Then he hops in. They've both got leathery skin from having been out in the sun a lot. Golf, tennis, sailing. They're in okay condition physically, considering their primary source of nutrition is alcohol. Dad hoists the mainsail and Mom raises a plastic martini glass toward me. "Going sailing, darling!"

A bolt of lightning in the distance. They haven't seen it. "Look! It's going to storm! You should wait!" I yell.

Dad hoists the mainsail and a huge burst of wind catches it dragging the boat across the lake. "Woo-hooo!" Mom shouts. Shit. She's drunk.

Dad ties down his line to light a joint. "Be back before that, bud!" I hate it when he calls me that. We've never been buddies at all. I fume and cross my arms as they sail off stupidly into wildly whipping winds. There are only a few other boats on the water and those are coming in, not going out, for fuck's sake. I rake my hands through my hair in frustration. I should have stayed at college. What the fuck was I thinking? That they'd remember today's a special day?

I slam back into the screened porch and the door bangs behind me and then I head into the kitchen and drink the first of six beers. It's my nineteenth birthday and nobody gives a damn but me. I hate my parents in this moment and wish they'd never been born, and also that they'd never had me. I drink the first beer quickly in two long gulps, and then a second one, a third. My head feels a little heavy and I sit down on the couch, carrying the six-pack holder with me. Maybe Dad did know it was my birthday, and this was his gift?

There are three beers left. I drink them in rapid succession and then—it's morning, sunlight streaming through the living room window and hitting me in the face as I'm stretched out on the couch. What the fuck? I struggle into a sitting position, set my bare feet on the floor, accidentally kick an empty beer bottle. It clatters and rolls under a chair. Through the windows, I see the downed trees, and all sorts of debris scattered across our property. "Mom? Dad?"

I call and stumble into their bedroom. The bed's still made, they're not here. Fuck no.

I dash down the hall and onto the screened porch, slam through it and out the door. Hold my hands up to my forehead to shield my eyes against the morning glare. A sailboat's capsized where the body of the lake meets the entrance to our cove.

DIANE
THE OLD GIRLFRIEND

Now

I've packed my things and am loading my car, ready for the long drive that will take me home to Arizona. Cass is dead and a manhunt's underway for Allen Wilson, I've warned Sadie. Now it's time to go. I've been lucky until now that no one has seen me besides Kate and Sadie, but I can't count on my sister not to talk. Sadie either, if it comes to that. Or for my luck to hold.

I opt to leave under the cloak of night where there's less chance of me being noticed. Better safe than sorry in blowing this town. Every time I went into a place somebody whispered. I wasn't sure about the guy at the diner eating his lemon meringue pie, either. I thought I recognized him from somewhere, but it was hard to say.

I realize my teenage drowning caused a stir. I've seen the newspaper clippings and paid attention to the stories at the time. For a while the police suspected Allen and then they ultimately let him go free. Maybe they were right to do that, who's to say. But it wasn't right for him to escape his due punishment for how he wrecked my life. He's paying in spades now.

I throw my bags in the trunk and slam it shut peeking up at the moon. Hands tighten around my neck and I whip-turn in the shadows, slam back against my car. My shoulders burn against the driver's door I've just unlocked with my electronic key. My God, that face. It's been so long, you'd think I'd have forgotten. But no. I recall every detail. The curl of his lips, the devil's gleam in his eyes. "What?" I struggle with the word. Gasp. Choke.

His death hold on my throat intensifies, aches. "Why?" I flush hot, feel I'm going to retch. Bile rises in my throat but he forces it back down, gripping harder. The exterior lights of the motel seem to flicker. One tall streetlamp has a shot-out bulb. I'm losing consciousness. Fuck. This was a mistake.

"You couldn't just stay dead, could you?" he growls between clenched teeth.

The more I fight, the weaker I become, his fingers digging in like bony pebbles.

I try to fight him off, kick and scream. I rasp out a breath, clawing at his arms, his hands, his wrists. How did he find me at this out-of-the way spot? He must have followed me to the nondescript motel, its wind-stricken facade and ratty paint-peeling doors hidden behind a thicket of trees. Now, no one else will find me. He'll dispose of my body.

He's going to kill me for real.

Then I see her over his shoulder, coming toward us at a hurried pace.

My pulse pounds and I cling to hope.

She's going to help me.

Then I see her gun.

SADIE
THE WIFE

Now

I huddle the sofa blanket around my shoulders to ward off the chill and lift the remote from a side table to turn on the gas fireplace. The fan-shaped window above it frames the trees, and—through their spindly branches—the pitch-black night. Within seconds of Allen leaving, the police were at my front door. The backup patrol stationed in front of Cass's house hurrying across my back lawn, their flashlight beams training toward the house. Officer Patel and her partner Brady asked all the questions.

"Everything okay in here?" Patel asks staring over my shoulder and into the foyer. She glances up the front stairs. "Are you alone?"

"Yes, I'm"—I lick my lips fabricating my story—"fine. I just thought I heard something out back." The other police team sees us standing in my foyer and raps at the patio door. I let them in while Patel and Brady follow me, carefully surveying the house.

The others join us from the backyard and we congregate in the breakfast nook beside the kitchen table. "A nine-one-one call came in from your number, but then got disconnected," Brady says. He stares at me in my pajama pants and sweatshirt, my bare feet chilled against the hardwood, before asking, "Did you place it?"

"No." Stupid lie. They obviously have my number. "What I mean is, it was an accident. I thought I heard something out back and got up to look. The gate was slightly ajar and that spooked me."

"When we cut across the yard," an officer says, "everything looked clear. We can check again."

Patel nods. "Yes, do that." She glances at her partner. "We'll do a quick tour of the house." I start to protest but she stops me. "Just to make sure." I have a very real sense that I'm in danger. That someone is out to hurt me. I don't want it to be Allen, but I can't shake my concerns. I wish I'd thought to ask him where he's been staying. Surely not out in the cold. The temperature's low tonight, we're expecting a springtime frost.

"Okay." I swallow past my fear. "Thank you."

Once they've surveyed the house, the four police officers stand by my patio door. They didn't even go in the garage, just took a quick peek at it through the kitchen door. "We'll do a full check of the yard," Patel says. She directs the others. "You two take the backyard and maybe poke around Cass's place to make sure nothing seems disturbed. Be sure you latch the gate when you go through it." She speaks to her partner next. "We'll take the front and the side yards. Sadie," she says and I meet her amber-colored eyes. "Are you sure you feel safe here?"

I'm not sure what I feel or think anymore. I numbly nod. "Think so."

"Well, if you change your mind," Patel answers, "we can move you somewhere else. A safe house if you'd like." But I know, if they do that, Allen will have no way to contact me again. Maybe that's for the best. Maybe I shouldn't be speaking to him at all under these circumstances. Still. My heart hurts. Doubts. There was that lingering ache in his voice. The way he said he'd love me under any kind of circumstances. Can I trust that's true?

How much does Allen really know about what happened between me and Cass that night? How much will he blame me for what I did? How much should I blame him for what he might have done later? I shiver and pull the sofa blanket tighter, securing it around my shoulders and staring out the back windows at Cass's house. Not a single light is on.

Cass is gone.

But are things really over?

DIANE
THE OLD GIRLFRIEND

Now

One minute I was outside my motel room, the next second I was being pistol-whipped. Then I was out like a light I'm guessing until they drove me here. I don't have a recollection of the time in between. Merely of being dragged out of a vehicle and hauled in this direction toward the cliff. There were two of them, but now just one. The she-devil. Oh wait. There he is in the distance. Watching. What a bastard. Like I could ever count on him. Like I could ever count on anyone. *Fuck them. Fuck them both!*

The pistol barrel pushes into the base of my skull prodding me toward the precipice, as I inch forward, my heart hammering. I don't want to beg but then I think of Nellie. "Please don't do this." The night is inky black, the moon occluded by clouds. Wind whips through my hair and through the trees. An old footbridge sprawls below us connecting one side of the river to the other, white-tipped rapids rushing below.

She doesn't answer. Presses a hand to my back, shoves.

I lock my knees, guessing I'm probably stronger, faster.

But I'm queasy and feeling weak from that earlier blow to my head.

Will this be it then? How things end?

O'REILLY
THE COP

Now

The chief calls me into her office first thing Tuesday morning and releases a weighty breath. "We've had a new development," she says. "A Jane Doe's washed up along the banks of the Haw River. Some kayakers found her this morning just after dawn. We're running forensics to hopefully identify the body."

Holy cow. "You think it's related to Cass's murder?"

"Not sure yet."

"Young? Old?"

"McMann's guessing in her thirties. The body was pretty beat up and had been in the water awhile. McMann didn't want to speculate until she had something concrete. Given our other ongoing investigation, she's rushing her results."

The chief stops me before I go. "Feel free to tell Captain Rodriguez, but otherwise—until we know more—I'd appreciate your keeping this close to the vest."

"Understood."

SADIE
THE WIFE

Now

I go to answer the door not really expecting anyone. Maybe it's a package delivery, or another check-in from the police, Captain Rodriguez and Deputy Chief O'Reilly? Instead, an older nun stands there dressed in a black habit, her head and hair shrouded from view. "Sadie?" A kind smile, eyes crinkling at the corners, within a roundish face marred by wrinkles. I guess she's in her seventies. "May I come in? I'd like to talk."

"I'm sorry. What's this about?"

"I'm Sister Mary Catherine Ward from Our Lady of Our Savior. I'm the pastoral minister there."

My pulse tick-tick-ticks like a tiny clock, panic threading through my veins. That's the school where Cass taught. What on earth can she want? "Yes?"

"I'd like to speak with you for a moment about Cass and your husband, Allen."

Air leaves my lungs with a whoosh. I can barely breathe. "What about them?"

She pulls a photograph from her purse and I gaze down at the little girl in a school uniform. My heart slams against my chest. She looks so much like Emma, and . . . no.

My legs go weak and my head light. I grab onto the doorframe to keep myself upright. Stare at the older woman. "Who is she?"

"Barbara Marconi," the older woman says. "Her family calls her Bobby."

O'REILLY
THE COP

Val walks into my office and shuts the door. She's rubbing her temples and some of her pinned-back hair has come loose.

I can sense her mental wheels turning. She's onto something. "What's up?"

She blows out a breath, rubs the back of her neck and shakes her head. "How the fuck did we make that mistake?" Her scowl, that furrowed brow. She's scaring me.

"What, Val? What is it?"

She sinks down in the cheap chair with metal arms opposite my desk. "We're wondering about motives with Allen, yeah?" She steeples her hands together resting her elbows on her knees.

"Yes." We've been through this a thousand times. Val and I have talked it over. The chief and I discussed it. The entire team's weighed in. Why would Allen act out now against Cass, if it was him at all? Where's the missing piece of the puzzle?

"Allen and Cass had a history, we know that. Some kind of nonsense back in high school, but we got so focused on that we forgot about something else, about Cass's late husband Richard and her late son, the ones who died in that car crash."

"Right." I nod recalling the sad tale. "Bobby."

"Wrong. Not Bobby. The Thomases never called their son that. They called him by his full name, Robert."

"How do you know?"

"I had a hunch. Did a little poking around during my lunch hour at the school today. Spoke to the pastoral minister there, Sister Mary Catherine Ward. She seemed uneasy with my questioning and said she can't divulge confidences shared with her at the chapel. I got a *very funny feeling* she's hiding something, although I don't know what."

I lean back in my chair, hands behind my head, flabbergasted. "Then who the hell is Bobby, if not Cass and Richard's kid? The boy Cass invited Emma to play with?"

Val holds open her hands. "You tell me."

"Maybe Bobby isn't even real?" I venture. "Maybe he's a figment of Cass's imagination? We kind of suspected she had problems, though she'd never been treated for them and wasn't undergoing any kind of psychiatric care."

"Maybe we should have paid more attention to that," Val says astutely. "Could be there's another explanation." She sits back and crosses her arms.

"I'm all ears."

"Maybe there is a real Bobby, only he's not Cass and Richard's kid," Val says seriously. "Maybe Bobby belongs to someone else? Remember that thing Cass wrote in Allen's high school yearbook about wanting to have Allen's baby?"

"Come on, Val. That's reaching and you know it. Did you ask the pastoral minister about kids named Bobby enrolled at her school?"

There are bound to be dozens of students named Robert or Bobby at Our Lady of Our Savior, but not quite as many directly connected to Cass.

"I did, and here's the interesting thing." Val cocks her head. "When I put that question to Sister Mary Catherine point-blank, the old nun clammed up."

SADIE
THE WIFE

Now

I feel like I'm underwater, parting the sludgy sea with my hands, as I wade into the living room and sink down on the sofa. I motion for Sister Mary Catherine to take our most comfortable chair. She sits and arranges her habit, positioning its long folds over her knees. She crosses her feet at the ankles and sets the school photo on the coffee table between us. I stare down at the picture of the child, my heart hammering.

"Who is Bobby Marconi?" I ask, dreading the answer. Why do I feel like I can guess? Like I already know the answer?

Sister Mary Catherine smiles softly. "She's Robin and Leon Marconi's little girl, and Cass's niece." Then she clicks her tongue and adds briskly, "To the outside world."

My breath catches, I'm finding it hard to speak. "You mentioned Allen and Cass?" I ask weakly. Although I don't want to acknowledge what's coming, I've already figured it out. Allen and Cass? What? How? When? No. And then I do the math.

Her light eyes glisten. "I normally don't break confidences, but this situation is quite unusual with Cass being dead and your husband . . ." She lets the thought linger and I know what she means, with Allen a suspect in Cass's murder. Sister Mary Catherine tugs at the cord of the crucifix hanging around her neck, straightening it in front of her. A tortured Jesus on the cross drapes down her chest, heightens my awareness of suffering. Injustice. The inevitable cruelties of this world.

"She's Allen and Cass's child, isn't she?"

Sister Mary Catherine nods. "Yes."

Oh my God. Wait. *Bobby.*

My conversation with Cass comes back to me. Shortly after Allen and I moved into this new neighborhood, Cass and I arranged a playdate between our two kids, but when I took Emma to Cass's, this mysterious Bobby didn't seem to be anywhere around. Cass claimed her child was a year ahead of Emma in school at Our Lady of Our Savior, and that she was on the way home, but—now thinking back—Cass never said whether that child was a boy or a girl. Or who the kid's dad was who was driving her over.

I'm suddenly back in the moment, standing in Cass's foyer with Emma for the playdate that never was. Nearly eighteen months ago exactly.

I peek around the corner and peer up the stairs. Cass's too-empty and unfin-ished-looking house is giving me a creepy vibe. "So Bobby?" I ask her when the kid is nowhere in sight.

Her grin sparkles. "Will be here in a bit."

Tension stirs in my gut. I can't leave my daughter here to play with some kid I've never met before. What if he's horrible? A mean bully? Someone who might pick on her? And why isn't he already here anyway, since Emma's been invited over to play?

I protectively lay my hands on Emma's shoulders. "We'll come back later," I say, wondering if I should call the whole thing off. None of this is sitting right with me.

She stops me from opening the door. "Bobby won't be a minute. You can leave Emma with me if you'd like?"

Right. With many other people and under different circumstances, I might believe that, but not with her. Something about this feels off to me. Something about Cass feels off. "You know." I check my watch. "I'm really sorry to do this, but I just remembered something."

Her face hardens. Suddenly, she's not the sunny neighbor. "Oh yeah? What's that?"

My pulse skitters. Think, think, think. "We, uh, have dental appointments."

Emma wrinkles up her forehead. "We do?"

I wince apologetically. "Yeah, sweetie. I'm sorry. Mommy forgot."

Not long afterward, Allen and I learned from the police that Cass had lost her husband Richard and young son in an auto accident years before. We all assumed that child was the Bobby Cass had talked about and that Cass had partially lost her mind. "So the boy who died with Richard?" I ask Sister Mary Catherine. "Cass and Richard's little boy?" My stomach sinks because I already know the answer. "His name wasn't Bobby, was it?"

She frowns sympathetically. "No, they called him by his full name, Robert."

"Why did Cass pretend the girl was her sister's? How in the world did they pull that off?"

She sighs. "How much time do you have?"

CASS
THE MISTRESS

Before

There never was a formal adoption. Robin and I worked everything out in advance. In those days, we looked so much alike we could have passed for twins so it was easy. Robin and her husband Leon had been trying to get pregnant for five years with no success. After three rounds of in vitro, they were running out of steam and out of cash.

I couldn't handle a baby on my own and didn't want one. I couldn't bear getting rid of it either and living with my Catholic guilt. Raising the child as hers was Robin's idea to begin with, but then I saw the potential in the situation. I could stay involved in the child's life, but not as a mom, as a trusted aunt. It was the next best thing to being a mother, and I wasn't about to try parenting solo. Biologically, I was old enough, but psychologically, I wasn't ready.

Allen had gone back to Teresa and then on to Sadie in a matter of a few short months. And, by the time I discovered my pregnancy, Allen and Sadie were already engaged to be married. Given the briefness of our affair, there was only a slim chance of Allen wanting to be present for our child, and he would never be the baby's live-in father. I could see that writing on the wall. Allen was too smitten with Sadie to ever leave her.

I'd seen them together around town, and while I was always careful about them not seeing me, to me it was obvious they were very much in love. Allen looked at Sadie in that adoring way I'd always wished he looked at me, and in a way he'd never looked at Teresa either. It was pretty clear to me he'd found his one.

So Robin and I arranged for me to pose as her, Robin Marconi, during my prenatal checkups. She always drove me to my doctor's visits and let me use her driver's license and insurance and debit cards when I checked in. I'd Venmo her the reimbursements later. Sometimes she'd fight me on that, arguing that she and Leon should pay the bills. But I wanted to at least do that one thing for my baby to help give her that good start.

We worked out a similar deal during my hospital delivery. My obstetrician had only ever known me as Robin, and nobody who checks in medical patients looks that closely at ID photos anyway. Robin and I took pains to dress similarly and do our hair the same way and laughed when people often asked us if we were twins.

My sister and I hid our agreement from our parents. I got a job tending bar in a neighboring town, dressed in baggy clothing to disguise my pregnancy, and limited the times I saw them, making up excuses about this or that. On the few occasions we got together, I believe my folks thought I'd put on weight but they were too polite to comment on that. Robin, in the meantime, had begun wearing prosthetics to make her look pregnant and they were very convincing. Her coworkers at the bank where she works even threw her a baby shower, and our parents were fully on board, buying her and Leon a baby pram and lots of toys.

Even later, after I married Richard, I never told him. It was too big a secret to risk having exposed and I wasn't sure how he would take it. When he wanted to name our boy Robert after his dad, I agreed as long as we used the full name Robert and didn't call him Bobby, explaining that moniker was already in use by my niece, and he easily understood and agreed.

When I delivered Bobby, which both Robin and I thought was such a cute nickname for Barbara, everyone at the hospital knew me as Robin Marconi, and I completed the paperwork for the birth certificate as such. All the while my heart was breaking at not keeping my baby girl. Once I held her in my arms and stared into her sweet little eyes, it was all I could do not to weep with remorse and tell Robin I was calling the whole thing off.

A deal is only a deal until you break it, and I was sincerely tempted to change my mind, but I didn't want to do it alone—that whole scary single-parenting thing. If Allen couldn't be mine as a husband and father, I prayed that maybe he would at least want to become involved in his child's life somehow.

I broke down that night and reached out to Allen by text. I didn't tell him what was going on, only that I was in the hospital and needed to speak with him ASAP. It was urgent. I thought maybe if I got him there, and he saw his precious child with his own eyes, he'd forget all about Sadie, Teresa, and everyone else, and come back to me. We could be a family. Because, miracle of miracles, even though I hadn't planned it, I'd actually had his baby like I'd always wanted. She was the most beautiful child with his nose and deep-blue eyes. I knew he'd fall in love in an instant.

He and Sadie were newlyweds and hadn't even known each other that long. Their abrupt marriage seemed like a rash decision when viewing it from the outside. Maybe I'd thought they were in love, but perhaps I'd been mistaken. Maybe Allen would feel differently about me now that we had Bobby. I didn't realize Allen and Sadie were already expecting Emma at the time.

Emma was born prematurely and she and Bobby are only six months apart, with Bobby being older. So my reconciliation plan probably wouldn't have worked. Allen was having a family with Sadie. But I'd already sent the text, and so I waited and hoped. Robin was furious I'd reached out to Allen. She took my phone away and said I needed to rest. We couldn't have anyone knowing about our pact, she made me swear.

But I still secretly hoped Allen would come, as I waited in vain at the hospital all through that agonizing night. And, when he never showed, I knew that Robin was right.

I had to move on.

ALLEN
THE HUSBAND

Before

Sadie and I have only been married about a month when I get a surprise text from Cass in the middle of the night. It's urgent and she has to see me. She's in the hospital. My heart pounds anxiously. Is she all right? I peek at Sadie sleeping soundly beside me, her hand resting on her belly. She's started showing now in her pregnancy but only slightly. I'm so happy about having a family, so happy about being with her.

But now Cass? What on earth can she want and why would she text me? She has a sister in town she's close to, Robin. And parents too. It doesn't make sense. I debate whether to answer or simply ignore her. That's a legit nonresponse to an ex-girlfriend, when you've both put your past behind you. I delete her text and lie back down, but my pillow feels lumpy, the sheets and duvet too hot. I can't get comfortable and I don't want to wake Sadie.

Then I understand why I'm restless. It's guilt. I didn't end things in the very best way with Cass when I went back to Teresa. She seemed to take it okay, but it's hard to know what she was actually thinking and feeling inside. Maybe I screwed up badly. Could have handled things better? I'm suddenly racked with fear.

What if something terrible's happened to Cass and she's seriously hurt, or worse—dying. That would be so fucked. And for me to ignore her would be even worse. Maybe she just wants to settle something. Say what she couldn't at the moment of our breakup because she was too stunned. I could read it on her face. Cass was very caught off guard when I told her it was over. In another way, she appeared almost resigned, like part of her had suspected she and I couldn't last. And we couldn't—can't.

I cast a look at Sadie. I'm with the love of my life now, my fated match.

But if Cass is in serious trouble and I ignore her, I'll have to live with that knowledge for the rest of my life. I don't want to be that kind of asshole. I also don't want to disturb or distress Sadie. Maybe it's best to first learn what's going on with Cass and see what she wants.

I get quietly out of bed and dress without turning on any lights.

Then drive to the hospital.

Cass's name isn't on the register. The person at the reception desk claims she never checked in.

"Can you look again?" I ask the woman with a glasses chain around her neck.

"We've got more than one Curtis, but no one with the first name Cass or Cassidy, sorry."

What the hell? I assumed Cass was a patient from what she wrote, but maybe she's here with somebody else. I spot her sister Robin by the elevators.

As I approach her, she wears a furious scowl. "Allen, what are you doing here?"

"Cass texted me. Where is she? Is she all right?"

"You're supposed to be out of the picture," she grates out. "You've got nothing do with this any longer." Why is she so angry, incensed?

"Any longer?" I'm flummoxed. "What does that mean?"

"You left Cass, remember? Broke her heart."

Ah, got it. She's being protective of her sister, but to a seriously harsh extreme. I purse my lips and frown. "I'm sorry about that, I really am, but Teri and I, we thought—"

"And yet," she fumes, "you left her too."

That's ballsy. "My personal life is none of your business, Robin."

"And Cass's personal life is no business of yours."

She shoves me hard in the chest and I blink. Hold up my hands. "Hey!"

"Leave now, Allen, or I'm calling security."

"But she—" I raise my phone then remember I deleted her text. "Cass is the one who contacted me."

"Well, if she did, that was obviously a mistake."

Robin's husband Leon walks over. "You heard the lady," he says, looking ominous. He's a big guy, heftier than me. He holds two cups of coffee like he's just been to the cafeteria. "This is family business here, and you're not family."

I text Cass from the parking lot but she doesn't answer.

I can only assume that Robin was right, and Cass regrets reaching out. We've been over for months and she might have had a weak moment and now is sorry she texted me. Family business, Leon said. It could be that one of Cass's parents is ill. That would explain Cass's sister and brother-in-law being here and also why Cass wasn't registered as a patient herself.

I glance up at the hospital through my windshield.

I hope she's okay.

SADIE
THE WIFE

Now

"Did Allen know?" I ask Sister Mary Catherine once she's relayed Cass's story.

"No. Cass never told him at the time. When she told me it was after her husband and son had died and in the strictest confidence. I normally don't break confidences, but this situation is so unique with Cass now being—murdered." Her breath shudders on the last word and she folds her hands in her lap, appearing chagrined. "I'm really sorry you're in this situation, Sadie. But I do have to wonder whether you're in danger. That's why I came to you and shared this secret. Someone was blackmailing Cass, she told me, and that person wanted her to reveal the truth about Allen and Bobby."

"For what purpose?"

She sadly shakes her head. "I believe the purpose was to destroy your marriage, break you and Allen up."

"How can we be sure Cass wasn't lying? Maybe she wasn't being blackmailed but used that as an excuse, because she wanted things out in the open herself?"

Sister Mary Catherine shakes her head. "No, I don't think so. Cass was happy living with her secret up until then. Things had worked out for Robin and Leon, and most importantly they were going great for Bobby. She was a well-adjusted child in a loving home. Cass loved her child, Sadie. She never would have wanted to uproot her or cause turmoil in her life. Besides that, she showed me one of the texts on her phone. It was chilling.

"I urged her to go to the police but she didn't want to do that. She wanted to talk to Allen first. She thought if he knew, then he could talk to you and maybe there was a way to avoid the disaster of Bobby's true parentage becoming public. She didn't want the scandal for the little girl, or for Robin and Leon."

I gasp. "So that's why Cass invited Allen over? What she wanted to talk about? She wanted to tell him that he was Bobby's father?"

"That would be my guess, and Sadie," she petitions with raised eyebrows, "I want you to know I'm going to the police with this information because I believe it might be relevant, might have given Allen a reason to harm Cass, if he didn't want the truth coming out. They've already sent officers to our school and I spoke with one of them today. I'm going back to the precinct now to deliver the whole story."

"What about Robin and Leon?"

"I've consulted with them and they agree I should move forward. They gave me their blessing in finding Cass's killer. Whether they'll continue to shield Bobby from the truth is up to them as her legal guardians."

"But they're not technically 'legal,' are they?"

She frowns and says, "No, but they're willing to live with the consequences, and proceed with a formal adoption if it comes to that. They believe their parents will support them, and I trust Allen won't stand in the way."

"I can't speak for my husband, I never have."

"We'll have to put this in God's hands then," Sister Mary Catherine says.

"Sister, thanks for coming by." My heart aches when I add, "And thank you for telling me about Bobby."

She stands and holds one of my hands in her soft and wrinkled grasp. "God bless you, my child. And please be careful. If Allen did harm Cass and he learns you're aware, I'd hate to think of what might happen if he came after you."

Before she leaves, I stop her. "Sister Mary Catherine!" She turns around from where she stands on my stoop, and I'm in the doorway.

"You mentioned someone blackmailing Cass. Did she ever learn who that was? Did Allen?"

"Not to my knowledge, no." Her forehead wrinkles when she adds, "But if Allen were to discover her blackmailer, I suspect that person would be in heavy danger too."

KATE
THE EX-CON

Before

When Diane tells me what she's done I can't believe it. "You what? Blackmailed Cass?" We sit in a worn booth with a beige Formica-top table and torn vinyl seats. The diner's mostly empty. A guy who looks like a trucker sits at the counter nursing a coffee and wolfing down a fluffy meringue pie. He looks a little like the yardman our folks used to have, but I'm not sure. It's been so long, I'm probably wrong about that. He doesn't seem to notice us anyway.

Diane takes a forkful of scrambled eggs. We're both eating breakfast at nighttime, a thing we liked to do when we were kids. On the good days when our parents acted normal. Those were few and far between. That almost made it harder because we kept holding out for those tiny glimmers of hope like little rays of sunshine peeking through our childhood storm. If they'd always been evil, we never would have learned to hope and pray they could be different.

"I honestly never knew the whole story," she admits. "Only enough of it to get her spooked. But there was clearly something going on between Cass and Allen that went way beyond the two of them having gone to the same high school."

I butter my toast and add grape jelly from a small packet. "What made you think so?"

"Dot did some asking around about Allen in prison, because—you know—she didn't believe it was over until it was over and was kind of mad about how things worked out. Had he really paid his dues for the things he'd done? Ruined people's lives? Dot wasn't convinced. She knew how he'd handled me, so she and I talked about next steps."

"You visited her in prison more than once then?"

"No. We communicated by phone. I always got in touch with her.

"One guy in lockup used to work at the check-in desk at the hospital. He later got arrested for stealing and fencing medical supplies. He claimed a woman matching Cass's description checked into the emergency room one night. He didn't know what was going on, but she looked like she was in a lot of pain. Doubled over in her overcoat. It was snowing out, December."

"What was her complaint?"

"Another intake specialist processed her at a separate bay, but this guy—Dot's contact—recognized Cass in retrospect when she was named a person of interest in Emma's kidnapping case. He didn't see her medical records, but he's sure of two things. It was Cass that night because the woman with her quietly called her that when she thought no one was listening, and this other woman looked a lot like Cass. Probably her sister."

"When was this that Cass went into the ER?"

"Roughly eight years ago, give or take. Cass was admitted to the hospital overnight and she only had one other visitor: Allen Wilson. Dot's contact saw the sister and Allen arguing near the elevators. The sister was furious at Allen. She started shoving his chest and shouting. She wouldn't even let him see Cass. Told him to get the hell out or she was calling security."

My chest tightens. "You think Allen hurt Cass? Put her there?"

"Jesus, Kate! I believe he's dangerous. He tried to kill me."

That's what I believed vehemently for so many years.

Allen's a murderer. Katherine inserts her opinion. *A cold-blooded killer.*

Is he, though? I rub my temples at the little snatches of memory. Allen and Diane laughing in the waves, playing, splashing, *kissing.* My secret discovery of the flat round case of pills I found in Diane's drawer later. When I got older, I understood what those had been: birth control pills.

I tiredly tell Katherine to go away. I'm growing weary of her interference, although she bothers me less and less these days. In some ways, it's like her voice is fading. Not as dominant as it used to be. Maybe my meds are working, or maybe I'm getting stronger. Possibly both.

Diane takes a bite of sausage biscuit. "He likely killed his parents before."

"I've heard the rumors."

"Cass now. Sadie's next."

"Sadie? Diane, that's doubtful."

"If she learns too much, she'll be in danger. Maybe she already is. I tried to warn her."

"When?"

"Earlier today."

I'm not following something. "I don't get your point in blackmailing Cass. What were you hoping to gain?"

"I wanted to force whatever was going on between Allen and Cass out into the open, because I knew there would be repercussions from that, like the end of Allen's marriage. An eye for an eye. He utterly destroyed mine. And there was something going on between them, or else Cass wouldn't have reacted the way she did, which was scared shitless."

My mind's boggled by what she's saying. "You *baited* Allen to kill Cass?"

"No!" Diane protests. "That wasn't my intention. I didn't think he'd go to that extreme, Jesus, and fuck up his current life. I did think I could make him buckle under pressure and reveal the truth to Sadie, and Sadie wouldn't have it. She'd leave him or better yet throw him out of their house. Allen was already with Sadie when he tried to see Cass at the hospital, so it's pretty clear he was being unfaithful, sneaking around and still in contact with Cass."

"That sucks."

"Right? That alone would be a secret he'd want to keep. I expected to see Allen leaving his house with a suitcase, not a backpack, this morning. That was the moment I was waiting for. And I don't mean a suitcase bound for Aruba either. That asshole didn't deserve to have that kind of trip, enjoy the sunny Caribbean with his perfect wife, continue his life unscathed."

I finish my meal and set down my fork. "How did you even know about Sadie and Allen's trip anyway?"

Diane heaves a breath and pushes aside her plate and sets her arms on the table. "I work as a travel agent in Phoenix for an online company and have access to all sorts of airline data. I've kept tabs on Allen over the years, a record of his comings and goings. He doesn't travel much, mostly on business."

"Christ, Diane! You've been cyberstalking him? Why?"

She shrugs. "Call it morbid curiosity. Allen doesn't belong to social media sites. It was hard to know what he was doing, but I was able to track his travels. That gave me some insight into his life. Honestly, his trips weren't very exciting until recently. The Aruba trip caught my attention because Allen wasn't traveling alone. He was going with Sadie. The idea that they were still together and taking a romantic vacation made my blood boil.

"After all this time, Allen was like a cat who'd landed on his feet. A cat with nine lives that had faced certain death time and again only to rise like a phoenix from the ashes. When I discovered they were taking that trip, I couldn't stand it. There he was leading his perfect life while my life was totally fucked. Cass's number was easy to find through travel records.

"I sent her anonymous texts, telling her that her time was running out. That I knew about her and Allen's affair and that I knew about the hospital. If she and Allen didn't tell Sadie the truth, I'd expose them both by making the whole sordid thing public."

"And yet, you didn't know what that 'whole sordid thing' was."

She leans forward and says, "Cass was too scared to call my bluff. She texted for me to hang on, that she'd take care of it. When I asked her when, she said soon. I brought down the hammer then insisting on a showdown before Sadie and Allen left for Aruba."

I sit there silently fuming and seeing Diane with brand-new eyes. If it hadn't been for her, people wouldn't have been pushed past their breaking points and Cass wouldn't have died. "And then Cass was murdered."

Diane sits back and finishes her coffee. "Yes."

"Why haven't you gone to the police?"

"For the love of God, Kate. I can't put myself on their radar, can't let Allen—or anyone else in Chapel Roads—know that I'm alive."

I know she's talking about our parents, and I don't blame her.

"Please swear you won't say anything," she begs, "about me blackmailing Cass. What can it matter now? The woman is dead, and I didn't do it. The police suspect the right person: Allen."

O'REILLY
THE COP

Now

The chief has us come in one hour early for our Wednesday-morning briefing. She's got Jane Doe's morgue photo on the board. It's not a pretty one, with lots of bruising around the victim's face.

"We've received the full coroner's report," Claremont says once we've all settled in. "We also got a match on the ID. Dental records show this person was Chelsea Walsh of Phoenix, Arizona." She waits until that sinks in.

Holy cow. "Not Walsh as in Caleb Walsh?" I ask. "The sex offender initially suspected in Emma's kidnapping?"

"One and the same," the chief responds. "This woman was Caleb Walsh's ex-wife, but that's not all." She heaves a breath and stares at the board and then around the room. "Our search pulled two matching sets of dental records for Chelsea, only the first set was two decades old and belonged to a local teenager."

Val's eyebrows knit together. "Not Chelsea?"

"Chelsea went by a different name then." The chief shakes her head. "Those sets of dental records belonged to Diane Martin."

Bev's hand shoots up. "Wait. Allen's teenage girlfriend? The one everyone thought died in a riptide?"

Chief Claremont clicks her tongue. "That's right."

A low murmur fills the room, people gasping, conferring with one another.

Val writes something down in her notebook, looks up. "How was she still alive?"

"She apparently survived the riptide," Claremont says, "and lived under the assumed name Chelsea Walsh." The chief crosses her arms. "What we need to find out is what she was doing back in Chapel Roads."

"Cause of death?" Patel asks.

"McMann believes she fell from a great height and lost consciousness. Likely from a bridge or potentially a cliff," the chief says. "But she wasn't dead when she hit the water, merely passed out, because she aspirated a lot of water into her lungs. A bit ironic considering how she was supposed to have died years ago.

"Official cause of death—drowning."

TERESA
THE EX-WIFE

Now

I decide to check on Sadie in light of this morning's news. I'm glad about that cop car sitting here on Sadie's street. There's another police cruiser in front of Cass's place. I drove down a nearby cross street and peeked to check. But I'm not all that sure the police surveillance will do much good. It's like they've spun a web and are sitting here silently waiting to catch a fly, but will a fly return once it knows the web has been spun?

I pull up Sadie's driveway and park my SUV in front of her garage. I texted I was coming so this visit isn't a surprise. What surprised me was when I asked if I could come by and check on her, Sadie said okay without hesitation. After what went down between us at the station on Sunday and during our ride when I brought her home, I sensed us growing closer. Sadie's finally starting to trust me, as she should. I'm pretty much the only one she's got at the moment. Damn Allen for all the trouble he's caused.

She opens her front door and it's almost hard to recognize her. Her blond hair is stringy and falling partially into her face. It doesn't look like she's washed it or showered. She wears worn jeans that are torn at the knees and a black cardigan sweater over a black long-sleeved T-shirt. It looks as if she didn't sleep a wink last night.

"Teresa," she says. Her voice is tired and so are her eyes. "Thanks for coming by."

"Of course." I pull her into a hug. Although it still feels foreign to embrace her, I intuit it's the right thing to do. She confirms my instinct by hugging me back, so tightly I almost choke. "I'm so sorry you're going through this." I hold her tighter. "What a nightmare."

"Yeah." She sniffs and breaks out of our hug. Dabs her eyes and nose with a tissue, then shoves it back in her sweater's pocket. She looks at me compassionately. "I know you're going through it too. This can't be easy for you and Forrest." My heart aches at the thought of my son and the anger he holds toward me. I guess I wasn't aware of how much.

I gently shut the door behind us. "Have you heard from Allen?"

She shakes her head no. She appears to be avoiding my eyes though. I wonder why. Maybe it's just too painful for her to think about Allen and all he's done. She's about to learn he's done something worse now: committed a second murder.

I want her to have the update from me before the police tell her about it, because I know it will come as a shock, and all things considered maybe this revelation is better coming from me. I saw an early report on the six a.m. news, so it will soon be all over town. Chapel Roads is small and people talk. Sadie leads me into the kitchen and fixes me a coffee. We both carry our mugs to the den and I sit on the love seat, while she takes the sofa.

"Sadie," I say, "I have something to tell you. The police will probably come by later but I want you to know first, because it's already made the news."

Sadie blinks and sets down her coffee. "Teresa," she asks, visibly worried. "What's wrong? What's happened?"

"Remember when you told me about Allen's old girlfriend being in town and coming to see you? Diane Martin? The woman who claimed Allen had tried to kill her, and insisted that he'd probably killed Cass?"

She appears lightheaded, unstable in her seat. Gripping her arms across her chest, rocking forward and backward. "That's what she claimed, sure, but Allen was investigated and he was cleared of any wrongdoing in Diane's supposed drowning years ago. Besides that, Teresa, she *lived*. Now I'm suspicious of what Diane told me. Why did she come to my house, and why had she been spying on Allen? Her motives couldn't have been good."

"Sadie," I say urgently, "I'm sure you're right about Diane. Her showing up in town like that is fishy and maybe we'll never know why she was here, but we have to look at this in the greater context. Allen's parents died in an accident, and Cass has died under mysterious circumstances—"

"Teresa, stop!" Her eyes are big and watery. "I hear what you're saying, but how can you believe that? You were married to the man. You loved him."

That's where she's got it wrong. Putting things in the past tense. "I'm afraid things have gotten worse."

"That's impossible. How could they get worse?" Her breath shudders. "Allen's in hiding. The police are after him. He's wanted for—"

"Diane's dead," I say, stopping her cold.

Sadie gawks at me, going pale. "Wh-what did you say?"

"A body washed up on the banks of the Haw River very early yesterday morning. There was no identification on the body, but they've now traced her through dental records, although they're decades old. I always knew there was something off about that story and Diane going missing. Maybe a riptide did get her, or maybe Allen tried to harm her like she said and she swam away. One way or another, she's survived all this time under an assumed name."

"What name?"

"When the police ran the dental records to identify her body, they found two sets: one belonging to Diane Martin and the other to Chelsea Walsh."

Sadie blinks. "Walsh? What the hell?"

"Right. Her ex-husband Caleb was the guy Allen got locked up in jail, when he was a jury foreman that time. It was all over the morning news. A big story. Now the police are after Allen for questioning in her mysterious death too."

"Deputy Chief O'Reilly texted me earlier about stopping by. Said he'd be busy this morning, but that he'd text me later with a time."

"Then it's probably to talk about that. He probably wanted to tell you in person before things got out in the media."

"How did it already make the news?"

"Someone probably blabbed at the police station. People leak juicy stuff all the time."

"Oh my God." She stares at me blankly. "Diane predicted this. Predicted that Allen would kill her. She said, 'Allen tried to kill me once. If he learns I'm alive, he'll want to finish the job.'"

I wrap my arms around her and pull her to me as she sobs. "Sadie," I whisper softly. "I'm so sorry. What a monster."

"He couldn't have done it, Teresa! Because that would mean . . . he'd also killed Cass." She's shaking now like a leaf and I hold her tighter. She stares up at me with red-rimmed eyes. "Teresa," she says in warbly tones, "I have a confession to make. Allen came to see me."

My heart thumps painfully. "What? When?"

"Really late on Monday night." She starts breathing hard, gasping for air.

"Sadie, how terrifying. He didn't hurt you?"

She vehemently shakes her head.

"The police didn't see him either?"

"No. He came in through the garage using a key."

"What did he want?"

Her breath shudders when she says, "He tried to deny everything, said he was going to take care of things for me and Emma. But I don't know how." Her voice rises shrilly. "How can he make things better if he's done the unthink—" She cups her hands over her mouth, her eyes opening wide. "Oh my God, it's my fault. He didn't know anything about Diane being alive—or in town." The blood drains from her face. "I told him."

I pull her into a hug. "You can't blame yourself. You didn't know how far over the edge he's gone. You need to be very, very careful. Be sure to lock your doors. Do you want to come and stay with me? Forrest has gone to his grandma's for spring break, and I've got space."

She pulls herself together and dries her eyes. "No, I'm all right. The police are here."

I brace her shoulders with my hands, look at her sincerely. "Are you sure?"

She nods.

"Well, I'm here for you, if you need me."

"Thanks, Teresa. You're really good to say that. I never thought. I mean, expected—"

"That of me?" I frown and answer, "I guess we're both in this together now."

She stares into my eyes, so very grateful, and I'm glad. I want her to be grateful for my efforts. I'm going out on a limb, though I don't have to. But if my friendship helps her understand what sort of man Allen really is then that's all for the better. Sadly. "We have our kids to think of," I say, winding down our conversation. I finish my last sip of coffee. "Forrest and Emma."

Sadie stares out the window at Cass's house. "Yes. We do."

"Sadie," I say seriously. "Maybe you should go to the police about Allen being here Monday night and tell them what he said. I'll go with you."

"I appreciate that, but I can't bring myself to do that yet."

"Sadie! What about Diane? And Cass?"

She sighs heavily and stares at me with weepy eyes. "You didn't see his face, Teresa. He seemed so crushed that I would believe him capable of murder."

"Of course he did, Sadie. That's who Allen is: a great actor, someone who covers things up. He's been successfully giving performances his entire life and they're only now catching on to him. Sadie, listen to me," I say direly. "We can't trust him. You shouldn't trust him, okay?" I open my purse and take out the Walther PPK I've stashed in its hollow. "That's why I want you to have this."

Sadie's face goes white. "A gun?"

"You told me Allen broke in here Monday night, Sadie. Maybe it was him that first time too but he got scared off by the police."

"But Allen wouldn't harm me." She trembles like she's not sure.

"Maybe that's what Cass thought too? Now look what's happened to Diane. Can you really take that chance? What about Emma? What if Allen does to you what he did to them? When he's finally caught and thrown in prison, where will that leave your little girl?"

She looks like she's in a trance. "With Pat and Gayle." I can tell that's not what she wants. What she wants is for Allen to come home and for all of this to have been a horrible nightmare. She's not going to get that luxury.

"I empathize, really I do. I know what it's like being disillusioned by Allen. But Sadie, your life is at stake here. You have to consider your future—and Emma's. I know you went through hell during her kidnapping. It would be devastating to lose her again, and not because she'd been taken away from you, but because you were taken away from her—by her daddy killing you. Imagine a child having to live with that. Allen's done some terrible things. We can't stick our heads in the sand any longer. We need to face facts and be prepared."

She takes the weapon from me carefully like it's a snake that might bite her. "Where did you get this?" she asks looking up.

"My mom bought it for me after Allen moved out. She said she worried about me and Forrest living all alone out in the woods." I fish a magazine from my purse and hand that to her as well. "Have you ever shot one of these?"

She stares at me blankly. "No."

"Don't worry. I'll teach you."

O'REILLY
THE COP

Now

Val and I are assigned the unsavory task of informing Diane Martin's a.k.a. Chelsea Walsh's family of her sudden death. Since I used to date Diane's sister, Kate Davis, the chief thought maybe the news would be better coming from me. I can see things both ways, but I deferred to her wishes, which were more like orders. We're speaking with Diane's parents first. Claremont contacted the local police in Miami, and they'll send an officer out to Diane's brother's house to deliver the news in person.

We found information on Mark Martin in Diane's rental car. A small notebook in the glove box had his name and phone number written on it, along with a girl's name, Nellie. A quick records search revealed Nellie to be Caleb and Chelsea Walsh's child, the infant girl that Chelsea left town with when she divorced Caleb and moved to Arizona during the heat of Caleb's highly publicized trial.

Diane had apparently already packed her belongings and checked out of her motel, intending to leave town, when something must have happened to her. Whether her death was self-inflicted or homicide, we're not yet sure. Once we'd positively identified Diane's body under her current assumed name, Chelsea Walsh, it was easy to track down active rental vehicle records. We got the plates, we found her car in a small church parking lot near Bynum Bridge on the banks of the Haw River.

"You sure you're okay with this?" Val asks as we stand outside Diane's parents' home. It's a massive place that looks a bit like an Italian villa with white stucco walls and a red tile roof. There's lots of landscaping and a pool around back, all very nicely done. These folks are living high on the hog.

I shove my hands in my uniform pants pockets and roll back my shoulders. Stand up straighter on the stoop. "Yeah, I'm good."

Val rings the bell and we wait.

No answer.

She tries again and we shoot glances at two vehicles in the driveway. One is a pricey sports car, the other a luxury SUV. Looks like someone's home.

Val knocks to no avail.

"Mr. and Mrs. Martin," I call. "Please open up! Police!"

Val cups her hand over her eyes to combat the glare and leans very close to the colorful stained glass panel in the front door. "Christ." She stares at me frantically. "There are two bodies on the floor in there! We've got to go in!"

Val calls for backup as I ram my shoulder against the door. It's only locked at the knob and not dead bolted, so it pops right open, swinging wide, and I stumble into the hall with a polished marble floor. Val dashes to the bodies sprawled out in the living room, looks like an older man and an older woman, and I'm fast on Val's heels. Both individuals lie on their bellies in large pools of blood. A gun rests on the floor beside them.

Val sets her hands on her hips, viewing the scene. "Murder-suicide?" she asks, looking up.

"Either that, or just plain murder."

DIANE
THE OLD GIRLFRIEND

Before

I'm appalled they would do this, attempt to murder their own child. Appalled and sickened as Mom drives me closer to the cliff with Dad's gun. She wants me to jump and fall to my death, but I'm not going to give them the satisfaction. If they're going to kill me, they're going to have to put a bullet through my head so the forensic evidence can be used to lock both their sorry asses away for a long, long time, if not forever.

But that could never be enough payback for the hell they put us kids through. For killing their own kid, for fuck's sake, like they're about to do now. I don't even know how they found me at my motel. Then I remember the guy at the diner with his lemon meringue pie.

Fuck's sake, he was their gardener, Earl Rankin.

I knew I thought I recognized his face. He must have tailed me to the motel after I met up with Kate, then gone to my parents with the information about where I was. I'm sure he asked them for money. Some people will do anything for a fast buck no matter who it hurts.

I try to stabilize myself on the cliff and resist being forced closer to the edge, the river rushing below me. "Why are you so angry?" I ask loudly above the sound of the water and the wind. "Is this about the insurance money?" I try making sense of their fury in the cold blustery night.

Maybe the insurance money makes sense. Mark and I found the papers on the three of us kids back when Mark and I were teens. Kit-Kat was really little, like in the second or third grade. We'd never heard of parents insuring their children before and found it super spooky, wondering if they'd planned to beat us all to death in order to do a big money grab. Each was a two-million-dollar policy. Dad was an insurance agent. He wrote them himself.

"No," Mom sneers. "It's about you being a lying little bitch. You always had that in you, didn't you, Diane? And now you faked your own death, huh? Made your dad and me suffer needlessly. Then the others disappeared, Mark and Katherine, fell off the face of the earth.

"Do you have *any idea* how that made us look to our friends?" she spews nastily. "We lost *all of them*. While our peers celebrated graduations, weddings, *grandchildren*, we were left on our own—with nothing. People looked at us like pariahs. Like there had to be something wrong with us, because it couldn't be a coincidence, could it? One daughter being dead and the other two kids gone mysteriously missing."

Her face contorts freakishly as she continues her tirade.

"Some people secretly pointed their fingers at us, privately accusing us of getting rid of you three children. They didn't say it to our faces, but we could tell that's what they thought. The way people would get up and move to another table at the club or shift to a different pew in church. Move across the fucking street to get on the opposite sidewalk.

"*As if* we'd done something as abysmal as murder you. You never gave us the chance. You bolted like scared little lambs before the slaughter. But nobody knew that. They all blamed me and your dad. Whispered rumors we'd hidden your bodies somewhere in our house, maybe even in the cement of the pool we put in after you 'died.'" She holds up her fingers in quotes and quickly reestablishes her grip on the gun.

She's insane, unhinged. Thank God we got the fuck out. "You have no right to talk about suffering!" I shout. "Y'all put me and Mark through hell, and Kit-Kat, she—"

"Where is she?" Mom demands. "Where's Katherine? We know she's out there somewhere, hiding same as you. Is she here, in Chapel Roads?"

"Leave Kate alone!"

Mom glares at me. "She goes by Kate now, does she?"

Shit. I never should have said that. Kate's always had her problems, major thanks to our parents. She's done a stint in prison and had trouble with the law, but now she's getting her shit together. On meds and in counseling. She does *not* need the filthy wrath of our parents' acid rain pouring down on her now.

"Where is she?" Mom demands. "Are you two in touch?"

"No!"

Dad's in the background by their convertible, watching.

Father of the year—not.

The moon casts creepy shadows across their ugly faces. I always knew they were sick motherfuckers but never completely understood how deranged both my parents are until now.

"How about Mark?" Dad's gruff voice calls. "Where'd that son of a bitch go?" He sounds drunk or high, maybe both. Come to think of it, it's hard to recall him being sober.

I'll never say Florida, never give up my daughter. Nellie needs to stay protected. She'll be okay with Mark and Elena. They'll take care of her. My heart breaks at the thought of losing my little girl. Then a surge of anger rises inside me with hurricane force, and anger, I learn, is stronger than fear.

I can't let them do this.

I have to fight back.

"Answer your father!" Mom demands hellishly.

She waves the gun in my face and I grab her arm.

O'REILLY
THE COP

Now

Someone's got to do the honors with Kate and this visit is worse than the one I'd planned initially. Now three people in her family are dead, her long-estranged and previously presumed-dead sister, and both her parents. Val sits beside me in our car. "Are you sure you don't want me to come in with you?"

We're outside Kate's two-story apartment building. The grounds are nicely kept and she lives upstairs. It's in one of those communities with tennis courts and a pool hemmed by flowering dogwood trees. Most of the trees' blossoms are white, a few pink. There's a vibrantly purple redbud tree by the spot where we park our cruiser. "No, that's okay," I tell Val. "I think it's better if I go alone." I frown. "Given our grim update." She knows I mean about the Mr. and Mrs.

Val reaches out and takes my hand. "You're a good man, Shane."

I set my jaw and stare at Kate's building. "Hope so."

She squeezes my hand before letting it go. "Now, go in there and prove it."

"You're something," I say, smiling at her.

Val proudly squares her shoulders. "Don't I know it."

I laugh but it's melancholy, due to the task ahead. I climb the outdoor staircase to apartment 2-B with weighty footsteps and a heavy heart. There is no doorbell. Just a knocker.

Kate opens the door wearing shorts and a T-shirt and there's a tug at my heartstrings, tender and raw. I'm over her but also sad about the way things ended. Although I didn't feel like the chief gave me much choice at the time, I basically walked on Kate when she needed a friend. Our department psychologist helped me see that. He also suggested I contact the prison's mental health department to see if I could get the doctors there to arrange treatment for her. I did so, but it never would have worked unless Kate had agreed to it.

"Shane?" She checks out my uniform noting I'm clearly on duty. "What is it? Is something wrong?"

"I'm afraid so, Kate. I'm sorry." I glance over her shoulder and her tidy apartment appears empty. "Can I come in?"

She backs up a step. "Sure."

"Maybe we should sit."

She blinks then says, "Okay." Kate's not a stupid woman. She knows I bring bad news. She can see it in my slumped shoulders, read it in my long face.

"Is this about Diane?" she asks tentatively.

"What makes you say that? Have you been in touch with your sister?"

"Only over the course of these past few days." Kate sighs heavily. "I accidentally discovered she was in town and we met for dinner."

"So then, you were aware she was alive?"

"I learned about it in prison, yeah." Kate stares blankly out her window then turns back toward me. "Needless to say, it came as a shock."

"No doubt." I clasp my hands together and ask, "So you knew about her hiding and living under a different name in Arizona?"

"Yes." She picks up her phone from a side table. "I got kind of a weird text from her on Monday night and she hasn't returned my texts or calls since then. Is she okay?"

"Kate, I'm very sorry to have to tell you this but Diane's dead."

"Oh no." She gasps and covers her mouth. "What happened?" She appears shaken, hugging herself by her elbows.

"She drowned in the Haw River."

"Drowned? For real?"

"I'm afraid so." I consider her comment realizing it could be important. The timing of when Diane was last known to be alive could help determine what happened in relation to her parents, once the coroner predicts their times of death. "Do you know the time of the text she sent you?"

"Yeah, I can look it up." She thumbs through her phone and then looks at me. "Shortly after one a.m."

"And what did it say?"

She appears on the verge of tears. "'Sorry, not sorry.'"

"That's it?"

She nods and sniffs. "It's a thing we used to say to each other."

"How did you hear about Diane in prison?"

"It was through Dotti. Diane came to visit Dotti shortly after she'd been arrested. They'd apparently been collaborating on . . ." She bites her lip, suddenly silent.

"Collaborating on what, Kate?"

"Never mind."

"Kate? Do you know something relevant to what happened to Emma?"

She hangs her head and then peers up at me. "Dotti ran off at the mouth a lot."

"Would you feel comfortable talking to me about it?"

"If it will help you, yes. But Shane," she says. "I probably should also tell you about Diane and what she was doing in Chapel Roads. She wasn't here on a good mission; she was out for revenge."

Holy cow. "So you think she might have been the one who——?"

"——killed Cass? No, I don't think so. I think it was more about blackmailing Cass and stirring up trouble for Allen and his family. She learned that Allen and Cass had been involved and there'd been some kind of incident between Cass and Allen at the hospital, after Allen had married Sadie. Diane assumed an affair that they'd hidden from Sadie, and she wanted to destroy Allen's marriage.

"Diane couldn't let well enough alone, unfortunately. My sister really had it in for Allen, but it wasn't for the reasons she claimed. She apparently told Dotti Allen had tried to force himself on her when they were teenagers that night when she supposedly drowned at the beach."

"I'm listening."

"I was there, Shane. Still a kid, but I remember a lot of things crystal clear. Diane wasn't crying for help. She was laughing. They were drinking and smoking on the beach and it looked like they were talking, getting along. The next thing I knew they were tossing off their clothes and running into the waves, playing and splashing. Kissing one hell of a lot. And look, I know I was just a little girl, but it appeared consensual.

"Then later, after Diane disappeared"—she licks her lips—"I found birth control pills hidden in a dresser drawer in the room at the beach we shared. I don't believe she could have been averse to having sex while being on birth control, do you?"

"It does sound contradictory," I admit, "but she could have thought she was ready then changed her mind, which would have—of course—been her prerogative."

"Yes, that's true. But Diane's version of things is not how I remember the evening, and I haven't been able to get that contradiction out of my head. Mostly because it tripped me up during Emma's kidnapping. I was mad as hell at Allen myself about what had happened between him and Diane. I believed the news stories and speculation and trusted what my parents said. They fully blamed Allen for Diane's death, therefore so did I.

"I went over my memories of that night with my therapist because I was trying to glean a more accurate version of the truth. My personal rage against Allen had caused me to do some really bad things when Emma went missing, but with my therapist's help I came to understand that the basis for my anger was unwarranted. I'm okay with the police obtaining my psychiatric records from prison if you need them, because they show my understanding of Diane and Allen's situation at the time, and that predates whatever's happened here."

"I appreciate that, Kate, thank you."

"I'm not saying Allen isn't guilty of killing Cass, mind you, because I honestly have no information about that. In Diane's case, I do believe she was still angry about Allen being on the jury during Caleb's trial. The result of Caleb's conviction was pretty devastating for her. I don't think she ever forgave Allen for breaking apart her family, even though it obviously wasn't all Allen's fault. There are twelve people on a jury, not one."

I'm heartened by her clearheaded thinking and the eloquent way she expresses herself. It's so good to see her looking so whole and settled, despite the difficult news I've delivered. "Would you be willing to come down to the station and tell Chief Claremont everything you've told me? Give a formal statement about what you learned relating to Emma and this new information about Diane?"

She blows out a breath and then says, "Yeah, I can do that, but I'd like to meet with my counselor first, if that's okay." Her blue eyes glisten. "And, hey. I never got a chance to thank you for arranging for my care."

"Wait. Who told you?"

"One of the prison doctors. I guess they didn't think it was any sort of secret."

It wasn't but still I feel embarrassed that she knows. "I only wanted the best for you. I'm really sorry about how things went down."

"You were between a rock and a hard place," she says understandingly. "I get that. No hard feelings."

"Sounds like you're doing better."

"I am."

I feel terrible for laying this on her. "Then I'm very sorry to share more bad news."

"What's that?"

"Your parents, the Martins, we found them dead too."

"No shit." She doesn't look stricken. More like amazed. "Who did it?"

"That's what we're trying to find out."

She tsks and picks up her phone. "Do you think it was Diane?" She says that in almost an admiring tone, as if she's proud of her sister.

"Not sure," I answer. "When we have the timing of their deaths, and forensics on the gun, we'll know more."

DIANE
THE OLD GIRLFRIEND

Before

I stare down at the banks of the Haw River, its rushing rapids tumbling over boulders and jagged rocks. The black water glistens in the moonlight, reminding me of Allen and me running into the ocean. I know I'm going to die tonight, and I've finally made my peace with that, because, hey, there are a lot of things I can't undo, and that are basically out of my hands. That night, though, I foolishly believed myself in charge of the situation. I had a plan and was convinced he'd go along with it.

I was living in utter hell with my parents and Allen knew my situation was untenable because I'd told him about it. But Allen only thought of himself and his future. Not about the dark sins that were occurring within my very own house. He didn't witness the abuse I was living through firsthand, because my parents were skilled at hiding it. When our two families went on those joint beach vacations, my folks were on their best behavior, meaning they pretty much left us kids alone to focus on their own partying. That worked well for me.

The night I nearly drowned, Allen and I were down on the beach, drinking from a bottle of scotch we'd stolen from our parents' bar and smoking weed. The grown-ups never checked their liquor bottles or measured what was left. And, if any booze went missing, each couple would have assumed it was the other lushy pair of parents dipping in. I had a joint that I'd gotten from Mark, and Allen and I were passing it back and forth, having a low serious conversation.

I thought I saw someone up by the beach house. A shadow behind the structure for the outdoor shower off to one side of the deck. Then I convinced myself I was imagining things. Now I know that shadow I saw must have been Kit-Kat, or as she calls herself now, Kate.

I'd gotten birth control pills from one of my older friends, who'd had them prescribed from a parental planning center. I paid her in small amounts of drugs I'd pilfered off of Mark without him knowing. When I told Allen I'd gone on the pill he was stunned.

"Don't you think we should have discussed this?" Allen asks with such a look of surprise, my eyes burn hot. He's a teenage guy, for fuck's sake, why isn't he thrilled? Ecstatic? We're at the beach and our two families are sharing a beach house. Allen and I are dating and snuck out late at night, after everyone else was asleep. We're down on the beach and it's dark out, with a faint wafting moon casting shimmers across the waves.

"Diane," he says quietly passing me the joint after taking a long drag. "Maybe that's not such a great idea. I mean, come on? What's the big rush?"

My heart strums unevenly and hurt wells in my throat. I hold the joint in trembling fingers, fighting back my tears. "I thought you said you loved me?"

"I do. Hey." He leans closer, his breath on my cheek. "But something like that's important, we both should be ready."

"I am ready," I tell him firmly.

He heaves a sigh and hangs his head.

"Allen?"

"I'm going to be very honest with you," he says. "I think we should wait. Something could happen. A mistake."

He's talking about a baby, the bastard. "Would that really be so bad?" I ask hoarsely. "The two of us having a kid?"

"No." His voice breaks sharply. "But not right now, Diane. Jesus Christ, we're basically kids ourselves. What about finishing high school? College?" Allen's always had ambitions of bigger things, of being his own man and stepping out from under his parents' dark shadow. He doesn't want his future tainted by anything unsavory. I suddenly wonder if he's cast me in that same lot as a person he should move on from. Maybe he doesn't want us to last.

"You don't have to worry," I say earnestly. "I've taken precautions." What I don't tell him is that, while I secured a few months' worth of pills, I haven't taken a single one. That's my backup plan with Allen, an unforeseen pregnancy. He'd have to marry me then. I know Allen. Even if he didn't want to, he would buckle down and do right by our kid.

I would be sixteen by the time it came along and him seventeen. I know the timing's not great, but I've got to get out of that goddamned house somehow and am scared to run away on my own. I've heard what happens to young women living on the streets. I could be abducted or murdered. Forced into prostitution, all sorts of horrible things that might actually be worse than the hell I'm living through day to day. But if I have Allen with me, I know everything will be okay. The two of us together could somehow make it work, build a life together.

Allen sits a long while thinking, the joint burning down to ash in his grip. Finally, he puts it out in the sand. "I don't want to disappoint you," he says looking up. "But I'm older than you—"

"Just by a year," I remind him sourly.

"Yeah, but still." He frowns. "I feel wrong about us making this call. If we're going to do it for the first time for both of us, it should be special, what we both want." And he doesn't want this. A knife plunges into my heart, twists.

I reach out and rub his arm. Run my palm up to his shoulder. "It could be fun," I tempt, leaning in and whispering against his lips.

"You know what could be fun?" he asks softly.

"Hmm?"

He suddenly pulls back and jumps to his feet. "Swimming!"

"What?" What the fuck?

"Come on, Diane," he coaxes, stepping out of his jeans. "Last one in the water loses!"

I scramble to my feet and out of my clothes, chasing after him. "Loses what!" I challenge playfully. "Her virginity?"

He laughs and keeps running, splashing into the waves. Cupping a bunch of water in his hands and dousing me with the chilly spray. "Hey! Stop that!" I cry.

"You'll just have to make me!" he bellows back.

He wades in deeper and the ocean rises and falls, my bare feet scraping against small shells, the sting of fleeing sand as the tide is pulled out—and then gets thrust back up against the beach in a gravelly roar. I leap through the salty swells calling after him. "Allen Wilson! Come back here!"

"Nope!" He laughs. "You'll have to come and get me!"

I bound into the surf and spring into his arms. Our bodies are slick and we're in past our waists, inching out farther from the shore with the roll and crest of the waves. Allen pulls me closer and his body's warm against mine. His chest is strong and muscled, his embrace tight. He runs his fingers through my wet hair and braces my head in his hands, kissing me deeply as we bob up and down in the water.

"How about we run away together?" I speak huskily between kisses and above the trilling sound of the waves, the light tingle of the wind against my damp face. "Just you and me?"

He stops kissing me to stare in my eyes, his face basked in moonlight. "What? We can't do that, Diane. Where would we go? How would we live?"

I shove his chest and joke. "You're chicken, aren't you?"

He blinks looking pale. "No. That's just stupid."

"I mean it," I insist hoarsely. "We should do it. Just you and me, tonight."

"Ha!" He steps back and splashes me soundly. "How much of that scotch did you drink?"

"Not any more than you did!" I splash him back, shouting. "Come on, Allen. Give me one good reason why not!" I sling water in his direction and he flings back the salty spray.

"I can give you many!"

I sweep my arms behind me preparing to splash him hugely. "I thought you loved me?"

"I do!" It happens in a flash.

A vise forms around my legs and ankles sucking me under before I can think or scream, whooshing me into a tunnel of rippling water moving at lightning speed.

A riptide hurls me out to sea.

KATE
THE EX-CON

Now

I won't lie, it was good to see Shane. It touched me that he did the right thing and apologized about our breakup. I've spent a lot of hours with Adelaide on that. I'll be glad to share the news. My heart feels heavy at losing Diane. I'd barely gotten to know her again. Though I didn't approve of things she'd done, I'd hoped to stay in touch and one day meet Nellie.

Adelaide opens her office door and the patient ahead of me leaves. "Kate." She shares a welcoming smile. "Come in."

I sit on her leather sofa and stare out the window at the spring-time trees: a budding magnolia lending its sweet scent to the air, a redbud with lilac blooms, a pink dogwood with star-shaped flowers, the Carolina-blue sky shedding sparkling rays of sunshine. Adelaide situates herself behind her desk in her chair. "You requested an emergency session?"

"I've had some news about my family."

"Oh, good!"

My expression alarms her. "Not good." She frowns sympathetically. "I'm sorry. What happened?" I tell her everything I know about Diane being in town and her blackmailing scheme, including her awareness of Emma's kidnapping back when it happened.

"I'm glad you didn't tell me any of this earlier," she says. "I would have had to go to the police."

"That won't be necessary now," I reply.

"Yes, and I'm very proud of you for making that call and for speaking to Shane." She pauses and then asks, "How did that feel?"

"Hard," I answer truthfully. But then I smile at the wistful memories. "Good too."

Adelaide smiles as well. "I'm glad."

"I learned something shocking," I volunteer, because the forensics came back in and the results were conclusive. "Diane shot both my parents and then killed herself."

"Oh my goodness, Kate." Compassion drapes every word. "How terribly hard for you."

"I'm sad about losing Diane, it's true." I shrug. "Not so much about my parents."

Adelaide exhales and nods. "I get that completely. You don't have to apologize for your feelings. Own them, please. You suffered years of abuse at their hands and so did Diane and Mark. It's no wonder you've had an uphill battle, all three of you children."

"Yeah."

"Have you spoken with Mark?"

"I have." I brighten at the thought. "He's invited me to come see him in Miami, and meet his family, and Nellie."

"That's wonderful."

"Yes."

"How are you doing on your medication?"

"Pretty excellent, actually."

"And Katherine?"

I stare at her astounded because it's happened so suddenly. And yet, on a very deep and instinctive level, I know I'm not wrong.

"She's gone."

O'REILLY
THE COP

Now

Kate's given her statement and Claremont is wrapping things up. "Kate," she says, "thanks very much for coming in today. This means a lot to us." Although the information about Dotti's collaboration with Diane won't affect Dotti's sentencing, it could have an impact with the parole board. Dotti's not getting out of prison anytime soon. She'll be in for the duration.

"I'm glad I could help," Kate says. She looks at Claremont and then at me. "I'm trying to do better." We both believe her. Kate's changed.

"One more thing," Claremont says before we stand to go. "So we can clear the books. You told us about Diane blackmailing Cass. Do you know if they ever met up?"

Kate shakes her head. "I don't think so. At least she didn't mention anything. Only that she'd been watching Cass's house and Allen's movements over those last few days before Cass was killed. She was waiting on the big eruption between Allen and Cass, expecting that to spill over into his marriage with Sadie. She wanted to muddy the waters and make things difficult for Allen. You could say she held a grudge, a very strong one. That was a weakness my sister had, wanting to make people pay."

"I know you had a tough upbringing," Claremont says.

"Yeah, that's true."

Claremont writes something in her notebook then sets down her pen. "When was the last time you saw Cass?"

"Me?" Kate thumbs her chest. "It was the day she died, I guess."

Claremont cocks one eyebrow. "Come again?"

"She came into Café Latte." Kate stops suddenly. "Shit." She winces at us. "Sorry."

"It's okay." Claremont holds up her hand. "What do you mean Cass came in? For coffee?"

"Yes, a double-shot latte." She crinkles up her face remembering. "That's weird now that I think on it."

"What's weird?" I ask her.

She stares at me and says, "She was with Teresa."

Teresa? What the fuck?

The chief and I exchange a look. I place my elbows on the table and lean forward. "What were they doing there together?"

Kate shrugs. "Drinking coffee? Teresa treated."

Claremont turns to me when Kate has gone. "I think it's time for a little chat with Allen's ex-wife."

"My thinking too."

TERESA
THE EX-WIFE

Now

"Thanks for coming in today," O'Reilly says as I take a seat in the interrogation room. Rodriguez is in here too. I don't know where Claremont is. Probably behind that glass.

"What's this about?" I didn't tell anyone that I'm here. I took a long lunch hour. Didn't tell Henry. I've been seeing a lot less of him this week in the evenings. I've had too much on my mind. This whole Allen situation is wearing. I'm ready for it to be over. I wish they'd find him.

"We wanted to ask you about your relationship to the murder victim, Cass Thomas?"

"Relationship? I didn't have any relationship with Cass."

O'Reilly taps his pen on the table, then twirls it around in his fingers. "We have a witness that saw the two of you having coffee." He adds more pointedly, "It was on the day Cass died."

"Oh, that!" I stage a laugh. "Well, honestly. I don't think it's important." What am I supposed to do here? Throw Sadie under the bus? They've already got Allen in the frame for Cass's murder.

"We beg to differ," O'Reilly says. "It could be extremely important. You were evidently one of the last people to see Cass alive."

"Don't be silly. There were lots of people at—" I gasp. "It was Kate Davis, right? She's the one who told you I was there."

"That part doesn't really matter." Says her ex-boyfriend. Might have expected that.

"Teresa," Rodriguez says. "If you're covering up for someone, maybe Allen—"

"Allen? Why would I cover up for him? A woman is dead, Captain Rodriguez. Two women if you count Diane."

Rodriguez and O'Reilly exchange a glance. There must have been some additional developments in Diane's case I'm not aware of, but neither one is sharing.

"I understand the seriousness of this case," I continue. "If I knew about what happened to Cass, I'd tell you."

"Sooo," O'Reilly asks again, drawing out he word. "Why were you having coffee?"

I blow out a breath. Maybe honesty is the best policy in this particular situation. That's not always the case, but maybe here. I've got to get them off my back by volunteering something. "Okay, I'll tell you the truth, but not to implicate Sadie in Cass's death. I want to be crystal clear about that."

"O-kay," Rodriguez says.

"I met with Cass to warn her about Sadie," I tell them.

"Sadie?" the two of them ask together. "Why her?"

I sink down in my chair. "I might have accidentally let it slip to Sadie that Allen and Cass were getting together that evening. Allen acted like he didn't know what Cass wanted to talk about. I don't believe they had anything going on between them but I guess you never know."

"So, back to Cass?" Rodriguez prods.

I press my lips together before speaking. "Sadie has a history of losing her temper around Cass. I honestly don't think she ever liked her. I was worried that she might show up at Cass's and go off half cocked. Accuse Cass and Allen of being involved."

"Sounds like she did that," O'Reilly informs me. "The two of them argued, but when Sadie left, Cass was very much alive."

I clap my hands together. "Well, there you go! I guess I was making mountains out of molehills and things never got as bad as I feared."

"What exactly did you fear, Teresa?" Rodriguez asks in low tones.

"Not murder! Gosh! No. Nothing like that."

O'Reilly thinks on this. "How did Cass take your warning?"

"With a grain of salt, I think. She didn't appear that concerned, but I'm still glad I spoke with her. My conscience is clear."

"And Forrest?" O'Reilly asks me. I hate that he's dragging my son into this. So unnecessary. "Where was he while you were on your little coffee date? Back at home?"

I resist the urge to scowl. "No, he was at his soccer practice. I dropped him off before driving to Café Latte."

"Why didn't you volunteer this earlier?" Rodriguez asks.

"I didn't think it was relevant."

O'Reilly's eyebrows arch. "Might not be."

They nod at each other. It seems my questioning is over. Now I have a question for them. "What about Allen? Have you had any leads at all?"

"Since he went by bike," O'Reilly answers, "he didn't have to use major roads or highways. If he knew where the CCTV cameras are— and I'm sure this time he does—he could have avoided those routes on purpose."

"Yes, but he's riding a bicycle and not a motorcycle. I mean, how far can he get?" I'm sure the police have checked hotel records, things like that. Sadie told me Allen took some cash but not much. "He has to be hiding out somewhere fairly close."

O'Reilly nods. "That's our supposition as well."

"Wait." A light bulb goes on in my head. "The lake house."

Rodriguez sits at attention. "What's that?"

"Allen's parents had a lake house. He held on to it as common property during our divorce, and I got our regular house, but then he sold it. Or at least he told me he was going to. I always assumed that he had. He's never mentioned that place once."

O'Reilly leans forward. "Where is it?"

"Lake Gaston."

"That's a bit of a hike," Rodriguez says, "but doable, I suppose. Allen seems in shape."

O'Reilly meets my eyes. "Can you get us the address?"

CASS
THE MISTRESS

Before

Allen's angry with me, I can feel it, although he's got no reason to be. Okay, yeah. Maybe I can see his point of view in not wanting to tell Sadie. But he's not thinking about how unfair he's being. Maybe he'll consider things more reasonably once he's cooled off.

I place our wineglasses in the dishwasher, feeling woozy. I can generally hold my liquor, and I only had one glass. I try hard not to look at him, because every time I do, he has that sway over me, that silent pull, and as much as I try to break free, I know I can't. Our secret keeps us bonded forever.

The dishwasher's nearly full and preloaded with a dishwasher tab. I press a button on the electronic panel on the lip of the door and shut it. I can feel him standing nearby beside the island in the center of the room. It houses a cooktop and has a bar with three stools on one side. "I think I should go," he says, as I stare at the floor, the tips of his loafers. The hem of his pleated khaki pants.

"But first," he says sternly. I look up and he's crossing his arms. "I'd like you to give me your word." I will myself to be strong. To live in *this moment.* Be grateful for what I have.

Stand my ground.

I meet his killer blue eyes, the ones I fell in love with in high school. He lowers his eyebrows ominously. "I'm serious, Cass." The harshness in his tone bristles the hairs on the back of my neck. Allen's always had this edge to him. Some would call it dark. But I know Allen's all bark and no bite. He's ticked off, that's all this is.

My gaze travels to his crossed arms in the cuffed sleeves of that blue button-down shirt. They guard his muscled chest, the chest I enjoyed feeling over me. Under me. The two of us skin to skin. I want to acquiesce. Have this conversation end smoothly. But no. There is too much at stake.

"I'm not going to make any promises I can't keep." I mean to say it boldly but my chin wobbles.

"You don't mean that." He steps toward me, then closer. "Cass!" he shouts when I turn away. His grip is on my arms now, pressing too hard, pinching just above my elbows. I wince and try to break free.

"Allen, stop!" The room seems to tilt and sway, and I blink to regain clarity. How strong was that wine?

Allen's eyes bore into mine, searing like daggers. "Swear to me."

"I can't." I didn't want it to come out like this. I wanted a way to break it to him gently, but he's thwarted me at every turn. Tuned me out when I've tried to open up. I've been trying to tell him for the past twenty minutes and now he's leaving. I've run out of time.

I can't stay silent any longer.

"Allen," I say. "We had a child."

ALLEN
THE HUSBAND

ALLEN
THE HUSBAND

Now

The lakefront stretches before me as the sun sinks lower and daylight starts to fade. I take a puff of my cigar, remembering, but not regretting, the choices that led me here. The moment I heard the sirens, I knew what I had to do. I had to dispose of the murder weapon, in order to protect my family. So I snuck out of the house and went to our neighborhood's playground where I'd hidden Cass's baseball bat under the slide.

I could tell Sadie was upset about something all evening, but Sadie doesn't always come out with her feelings right away. Sometimes, she sits on them and lets them stew, until the pot boils over. I figured she had something to say and was probably waiting until after Emma was in bed. We never have uncomfortable conversations, or argue, around our child. So I patiently waited for her to break the ice. It happened after I'd tucked Emma in. Sadie and I take turns with our duties. That night, I took care of Emma while Sadie washed up the dinner dishes. I can still see the moment in my mind's eye, Sadie's worried frown as clear as day.

ALLEN
THE HUSBAND

Before

I come down the back staircase and find her in the kitchen, drying and putting away the final pot from dinner in a cabinet. She doesn't turn to look at me. Doesn't ask how things went with Emma. She's been unusually quiet since returning from her errands and she's usually very bubbly in the evenings. I know Sadie. Something's wrong.

"Hey, Sadie?" I say as she walks into the den area.

"Hmm?" She doesn't turn to look at me. She sits down and picks up a magazine, leafing through it.

I follow her into the den and sit beside her on the sofa. "Is something going on we need to talk about? Because, if there is, hon, I'm here for you."

She blows out a breath and drops the magazine she's holding down on the coffee table, leans back and crosses her arms. She's not worried, she's angry—at me. "Why didn't you tell me, Allen?" A sideways glance that chills to the bone. "Tell me about you and Cass?"

Oh Jesus. Here it comes. "There is no me and Cass, Sadie." I soften my tone and say gently, "There hasn't been for a very long time."

Sadie glares at me with watery eyes. "You told Teresa, Allen? Teresa but not me?"

Oh man. On top of everything else, she's mad about that? "Why drag Teri into this?"

Sadie huffs out a hard breath. "Because she told me you and Cass had a thing, but she said it like she thought I already knew. Like she assumed you'd told me."

Shit. "Sadie, listen—"

"No! You listen to me, Allen!" She's shouting now, going to wake Emma.

I make a downward motion with my palms and she grates out in a whisper, "Don't you shush me." I've never seen her so ticked off. There are pink spots on her cheeks and temples.

"You fucked Cass Thomas, didn't you?" she hisses more quietly. "Not just once, but multiple times! Is that what happened with Teresa while Emma was gone? You said you slipped up once, that it only happened one time. Was that a lie, too, Allen?" She sweeps her hands around the room. "Has all of this been a lie? Our life? Our marriage? When will the next lie be the last lie? Or will they just keep coming?"

"Sadie . . ." My throat burns raw and I try to touch her arm, but she jerks it away.

"Don't touch me."

I sigh and bear the sting of her gaze, the look of utter betrayal in her eyes. "It wasn't like that at all, honey. Teresa and I were separated, and I was under a lot of pressure. This was *years ago* during the Walsh trial."

She blinks. "What?"

"Yeah, I know. I get it." My shoulders sink under the weight of her stare. "I should have told you about that, too, and way before Emma's kidnapping. Now, I'm sorry I didn't. Sorry I didn't mention that Cass and I had dated, but only briefly. I apologize for that now. I was separated from Teri at the time and headed for divorce. I ran into Cass at Smokey Joe's where she was tending bar. Sadie, honestly, it was just a fling. Cass wasn't even that into me."

She gapes at me in disbelief. "She *loved you*, Allen."

"Who told you that?"

A muscle in her jaw flinches. "Cass."

Shit, shit, shit. So Sadie went to see her. "What? When?"

She glares at me long and hard. "Tonight."

My heart thuds in a dull ache. "Sadie?" I ask softly. "Did something happen between you and Cass?" She turns away, avoiding my gaze. Fuck, no. I hope they didn't get into it. Sadie has her soft side, but she's also got a temper. A memory burns through me. Did her temper flare like it did when she lunged at Cass during Emma's kidnapping investigation? "Sadie," I ask calmly to keep the tremor from my voice. "Did you harm her?"

Sadie gapes at me. "Jesus Christ, Allen! How can you even ask me that? Cass is the one who came after me!"

"Sadie, please, keep your voice down." I dart a gaze at the kitchen stairs. Then I ask more quietly. "You two didn't fight—physically?"

"Of course not. We just had words." She frowns at the memory. "They weren't very pretty ones."

"Oh, sweetheart, I'm sorry. Sorry that things got ugly." Though honestly that doesn't sound like Cass. That seems more like Sadie.

I pull her into a hug and she sags up against me, lets me hold her. "Maybe we should schedule an appointment with our counselor to work this through?" I glance out the darkened window and at Cass's house, not wanting to stress Sadie further. She's already stressed enough. I need to be the voice of reason. Supportive. Calm.

"That might be a good idea," Sadie acknowledges. She's always had this issue: fear of abandonment. And that fear can manifest as jealousy. She told me about it when we first fell in love. After tragically losing her parents and being left on her own so young, she had trouble trusting that people wouldn't leave her and she was terrified to fall in love with me. And yet she did. I won't let her down. I'm not perfect myself. But I am the perfect one for her. I've always believed that and I still do.

All the while, I'm thinking I should check on Cass to make sure things didn't get too nasty between them. Up until now, Cass has been respectful of my wishes about not telling Sadie of our earlier affair. Now

I see that request was unreasonable. I should have told Sadie myself. And now it appears there is even more to tell her, but I don't want to do that until I learn the full story from Cass. How could she have hidden something so huge from me for all these years?

I should have been honest with Sadie about Cass's and my brief affair from the start. I didn't want to intentionally lie, but knowing how Sadie can react, I was trying to protect her feelings. Emma's disappearance came so quickly on the heels of our move, we barely had time to catch our breath before being thrown into the investigation for Emma's kidnapping.

Then afterward, we had my infidelity with Teresa to deal with. Heaping the story about Cass on top of that did not seem like the right thing to do at the time. Especially since Sadie already majorly distrusted Cass and had as good as assaulted her over the entire Bobby issue. I didn't want that happening again, over a relationship that had occurred so long ago.

"Can you tell me what happened," I ask gently, "between you and Cass?"

Her eyebrows knit together. "She answered the door and we talked. Then things got heated and we started shouting. She came at me in a rage and I picked up the . . . *Crap.*"

"What did you pick up, Sadie?"

She hangs her head. "Cass's baseball bat, but then I dropped it, Allen, I swear!"

"Did she chase after you?"

"How the hell would I know? I was scared for my life. You should have seen her, Allen. She was like this irrational, deluded person! Kept talking all this gibberish about how you and she were meant to be a family, and that—if I'd never come along—that might have happened."

"Oh boy." I hug Sadie to me again and this time she embraces me so firmly I can feel her heartbeats pulsing against mine. "Here's what's going to happen, all right?" I brace her by the shoulders and look in her eyes. "We're going to put all thoughts of Cass behind us this week and continue our lives as normal. Get on that plane to Aruba tomorrow and have a total blast, and Emma's going on her trip of a lifetime with her aunties Pat and Gayle." I decide that's the right thing to do. We'll face the issues relating to Cass when we get back. I want Sadie to have a good time. I can't selfishly ruin our trip.

"But Allen—"

I place my fingertip to her lips. "We've been through worse. We can weather this storm."

She smiles sadly but I've won her over. "Okay."

CASS
THE MISTRESS

Before

Allen lets me go with a shocked look.

I falter then get my bearings on spaghettilike legs.

"What *the fuck*, Cass?" He rakes his hands through his hair. "What the actual fuck?" His eyes are wide, his jaw slack. "You kept this from me? For all these years? Christ Almighty." He starts pacing the kitchen, glancing around.

His eyes dart to the built-in desk and my two baseball mitts. A baseball bat leans up against the desk on one side. I have a fleeting, odd thought I might need to use it. The notion comes from out of the blue like a self-protective instinct. I casually move in that direction—even though it's crazy to think this way, something inside me says I ought to.

Don't be foolish. Don't trust him.

Allen's face is pink now and turning red. He casts me a distraught look. "Why tell me now?" His voice grows raspy. "Why all of a sudden these true confessions?"

I start crying because the truth hurts so much. "I lost her." I press my hands to my chest and sob.

His eyes light with understanding. "The hospital. Fuck." He wheels on me suddenly. "You texted me that night, told me to come."

"You were already with Sadie," I say miserably, because I know now what I knew then. Allen was hers then and he would never love me.

"Cass." He softens his tone. "Cass, I'm sorry. I didn't know." He looks so genuinely thrown I actually believe him. "Your sister Robin was there with her husband Leon. They turned me away. Didn't say anything about . . . Holy mother of God," he says putting it together. "That's what this is all about? Why you want to tell Sadie?"

"I think she should know."

"Why now?"

"Because the truth is coming out, one way or another. It's out of my hands. Someone found out, got hold of the information."

"Who?"

"I don't know who, but they've been blackmailing me. Threatening to expose it themselves if we didn't let Sadie know first. And not just to Sadie, they said they'd make it public online. Think about what that would do to your kids, Allen: Forrest and Emma."

"Jesus Christ. What a mess."

I step closer to the desk and Allen sees the baseball bat. I reach for it but he grabs it first, hoists it high between us. I shrink back, my eyes on the bat. "Cass?" he asks breathing hard. "Cass, for Christ's sake, what are you doing?"

I get a horrid, sickening feeling.

I turn to run, but stumble.

Scramble to my feet.

Allen chases after me holding the baseball bat.

Pivots right in front of me.

Throws his back against the front door, blocking my escape.

His fingers tighten around the neck of the bat, his knuckles going white. He's got it up against his chest pointed diagonally at the ceiling. It wouldn't take a moment for him to lunge at me and smash the bat down over my head. My breath quickens and I inch back, my fingers splayed out, palms positioned downward. "Allen." I lick my lips, my nerves raw on a razor's edge. "Let's calm down." I move back a little more and he glares at me. "Discuss this reasonably."

"Do you know what this means?"

"Of course I do."

His eyes water. "This changes everything," he says like it's finally sinking in. I think he actually might cry.

"I know." My voice grows low and husky. Afraid.

His gaze darts to the baseball bat and he slackens his hold. "Christ, Cass. I'm sorry." The bat droops by his side when he holds it with one hand. Then he slowly puts it down on the floor. "This is *not* how it looks, all right? I would never in a million years hurt you. Christ. I just didn't want you to smash the ever-loving daylights out of me."

Allen's cell phone rings in his pocket and he takes it out. "One second," he says to me before answering. "It's Sadie." He holds the cell phone to his ear and says, "Hey, hon," in such a relaxed way you'd never guess he was here. "Wait. What? Right now?" He holds up his arm and checks his watch. "Okay. No worries. You can tell them I'm on my way."

He ends his call and looks at me. "I've got to pick up Emma from our friends' house. Sadie's stuck somewhere and has been delayed."

He grabs his car keys from my entry table and lowers his eyebrows. "This conversation isn't over," he promises. "I'll be back."

I nod, my heart pounding.

But, when the doorbell rings again, it's Sadie.

SADIE
THE WIFE

Teresa comes to see me Wednesday afternoon. She looks really shaken up. "I was just down at the police station," she says as we sit in the den. "They think they might know where Allen's been hiding."

"What?" My pulse spikes erratically. "Oh my God, are they bringing him in?" I don't want to believe Allen was involved in any of that. But I don't know what to believe anymore.

"If they can find him."

"Where do they think he is?"

"At his late parents' old lake house."

"I didn't know Allen owned a place like that."

"I didn't either," Teresa answers. "I thought he'd sold it. Sadie," she says, her eyes wide. "I want you to be ready. Once Allen learns the cops are onto him, who knows what he'll say or do. He's likely killed Cass and we don't know about Diane. Unless they keep him in custody, he could come after you next. You know too much. You can testify that Allen snuck out of your house in the middle of the night to see and possibly kill her."

I feel faint and my stomach clenches. "Why do you think he would have done that, Teresa? What was his motive in killing Cass?"

"I think Cass had something on him," Teresa says in a whisper. "Something dark."

I cover my mouth with my hands. "It was about Bobby." This realization hits me with such strong clarity it has to be correct. Cass had been keeping this unimaginable secret and she claimed she was being blackmailed, that she had to reveal the truth about the child or face the consequences of Bobby's true parentage becoming public. That's why she said she had to talk to Allen first and then let him explain the situation to me afterward. Oh my God.

"What? Which Bobby? Wasn't that the phantom kid Cass had? The one who died in—"

"No, no." I shake my head. "This Bobby is very real and alive. Cass's sister Robin and her husband, Leon, called her Bobby for Barbara and raised her as their own. But Teresa." I stare at her seriously, unsure of how she's going to take this. "The child wasn't Robin and Leon's. She was Cass and Allen's little girl."

Teresa's mouth drops open. "You're kidding. Allen and Cass had a kid? Unbelievable!"

"Yes. Cass and Richard named their boy Robert and they called him by his full name. He's the child who died in the auto accident along with his dad, Cass's ex-husband."

"Mind blowing. Wow." I can see Teresa's having a hard time processing this. It's a lot to take in. I was completely overwhelmed too. "How did you find all this out?" she asks me. "Who told you?"

"The pastoral minister from Our Lady of Our Savior came to see me. Cass had confided the story to her at one time. After Cass's death, and with Allen being named as a suspect, she felt that I should know the truth about Allen's daughter. Up until then, I was completely in the dark. Sounds like Allen may have been unaware he had this child until Thursday when Cass might have told him."

Teresa frowns. "And when he learned the truth about Bobby, Allen didn't want that coming out because . . ." Her voice softens. "He didn't want to lose you. Oh, Sadie." She takes my hand and my eyes brim hot. "I'm so sorry, hon. What a nightmare. What are you going to do?"

"I don't know." I hang my head, remembering my heated altercation with Cass, and not wanting to face the horrible truth. "Teresa," I say. "I don't think Allen killed Cass at two a.m. I think she might have already been dead. Or maybe he drugged her first and then bludgeoned her to death later." My stomach roils at the thought. But the baseball bat must come into play somehow, or else Allen wouldn't have taken it to dispose of.

"What? Why?" Teresa asks.

"I've been thinking and fretting about it. When I went to confront Cass about having an affair with Allen, she wasn't acting exactly right. She was behaving almost as if . . ."

I swallow hard and Teresa says, "Go on."

"As if maybe she'd been drugged."

Teresa gasps. "You think Allen put something in her wine? I know the police found Allen's fingerprints on the wine bottle. You told me that, so they were pretty clearly drinking together."

My heart grows heavy. "What other explanation can there be?"

"Maybe you should tell the police about the wine? You need to tell them that Cass was acting drugged and you think it might have been Allen who drugged her. Maybe it's time, Sadie. You have to think of your own safety and of protecting Emma."

Before these last several days, I never thought I'd feel kindly toward her, but Teresa is making so much sense and she's been so good to me. Helping me through this trauma. The last thing in the world I want to do is hurt my husband. But I simply can't allow him to harm us. Teresa's right. I have to go to the police. No more cover-ups and no more secrets. I'm going to tell them everything I know.

O'REILLY
THE COP

Now

We pass a campfire ring of rocks outside and enter the lake house with guns drawn, as dusk closes in around us. The campfire looks like it's been recently used, still emanating heat from its dying embers. It's shadowy inside the cabin under a canopy of trees. I flip on a light switch in the kitchen. No dice. The clock on the stove has stopped working and the microwave's panel is blank. I hold up a hand. We stop, wait and listen. No humming noises at all. The only sound comes from outdoors: the wind raking through the trees, the lulling sounds of the lake.

Rodriguez whips into one room, leading with her weapon. Patel and Brady are here, so's Claremont. The chief returns from the back of the house. "It's clear. Nobody's here."

There are cans on the counter, some bottled water. An unopened bag of chips. A covered pot sits on the nonworking stovetop. I lift the lid. Bring the back of my hand to the side of the pot. Still warm. It's canned beef stew. Likely heated on the campfire.

I peer into a bedroom and the covers are rumpled, some scattered dirty clothes on the floor. Try the light switch. "Looks like the power is off," I tell Rodriguez as she stands beside me.

"Chief!" Brady calls from a window. He points at the driveway and a figure biking away at full speed, standing on the pedals to move them faster. We pour out of the cabin en masse and start shouting.

"Stop! Hands up!"

"Police!"

TERESA
THE EX-WIFE

Now

"I'm sorry," O'Reilly says to me and Sadie, relaying the tale. "We ran after Allen as best we could, but he was faster on the bike and seemed to know where he was going. We couldn't drive our cars into dense woods. But don't worry, we'll catch him. Now that we've discovered the cabin, he has limited places to go."

O'Reilly asked the two of us to meet with him at the station so he could fill us in. We both sit in his office, which is a nice change from an interrogation room. We're being informed now rather than questioned. Still, I was hoping for better news. This has dragged on too long and is taking its toll on Forrest. The outcome's not going to be pretty, but the sooner we deal with it the better.

I glance at Sadie because she got here first. While the others were away, she gave her statement to Officer Patel, a person she knew and trusted from Emma's investigation. She's probably ready to go home. She's been down at the station for a couple of hours now at least.

I protectively lay a hand on Sadie's arm and ask O'Reilly, "Is Sadie in danger?"

O'Reilly frowns. "After what Sadie told Officer Patel earlier, she could be. We now fear Allen drugged Cass, likely by putting something in her wine."

"So you found poison in Cass's system during the autopsy?" I ask to confirm.

O'Reilly shakes his head. "It wasn't poison, it was Ambien."

"Sleeping pills," Sadie gasps. "That makes sense based on how Cass was acting."

"How disgusting." I turn to Sadie. "Allen really wanted her out of the way."

"Yeah," Sadie says sadly, "apparently so." She looks like she's trying to wrap her head around it. She sweeps back her hair from her face and tucks it behind her ears. Poor Sadie. It's hard to live in glass houses and have them come crashing down all around you.

O'Reilly spreads his hands on his desk. "We tested what was left in the bottle. That wine itself was clean. We're assuming Allen likely crushed the pills and put them directly in Cass's wineglass when she wasn't looking. She told him about Bobby and he didn't want her to talk."

"That's so horrible," Sadie says in a whisper. "I feel guilty if it was on account of me."

"Even if it was," O'Reilly says, "you can't blame yourself for a woman's murder. Only the murderer is to blame."

"Were there traces of Ambien on the wineglass?" I ask to clarify.

"Nope." O'Reilly rakes a hand across his buzz cut. "Both wineglasses went through the dishwasher, which is what makes this case so tough to crack. We know that Allen was there, because his fingerprints were on the wine bottle and elsewhere in the house."

I offer my opinion. "He must have drugged her first and then finished her off with the baseball bat when she was in a weakened state."

"That's what we're thinking too," O'Reilly says. "We just need to confirm it with the coroner, but for the moment everything clocks. Allen had a motive, means, and opportunity to kill Cass."

"What about Diane?" Sadie asks nervously. "Who killed her?"

O'Reilly leans back in his chair and sets his hand on his holster. "I'm afraid that's an ongoing investigation so I'm not at liberty to discuss that."

"But it *could have been* Allen?" Sadie wraps her arms around herself and trembles. "Oh my God."

"Did you tell them, Sadie?" I nod at O'Reilly. "Tell the police about Diane saying she worried about Allen 'finishing the job'?"

She nods, holding her stomach. "I did."

Sadie glances at me then volunteers, "Allen was acting really funny the evening Cass died. I was mad at him for concealing his affair with Cass and we had some words. I didn't know anything about Bobby then, and she didn't come up.

"I told Allen I'd spoken to Cass and told him how we'd argued, but not about how sleepy acting she'd been." Her face colors as she speaks to O'Reilly. "I should have come to the police with all this information earlier. Should have told you immediately that Allen was on the run. I didn't understand what was happening initially. Didn't want to face what Allen might have done."

O'Reilly's forehead creases in understanding. "You were in shock. What's important is that you're helping us now."

"So, the official cause of death was head trauma?" I ask O'Reilly.

He nods. "Allen allegedly disposed of that baseball bat for a reason. Sadie," he says addressing her. "I'm asking you to be careful," O'Reilly warns. "Stay aware of your surroundings at all times. Be alert when you're out on your own and walking to your car, and when you're at home be sure to lock your doors.

"You may think you know Allen," he says, "but people can surprise you. He might not be the man you think you married. There are a lot of suspicious circumstances surrounding one individual, and one too many coincidences if you ask me." He crosses his arms, considering her a moment. "Allen doesn't have anywhere to go tonight. The cabin's under watch and he knows he was discovered there, so I'm banking on him trying to come home, and Sadie." He stares at her. "I want you to be ready."

"Is it really safe for Sadie to be in her house?" I ask him.

"We'll have her surrounded by law enforcement, and having Sadie there might actually work to our advantage. Allen's more likely to show if he knows that she's there."

So their house is the mousetrap and Sadie's the cheese. Sounds dangerous. I'm glad I gave Sadie my gun. I shudder inside at the thought of Allen getting shot, but I can't let anything happen to Sadie. That would be worse. Allen needs to be held accountable for Cass's murder. Sadie doesn't have it in her to kill someone, least of all Allen, but she can hold him at bay until the police arrive.

"Now that I know Allen's guilty," Sadie says, "it feels a little creepy staying there alone."

"We can station an officer or two inside," O'Reilly says.

"Do you really expect Allen will show in that case?" she asks him.

O'Reilly frowns. "You make a good point and we do want to catch him."

Sadie sends me a hopeful look. "Teresa, I know this is a huge imposition—"

"Of course, you know I'll do it."

"I wouldn't want to put you in danger," Sadie says.

"We'll keep the situation closely monitored the entire time," O'Reilly promises us both. "We'll have an unmarked police van on Sadie's street with sound surveillance and recording equipment and will set up listening devices in your house. Patel and Brady will remain posted outside, with Gomez and Johnson near Cass Thomas's, and additional marked vehicles patrolling the streets. We'll post an additional unmarked car at the vacant house on Cass Thomas's street. The one directly across from the path leading into the woods. We believe Allen accessed the neighborhood by riding his bike down the greenway before, and he'll do it again. Next time, we'll see him coming. This will hopefully be over soon."

TERESA
THE EX-WIFE

Now

I don't mind staying with Sadie. I know she's nervous about Allen. I would be too. He wanted to protect their marriage but now will know she turned against him by attesting to Cass's drugged state after he'd been at Cass's house drinking wine. Cass was athletic and health minded. She never would have indulged in mixing that heavy dosage of meds with wine.

I toss my final things into my gym bag. Apart from basic toiletries and makeup, I'm only bringing stretch pants and a baggy shirt to hang out in and an old T-shirt of Allen's to sleep in. Okay, I get it. That's a little perverse given the circumstances. But I've had it forever and it's comfortable, softened from years of washing, and I like the way it hangs mid-thigh. Sadie would probably be creeped out if she knew where I got it. Maybe she'll think it's Henry's and won't notice the tattered stitching on the sleeves and hem.

Someone knocks on the door and I traipse down the wooden stairs. Due to its modern design, our staircase has no railing but it's never been a problem. I open the front door and—crap. It's Henry. He stands there in a plaid button-down shirt and jeans, wearing his tortoiseshell glasses.

"Teresa, thank God you're okay." He pulls me into a hug without bothering to come in. I'm glad we don't have close-by neighbors. I wouldn't want them looking and getting into my business.

"Henry," I ask, my eyebrows arched. "What are you doing here?"

I don't ask him in but he assumes it, walking past me and shutting the door. "I was worried about you with the news. So much going on. This thing about Allen. Holy shit. Things look bad for him, right?"

I frown and offer my opinion. "I'm afraid so."

"I didn't see you at the observatory."

"I took today off."

"I don't blame you." He pushes his glasses back when they slip. "I've tried calling and texting," he says. "My calls go to voicemail and you haven't gotten back to me."

I sigh and offer an excuse. "I know it's been bad of me, but I've been dealing with Forrest."

"Of course." He wears a worried frown. "How's the kid holding up?"

"The kid is with his grandma."

"I'm really glad. I know you're glad he's away from all of this too."

"Henry," I say. "I'd love to chat but—"

"What the hell, Teresa? Are you mad at me?" He appears so genuinely hurt I want to feel sorry for him but I can't. I've used up all my sympathy and I have a limited amount. Henry's so needy and his neediness is starting to drain me.

"Look, I'm sorry, but I'm really exhausted. The police have been asking me a lot of questions and now they're worried about Sadie."

"Oh no."

"Yeah." I gesture to the gym bag I brought downstairs with me. "I'm headed over there to stay with her tonight."

"So." He blows out a breath sounding frustrated. "They still haven't caught Allen?"

"No, but they're getting closer I hope."

His expression changes like he's decided something. "Tell you what. Why don't you let me come with you? I can stay with you and Sadie and—"

"Awkward, Henry. Thanks and no. The police will be stationed outside and at Cass's house on the street behind Sadie's so we'll be well looked after."

Doubt gleams in his eyes. "You're sure about this?"

"Yes, but thank you." I give him a perfunctory kiss. "I'll call you later when it's all over." I decide then I won't.

SADIE
THE WIFE

Now

Teresa's here and the vibe is kind of strange. We've never hung out just the two of us, but I guess there's a first time for everything and the circumstances couldn't be more fucked, which calls for wine. I ask her red or white and she says red. I open a Chianti and pour us each a hefty glass. We've ordered a pizza so an Italian wine fits. We sit in the den in our comfy clothes, but those don't help assuage the grip of the snug-fitting body armor underneath. It's hard to wrap my head around the two of us teaming up in order to trap Allen. But I'm not the kind of woman to let a cold-blooded killer run free. The police planted bugs all over the house and I'm wearing a wire besides. Nobody's taking any chances, least of all me.

Teresa's on the sofa and I'm on the love seat. "Well, this is weird," she says and I laugh.

"Yeah, who would have ever thought this?"

She shrugs and takes a sip of wine. "Not me."

"Me neither." I stare out the darkened window across my backyard. I can see the tiniest bit of the police cruiser on Cass's street at the end of her driveway, and the gate is latched. I'm in a horrible position but I'm doing the best that I can. I need to focus on the big picture and making things right for Emma, my little girl.

"Hey, Sadie," Teresa says thoughtfully over the rim of her glass. "I never thanked you for something."

"Yeah, what's that?"

"Stealing my husband," she sneers and for a second I can't tell if she's kidding but then she laughs. "No, sorry. Didn't mean that. I understand you didn't steal Allen."

Right, I think in my head. *Maybe you secretly believe that person was Cass.*

"What I honestly meant to say." Teresa rests her glass of wine on her bent-up knees. "Is thanks for how you are with Forrest. I don't know how you do it, but you're very good to him." She shrugs.

"He's the greatest."

"Not always."

I chuckle. "Well, he is almost a teenager."

"We're both fucked," she jeers and my eyes water. I didn't expect her to say that, to expect me to be a continued part of Forrest's life, but of course, why wouldn't I? I've bonded with him over the years, and I couldn't ever see just letting him go.

"He'll land on his feet," I say and raise my wineglass. "To Forrest!"

"To Forrest!" she cheers and takes a drink. "He hates me, you know," she says and frowns.

"Teresa, no. I'm sure that he doesn't."

"Oh, but he does. I haven't always been exactly present."

I don't comment immediately because Allen once told me that's why his and Teresa's marriage broke apart, because she couldn't be present for him. I sip slowly from my wine and wait to see if she'll add anything more. She looks wistful a moment staring out our fan-shaped window. "I like your house."

"Thanks, I like yours." It's true I appreciate its aesthetic. At the same time I've always been envious of Teresa's retreat in the woods, the house she and Allen built together.

"Do you think we'll make it?" she asks. I consider her in a new light, in the way Allen probably once did in the beginning and I understand her appeal. She's attractive and winsome. Something about her makes you want to rush to her aid, although despite her diminutive size she appears to possess a lioness's strength.

"I suppose we'll have to." I shrug. "I mean, what choice do we have?"

My phone buzzes with a text. It's Patel checking in. I send a thumbs-up and she texts back Test mic. Shit. I forgot. I lower my chin toward my chest and the area where Patel strapped the wire to my chest. "This is Sadie."

Sound crackles back, then Patel responds. "Great. We've got you." She runs Teresa through the same drill next. The overt police surveillance seems very intrusive somehow given my and Teresa's intimate conversation, but the police want to be sure there are no mistakes and that they can get to us in a heartbeat.

"All good?" I ask Teresa after she finishes her brief run-through with Patel.

She shares a thumbs-up. "*All good,*" she says a bit too loudly. She brings a finger to her lips and whispers, "Where's the gun?" I pull out a side table drawer next to the love seat and it's nestled inside. She mouths, *Can't be too careful,* and I agree. Although it's hard to imagine needing to use it with the police being this close. Much less using it on Allen. No matter what he's done, I could never shoot my husband. What a horrible thought and position to be pushed into. Some things you have to leave up to the law.

Still. Teresa drove home her point. The police didn't keep Allen from getting in last time. Why give them the benefit of the doubt when the stakes are this high? So the Walther PPK is just insurance, in case things go awry. My heart pounds erratically in my chest. I hope I'm up for this and will be able to see it through.

Teresa cradles her drink in both hands, her slim fingers wrapping around the wineglass. "Sadie," she says. "I'm really sorry about all of this. About how things have gone down with Allen."

"I know. Me too."

"But I am glad of one thing." She pauses to think. "No, two, actually. One, that we both have our kids, and two, that Emma came home, and that she's doing better."

I lift my wineglass in her direction. "That's three things but I'll drink to all of them."

She frowns. "What are you going to do about Bobby?"

A lead weight settles in my stomach. "That's a tough one, I don't know. Probably go and talk to Robin and Leon, once Cass's killer is safely in custody."

"That sounds like the right thing to do." She admires me a moment. "You're very good about that, Sadie. Always doing the right thing."

"Not always," I admit truthfully, "but I'm trying to do better." I pick up the television remote, needing to fill the time and not with conversation. Teresa and I can pretend we are cordial but there's a silent undercurrent between us. She may not sense it but I do and it makes me antsy. I don't want to be Teresa's friend. She's done horrible things to my family. I want Teresa to be held responsible for the things she's done, but there's no magic bullet that will make that happen tonight, and tonight I need Teresa's company. It's important that she's here, and I'm not alone. "So what'll it be?" I ask, switching on the TV to our streaming menu. "Rom-com? Thriller?"

She shakes her head. "No jump scares for me."

She's right about that. No need to set our nerves further on edge than they already are. We settle on a newly released romantic comedy, but I don't laugh at any of the scenes. My heart keeps pounding in my throat as I sit and wait for Allen.

TERESA
THE EX-WIFE

Sadie and I watch the movie pretending this is some kind of girls' night, but inwardly we're both on guard. If Allen doesn't show, I don't know what I'll do. It's hard to imagine going through this two nights in a row. Three nights, forget it. Four? I'll fall apart from nerves. And who knows how I'll ever sleep.

I'm not going in to work again tomorrow or probably for the rest of the week. Who am I kidding? I'd never be able to focus, and I honestly don't want to run into Henry. I feel like I treated him badly earlier tonight and I shouldn't have done that. It's not Henry's fault that he isn't Allen and that he could never replace the man I loved.

I heave a deep sigh realizing it's happened.

It's come on so suddenly my heart skips a beat.

I no longer love Allen.

Maybe it's because of who he is or what he's done. The choices he's made have driven him further and further away from me. And all the times I tried to draw him closer only exacerbated the problem by driving him back into Sadie's arms. And now that Sadie understands what a monster Allen is, she won't want him either. Good. Allen's finally going to get what he deserves.

Sadie puts the movie on pause and turns to me. "Want to take a break for a minute and clean up?"

"Sure," I say staring at her cell phone on the end table beside the love seat. The police are still listening and recording. Maybe they're getting more out of the movie than we are. Sadie carries our plates to the kitchen and I pick up our empty wineglasses.

"Want anything else to drink? Coffee?"

I shake my head, my nerves already on edge. "Better not."

"How about decaf or herbal tea?" She strides back into the den and I'm in the kitchen setting our wineglasses on the counter. I hear a noise and spin toward it. The doorknob to the garage turns from the other side. Shit. "Sadie!"

The door yanks open and it's Allen.

He looks like hell in beard stubble, his expression gaunt.

He wears jeans and a black hoodie. It looks like he hasn't bathed in days.

His eyes gleam wildly when he sees me, sees Sadie.

Fuck.

I back against the counter, suddenly afraid. Like he'll assume that I'm involved in setting him up and take things out on me. I'm here after all with Sadie.

"Allen," she says, "stay where you are." Sadie's gone as white as a sheet and she holds my gun with both hands, pointing it at Allen.

Allen's hands shoot skyward. "Sadie! What the fuck?"

"We know, Allen." Sadie's voice shakes. "We know that you killed Cass."

I'm inching my way out of the kitchen, my pulse pounding in my throat.

"And what's Teri doing here?" he asks glaring at me.

"How did you get in?" Sadie demands loudly. She's signaling to the police. Where the hell are they? Why aren't they here?

"I used the spare key we keep in the foyer. I took it."

Sadie sets her jaw but it trembles. "After murdering Cass."

"Sadie, stop! That's not true!"

"You drugged her, didn't you, Allen? Put sleeping pills in her wine?"

"What? No!" Allen's face is blank, so guileless.

"Then you went back later and when you saw she wasn't dead, you hit her with that baseball bat! That's why you had to get rid of it, isn't it?"

"Sadie, wait." He lowers his hands slightly and Sadie brandishes the gun.

His hands move back up—slowly.

"Just admit it, Allen! We all know!"

He glares at me suspiciously. "You've got the wrong person, Sadie. It wasn't me. Now put the gun down." Allen steps closer and I dash away, scooting behind Sadie. Fuck. Things are looking bad. Where the hell are the police? Wait! There! I stare down the front hall and through the sidelight I see them running up the driveway, and also out back: the second pair of officers sprinting across the lawn.

"Allen," Sadie says huskily. "The police have evidence. It's all coming out in the open about you and Cass and Bobby."

"Bobby?" Allen's face goes white and then it changes, turning pink and then red.

Sadie backs away bumping into me. "That's why you killed Cass, isn't it? Because she wanted to tell the world, wanted to tell me?"

The police burst in the front and back doors.

"Freeze!" Patel shouts. "Police!"

Allen rushes at Sadie.

She fires.

SADIE
THE WIFE

Now

Allen holds his stomach and doubles over.

Blood seeps through his fingers and he falls to his knees, crouches. Catches himself from falling to the floor with one hand. The other hand grips his middle, the sleeve of his hoodie turning crimson, soaking up his blood.

The gun slips from my hand and hits the carpet.

"Allen! *Nooo*."

I rush to my dying husband, unable to calculate what's happened. Disbelieving what I've done. He's clutching his middle, his breathing labored. "Sadie," he wheezes. He raises his head to look at me. "Sadie, I'm so sorry." Then he closes his eyes and slumps forward, collapsing on the floor.

"Everyone! Get back!" Patel's barking out orders. Brady has me by the shoulders and is tugging me away as I wail and sob and shout out his name. Teresa stands there staring like she's witnessed a horror show, like she can't believe what I've done. Bev Johnson takes her by the arm and leads her away.

Fifteen minutes later, Teresa and I are huddled in the back of an ambulance when a gurney's rolled out my front door. The body on it is covered with a sheet and I start crying.

Teresa takes my hand. "It's over."

TERESA
THE EX-WIFE

I'm back in my office at the observatory the following Monday, trying to make sense of everything that transpired last week. Sadie won't be charged in Allen's shooting. The police on the scene affirm she fired in self-defense. Allen could have wrenched the gun away from her. The other officers being present might not have prevented the worst-case scenario from going down. Allen might have grabbed that gun and shot Sadie. Hell, from the look on his face, he might even have shot me.

Henry appears in my doorway and I'm not glad to see him. I'm so tired I just want to be alone and have time to think. "You've got a visitor," he says and moves aside.

What the fuck?

It's Kate.

"Kate Davis," I say. "What are you doing here?"

Her eyes are red like she's been crying. "I heard the news about Allen."

I shut my laptop and ask, "Who told you?"

She frowns. "The police."

"But why would they tell—" I stop suddenly then say, "Oh, because he killed Diane."

"No," she says. "It wasn't Allen."

"No?" I was so sure it was him. "Then who?"

Before

I've got a lot of blood on my hands for a person my age. I guess I learned my taste for vengeance from my parents. I'm some sort of vampire with the thrill of destruction in my veins. I've lived with that duality my whole life, but now I've come to accept it. I want to do better in the daylight but then the darkness seeps in, and I know I've got to act out by striking back. By making some motherfucker pay for what they've done.

The three of us kids chose different paths. Mark went soft, belly up and into drugs, drowning himself in delirium, until he had the sense to leave home and finally get his shit together. Poor Kit-Kat was nearly broken, but I'm proud of my baby sister. She's pulled herself up by her bootstraps and is making a life for herself. So is Mark.

I couldn't completely beat it myself, that relentless early abuse. I hated what my parents did to me so much, I wanted to give as good as I'd gotten. I was never mean to Caleb, though. My ex-husband was a sweetheart of a man and a very kind soul. I hate that he got some shit breaks, which is why I enacted my payback on his behalf. My collusion in Emma's kidnapping wasn't honestly as much about Allen's teenage rejection of me, although that did sting. What I was maddest about was his treatment of Caleb because that blew up our family.

As vindictive as I acknowledge I am, I'd never hurt a hair on Nellie's head and what I'm doing now is not with that intent. I want nothing but the best for my baby girl, and I've come to understand that the best involves her moving on without me. Creating an existence without a screwup of a mom around who's done some unmentionable things, like kill her grandparents. And I did do that—very happily. I won't lie. The world is a better place.

I knew the instant we got to Mark's that he was a better fit for Nellie. He opened his arms and hugged me so tightly I almost wept. Emotion clogged his voice.

"Diane, my God, it's so good to see you." I didn't know I would need this, to feel my big brother's arms around me, but I do. Mark releases me and smiles down at Nellie. "And you must be Nellie. Hello. I'm your uncle Mark." His smile's so warm she leaps toward him in a hug. I'm stunned. Nellie's generally more reticent around people.

Elena welcomes us next, embracing us firmly. "Diane! At last." Her eyes twinkle at my child. "And Nellie. You're Clara's age, aren't you? Right around eight?" She smells of flowery perfume and has her ebony-colored hair swept up. She's got a light Spanish accent too. Mark told me her family's Cuban.

Clara bounds into the hall with her little brother Jaime. She protectively holds his hand. He's four. Both look more like Elena than Mark with their dark hair and eyes, though Clara's a bit lanky. She might get her dad's height.

They have a one-story house that is mostly windows. Huge sweeping glass walls provide views of manicured gardens, a tumbling fountain over cascading rocks, a gigantic green space with freshly mowed grass and a trampoline. Beautiful artwork's on the walls, bright splashes of color in the otherwise neutral decor, including a gleaming white tile floor with tasteful earth-toned inlays.

"Nellie," Elena says, "these are your cousins Clara and Jaime."

"Hi!" Clara grins, not shy at all. "Want to play?"

Nellie casts me a glance and I nod, then she shrugs. "Okay."

"Come on!" Clara says, taking Nellie's hand with her free one. She tugs Nellie and Jaime through the house and slides open a rear door. The kids burst onto the lawn in a gleeful procession. Nellie's running. Nellie's laughing. She's free. Then she's up on the trampoline, bouncing and giggling. I bite back my tears.

"You're really good to do this," I tell Mark and Elena.

"Of course," Mark says. "What are families for."

That's never the family we've had and he knows it.

Now I see a new sort of future for Nellie, should anything happen to me. A better and brighter world where she can grow and flourish among people who will love her and treat her kindly. I never could have imagined letting her go before.

But now?

Now my heart knows.

It's pitch black as I stand on the Bynum Bridge at midnight, the colorful graffiti on its walls and a footpath leading my way. The moon's a silver crescent like the rim of a thumbnail, but its faint light is enough to guide me as I traverse the shadows to the center of the bridge. This is pretty close to the spot where my mom tried to shoot me on that precipice overlooking the river. How fucked up is that? I guess I got the last laugh. I broke free from her and started running. It wasn't until I was a hundred yards away and safely in the woods that I realized I had my dad's gun.

I crouched silently in the underbrush until I heard them give up on their search for me and get into their car. They went home and hit the bottle if you can believe it. I did, because I'd seen them engage in that behavior so many times before. Drinking after doing some utterly stupid shit, then not remembering what they'd done the next morning, like beating their offspring to a pulp. I was so mad for me, and incredibly angry for all of us. I burst through the unlocked front door and found them slumped down in their chairs, glass tumblers in their hands. Melting ice cubes in pools of amber. Bourbon more than likely. It stank.

Dad raises his glass but he's too drunk to stand. Good. "What are you doing here?"

Mom slurs her words. "You little cunt."

Such sweet words from a mother. I raise the pistol and shoot her in the head. Blood explodes from her forehead, dribbles down between her eyes, trails down her nose. I'm a surprisingly good shot. I get Dad in the mouth next. He's got it open, preparing some obscenity.

Bang, bang, you're dead.

I stand there numbly as their bodies writhe forward, slump into unnatural positions, somehow wind up on the floor. Their evilness dragging their souls to hell more than likely. Okay. I release a breath. That's done.

The river rushes below me, skirting over rocks and gushing around boulders. It's louder in the still of the night. I hear crickets and a passel of croakers, those annoyingly loud frogs.

I don't want to go to prison and I'm not arrogant like Dotti.

I'm just ready for things to end.

Mark's a good man. He'll take care of Nellie. Probably a hell of a lot better care of her than I ever could. I climb onto the lip of the bridge, the stone wall overlooking the river. There's one person I need to contact so I send a short text, then drop my phone in the water. It lands with a plunk. My heart pounds one, two, three times. Best not to overthink this.

I jump.

TERESA
THE EX-WIFE

Now

I blink at Kate as she stands there just inside the doorway.

"Oh my God, that's shocking."

She steps closer to my desk and tilts her head. "What's shocking is that you got away with Cass's murder."

I laugh with disregard. "What on earth are you talking about?"

"I know what you did, Teresa," Kate says sternly. She puts her hands on my desk and leans forward. "I know that you killed Cass."

I scoff. "That's ridiculous. Everyone knows it was Allen. The police have closed the case."

"Well, maybe they shouldn't have."

"Whatever you think you know is wrong, okay? Why would I kill Cass? What would my motive be?"

She shrugs still angling toward me, her elbows locked. "Maybe you wanted her out of the way? Maybe you were jealous of her like you were of Sadie?"

"Don't be ridiculous. I had nothing to do with Cass's death and I've been nothing but present for Sadie. You can ask the police. Ask her."

"Maybe you found out about Bobby," she continues, "and it was too much to take. You wanted Allen to come back to you, didn't you? You hoped to have another child."

"Who the hell told you that?" I never told anyone. The only person who had that information was Allen, and now Allen's dead.

"But Allen wouldn't have a kid with you, would he? No." She narrows her eyes and adds cruelly, "He had one with Sadie, though. Then, when you learned he'd also had one with Cass, another little girl, it pushed you over the edge. You couldn't take it."

My stomach knots. "What the fuck, Kate? That's quite a theory. And very ridiculous. No one on earth will believe you, an ex-con with mental health issues."

"Talk about the pot calling the kettle black." She sneers. "At least I'm getting help. You should probably look into it."

"I think you need to leave now." I pick up my cell phone. "I'm calling security."

"Great," she says breezily. Her shoulders hunch forward. "They can bring the police."

I grip the cell phone so hard my knuckles ache. "And get *the fuck* off my desk."

She raises her hands like she's touched a hot stove. "Oops. Sorry, but actually *not sorry* about what I told the police."

"What?" I go a little faint. "What do you mean what you told the police?"

She folds her arms in front of her. "I let them know, Teresa. Told them about what I saw at Café Latte."

My heart beats like a kettledrum.

"We were just having coffee."

"Yeah, but you treated Cass to her order."

"So?"

"You thought my back was turned, didn't you? But here's the thing about coffee shops: all those shiny and reflective surfaces, stainless steel everywhere, and oh! How can I forget? The mirror mounted over the cappuccino machine that captures what's happening at the creamer station."

Fuck. "Kate, listen. It's not what you think. I was just adding sugar."

"Sugar?"

"Yeah, to Cass's latte."

She wrinkles up her face. "A health-conscious woman like Cass doesn't seem the loads-of-sugar kind."

"You're absolutely right. I used artificial sweetener."

"And stirred it in and then replaced the lid on her cup?"

I scoff. "What the hell, Kate? I wasn't going to carry Cass's latte across the room and outside without making sure the lid was on tight. Where are you even going with this? Why the hell does it matter whether I had coffee with Cass, or not?"

"You know what I think?" She gets a suspicious twist in her lips. "I don't believe you added any kind of sweetener to Cass's cup at all. I think you stirred in Ambien."

She waits for me to react so I put on a show, strictly for her stupid-ass benefit. "Bravo, Detective!" I mock her by clapping my hands. "Well done! You figured out what nobody else did, but here's the sad truth, Kate. You have a bad history with the law and a bum reputation in this town. No one on earth is going to believe you."

"Oh, I beg to differ about that." O'Reilly appears in the doorway.

Double fuck me.

Rodriguez shows up next. "Kate's wearing a wire," she says smugly. "We heard the whole thing." My face grows hot.

Patel appears with a pair of handcuffs. Brady's at her side.

Then, to top it all off, Chief Claremont walks in.

"Teresa Wilson," she says curtly. "We meet again."

TERESA
THE EX-WIFE

I duck my head and Claremont puts her hand on top of it, shoving a bit as I climb into the back seat of the cop car, hands shackled in front of me, like the common criminal I guess they think I am. I could have protested my innocence but decided I'd be wiser to wait and opt for a lawyer. Because the real truth is, they're all wrong about so many things.

I didn't mean to kill Cass Thomas. The dosage I carefully selected wasn't supposed to be fatal. I didn't know Cass's exact weight but I could guess it close enough. She was a bit shorter and plumper than me, but athletic. After the trauma of Emma's kidnapping, I had difficulty sleeping at night, so my doctor prescribed me Ambien. I took them for a while and there were a couple of really bleak nights where I was tempted to take too many, but I could never do that to Forrest, leave him without a mother.

Still, the idea lingered in the back of my mind, so I began stocking up, asking the doctor to refill my prescription without taking them. I was so distraught over Allen staying with Sadie, I didn't know which way to turn. Not to Henry, no. He was fine as a placeholder but he wasn't the man I desired, the person I loved. There were a few brief moments when Allen and I were together that he gave me hope. But then he crushed it just as surely as someone putting out the butt of a cigarette with their heel.

He couldn't extinguish the embers, though. Couldn't completely snuff out my feelings. I know that's what he intended to do, but those old dreams flickered, refusing to die. If I could just think of a way to get rid of Sadie, I could have Allen for my own. But I couldn't kill his new wife. As the ex-wife, I'd be a prime suspect, someone too close in his inner circle, a person who might have a motive because she still carried a torch for the man who'd left her.

Claremont slams shut the door and I jump in my seat, not expecting the eerie echo of my whole life going down the drain. I stare out the window as the others drive away. O'Reilly with Rodriguez and Officers Patel and Brady. Kate sitting in the back of O'Reilly's cruiser, appearing enormously pleased with herself, *conniving witch*. I didn't intentionally try to kill Cass, and I couldn't bring myself to kill myself either. Because, well. Forrest. My son needs me around to look after him and help him grow into a respectable man.

I stare out at the trees passing by in a blur and wonder why they look that way. Then I realize I'm probably crying. My eyes are hot and Cass is dead. Sadie's not, unfortunately. I toyed with the idea of offing her, but then harsh reality set in. Her being deceased would be no guarantee that Allen would reconcile with me. He'd probably build her a shrine and anoint her as sainted Sadie. Mourn her loss for eons, maybe even assuage his sadness by doing something unfathomable like going back and fucking Cass.

I despised Cass for interfering in our marriage. If she hadn't intervened with her round ass and big sexy tits, maybe Allen would have come back to me for good. That's when the idea hit me. It wasn't Sadie who had to go; it was Allen's former lover, neighbor, and old high school friend. I sniff and rub my forearm against my damp cheeks, not wanting Claremont to know that I'm crying. She's got another cop riding with her up front. His name is Gomez. He looks in the mirror and sees me.

But I don't care about him because I don't know him from last time. He wasn't around for the whole Emma scene, at least not that I knew of. I almost got Allen back before Emma went missing, but then that illusion blew apart, thanks to Sadie. No matter what the fuck I said, or how great I fucked him, Allen invariably landed back in Sadie's arms. It took me too long to see that but I finally did. That's when I crafted my master plan.

If I could successfully implicate Allen in Cass's murder, his and Sadie's marriage would surely break apart. Sadie's not stupid. She's not going to stay with a cold-blooded killer and put Emma at risk. But even for me, and hating her like I do, arranging Cass's death was too big a pill for me to swallow. So I opted for the next best thing to homicide: Cass's *attempted murder*.

I knew Allen was seeing Cass again, and I could guess why. It had to do with their secret bond, their love child Bobby. The knowledge burned me to the core like a searing-hot poker jammed through my heart. I had a pill cutter and a pestle and a mortar, so an easy way to break down the sleeping pills and convert them to a powder.

My first thought was to frame Sadie for Cass's murder to get her out of the picture. She'd attacked Cass once before. Allen told me about it, and the police were aware. So, in the light of Cass's attempted murder, they'd be watching Sadie closely. Maybe a court would convict her, if I put the whole thing together deftly enough.

But then Allen came over that day *gushing* about their second honeymoon trip, and how great it was going to be. He was clearly head over heels about Sadie, worshipping the ground she walked on. His obvious enthusiasm about their vacation made me literally sick to my stomach. He and I had talked about going to the Caribbean but we never did. Never set foot outside of the state of North Carolina on a couple's trip, or did anything that exotic. We vacationed in the mountains and had honeymooned at the Outer Banks.

After Allen left, I raced to the toilet and threw up.

When I was washing my face at the sink afterward, my gaze fell on my bottle of sleeping pills, and then I knew. Allen would never be mine again, that thinking was delusional. And, if I couldn't have him, I didn't want Sadie to have him either. I wanted her to suffer a loss similar to mine. I needed to see Allen wrenched away from her in a heartbeat so abrupt she felt like her whole world had been yanked out from under her. Destroyed.

If Allen were convicted for Cass's attempted murder, he'd be locked up in prison for a long time, but I had to make sure the police would pin it on him. Had to wait until I was certain the two of them were going to be together and make my move then.

I considered tampering with a bottle of wine but that was really difficult. I couldn't open then reseal a brand-new bottle without the results appearing suspect. And then, I'd have to somehow get that bottle to Cass. No. I'd have to break into Cass's house, find an open bottle and dump in the powder, *then* count on her to drink some, but then Allen might drink some, too, and if both of them were found unconscious that would mess up my plan.

That's when I had the brainstorm about meeting Cass for coffee to warn her about Sadie. It was a natural thing, one woman looking out for another. I thought Kate might have overheard our conversation at some point, but I honestly never considered those reflective coffee shop surfaces or remembered the mirror over the bar.

So I had no way to know that Kate was watching, no way to tell that she'd seen—me briefly remove the lid of Cass's tall double-shot latte and stir my powder in.

O'REILLY
THE COP

Before

It takes me and the chief and Rodriguez about an hour to devise the sting. We're aware we have to act quickly to catch the real killer. It all started back at Allen's parents' lake house when he was on the run.

Allen climbs onto his bike and starts pedaling toward the trees.
"Stop! Police!"
Allen's foot hits the ground and he peers over his shoulder.
"We just want to talk!" I shout. "It's about Sadie! She's in trouble!"
He hangs his head and we know we have him.
Allen will do anything for the woman he loves.

SADIE
THE WIFE

Before

I sit with Officer Patel in the interrogation room. Another officer is with her, someone I haven't met before, Bev Johnson. Everything I say is being recorded but I expected that.

"Can you please go over that part again very carefully?" Patel asks. "The bit that happened after you and Cass struggled and crashed into the window."

My pulse threads unevenly. "I didn't kill Cass Thomas. She was very much alive when I left her."

"We know," Patel says and I'm stunned. "You're not a suspect."

Relief swamps through me, but what about Allen? I assume he's still presumed guilty. I go queasy worrying about Emma and what this will do to our family.

Patel's rapidly typing notes on her tablet. "You last saw her around six thirty, correct?"

"That's right," I answer, grateful this isn't coming back on me. But still, my heart aches for Allen. I'd give anything to believe he's innocent. My mind keeps saying I should give up hope and view things rationally the way the police are, but I can't.

"Cass texted her sister Robin around six fifty in the evening saying she wasn't going to meet up with her as planned early the next morning for breakfast, because she thought she was coming down with something and was going to turn in early. She wanted to get a good night's sleep."

Patel checks her notes. "According to the statement you gave us earlier, you and Allen were at home having dinner and putting Emma to bed at that time." She must know if one of us had been determined to do it we could have snuck over to Cass's house to do her in, but this obviously isn't the tack she's taking. Patel is onto something else.

"At the moment, we're not as focused on the head trauma as we are on why Cass behaved as if she were drugged while you were speaking with her. Can you go through your story again?"

"But Allen? I don't think he would have done something like that. Teresa wanted me to come and tell you about the wine, but that honestly sounds so unlike him. He would have had to get some sedative in advance and plan it. We don't use sleeping pills. We keep nothing like that in the house. And anyway, aren't those pills by prescription?"

Patel nods. "They are." She writes some things down then muses, "Teresa thought you should tell us about the wine? Hmm, that's interesting."

"Interesting?" I ask. "Why?"

She glances at Johnson who's been totally silent but listening. Maybe she's in training, or junior to Patel. "Can you run out and do me a favor?"

Johnson nods. "Sure."

"See if we can't get a quick bead on who Teresa's doctor is, and expedite a warrant to access her prescription records."

I'm stunned by where they're going with this. Teresa? Oh my God. Doubts niggle at me when I consider her actions these past few days. She's been keenly intent on casting Allen in a bad light and inspiring me to fear him. Could Teresa have been covering her own tail? Could she really be involved? Could she have killed Cass?

Although she's tried to hide it, Teresa's always coveted my relationship with Allen. Was she worried about the same thing I was, that Cass and Allen were getting back together? What if she somehow learned about Bobby? She never would have been able to stand that. I admit that I'm jealous and my emotions sometimes get the better of me, but Teresa takes things to the next level. She's envious and devious, a dangerous mix.

"I know what pharmacy Teresa uses," I say because I've picked up prescriptions for Forrest there many times before.

"That would be very helpful, Sadie," Patel says.

I volunteer the information and Patel instructs Johnson, "See what you can find out."

Once Johnson's gone, Patel motions with her hands. "Go on with your story, please."

"Okay." I take a deep breath recalling the scene. "After we crashed into the window, I stood and pulled myself together walking toward the kitchen island in a daze. I couldn't believe what I'd done. How I had totally flipped out and taken a run at her. I lost my temper, but not my mind, I assure you! I didn't mean to hurt Cass and certainly wouldn't have killed her."

"I'm afraid I need details," Patel says.

And then, I'm back in the moment so vivid as if it were now.

My blood's pumping hard and my breath is heaving. "Cass," I say miserably. I tug at my sweater and smooth down my hair. "Cass, I'm so sorry. Fuck." I can't believe I lost my cool like that, that I let my jealousy drive me over the edge. What was I thinking getting into a brawl with Cass? How is that helping anything? Allen lied to me, yes, and I'm angry, but that's on him. Didn't matter that their affair was nearly a decade ago. He should have told me.

Cass grabs the baseball bat off the floor but she falters on her feet, weaving around and grabbing onto things. The center island, a kitchen counter, the refrigerator. She rubs her forehead, then the back of her neck. "I think I—need to sit down." She stumbles toward the living room catching herself on the doorframe.

"What's wrong with you?" I ask concernedly. "Are you drunk?"

She shakes her head and sinks down in a chair. "I think it was the wine. I took some allergy meds earlier. Shouldn't have mixed the two." She yawns and I eye her worriedly.

"Do you need to go to the hospital or something?"

Cass waves me away but she still looks woozy. "No, I just need to sleep."

"Are you sure?" I don't want to leave her like this right after we've fought. What if something happens? What if she's really sick?

"Sadie," she says seriously although she slurs her words. "I think the best thing you can do is go."

"And so you left then?" Patel asks to confirm.

"Yes."

Officer Brady appears at the door to the interrogation room. "Officer Patel," he says. "If you have a moment?"

"If you don't mind waiting, Sadie," Patel says, "I'll be right back."

About ten minutes later, Patel reappears. "Deputy Chief O'Reilly wants to speak with you for a bit when we're done here. But he's otherwise disposed so it could take a while. Would you like a cup of coffee?"

"I'm not in trouble?" I ask nervously.

"No." Patel shares a cryptic smile. "It's good news."

O'REILLY
THE COP

Before

The chief and I have got Allen in the interrogation room and he's agreed to cooperate fully. He's waived his right to an attorney and has state-appointed counsel at his side.

"You said Sadie's in trouble?" He looks haggard, his face sagging, and also like he's lost some weight. He's sporting beard stubble too.

"She may or may not be," I answer, "depending on how things go here. We do know she met with Cass Thomas on the night Cass died. We have forensic evidence placing her at the scene and very strong evidence the two of them struggled. We found fibers from Sadie's Shetland sweater in Cass's broken window glass."

Allen rakes a hand through his hair. "Jesus Christ."

"We've got a couple things to ask you," Claremont says. "First, why did you do it?"

Allen squares his jaw. "Cass and I had a relationship years ago and she had a secret, one I didn't know about until that night."

"You're talking about the baby," I say and Allen blinks.

"Yeah," he admits hoarsely. "That's right."

"And so what?" Claremont asks leadingly. "You didn't want Sadie finding out?"

"You don't have to answer that," Allen's lawyer says.

"It's all right." He stares at Claremont and then at me. "Yes, that's it. I didn't want Sadie knowing. What Cass and I had was so long ago, and Sadie's and my marriage was just getting back on track."

"After Emma's kidnapping?" Claremont asks quietly.

"Yes."

"Can you tell us what happened the night Cass died?"

"Yeah, she . . ." Allen clears his throat and continues, "Cass texted that she wanted to meet up because she had something to discuss. Turns out she wanted to tell me about her pregnancy and the kid she'd lost."

"You didn't know you two had a child together until then?"

"Absolutely not."

"What happened next?" the chief asks.

Allen sighs heavily. "We argued over whether or not to tell Sadie and then I got a call from Sadie about picking up Emma, and so I left."

I lean forward and set my elbows on the table, staring into Allen's eyes. "But then you went back?"

"Yes."

"When was this?" I ask, assessing his body language. How he set his jaw when his cheek flinched. He's working hard to keep calm, stay under control, his hands resting on his thighs under the table. His shoulder blades back against his chair. He sits rigid. Too still.

"Very late," Allen says. "In the middle of the night. I think it was around two a.m."

"Did anyone see you leave? Was Sadie awake?"

"No."

"What did you do when you went back over to Cass's?" I ask him.

He doesn't answer right away, staring off into some point in space.

"Allen?" Claremont asks.

He looks right at the chief. "I killed her."

Allen's counsel sighs and holds open his hands.

"It's okay." Allen glances at the guy. "I want to finish."

"Oh?" the chief asks. "How? How did you kill Cass Thomas?"

"I hit her with a baseball bat."

Allen's lawyer shakes his head, taps some notes on his electronic tablet.

"Where's that baseball bat now?" I ask Allen.

His eyebrows rise. "Somewhere at the bottom of the lake."

"Don't worry," the chief says lightly. "We'll find it."

The blood drains from Allen's face. "What?"

The chief gathers some papers and stands. "Thanks for telling us where to look."

"Fuck," we hear Allen say as we leave.

We shut the door so he can confer with his attorney.

"He's lying," Claremont says. "Protecting someone."

We both know who we think that is.

ALLEN
THE HUSBAND

Before

Sirens pull me from a deep slumber. A low whooping sound and short sharp yelps. A fire truck and maybe police? A rising-falling wail.

An ambulance. Shit.

This won't look good.

I sit up in bed and scrub my fists against my eyes, suddenly wide awake. Sadie's not in bed beside me. She must be downstairs. It's still dark outside. I slowly peel back the covers and creep out of our room, head into my office where I'll get a clearer view through the hazy rain.

Flashing red and blue lights clog Cass's driveway.

First responders smash in her deck-side door.

Rush into the house.

Switch on the lights.

Fuck me.

Sadie's there standing in the rain and chatting with a police officer by our back gate. I have to think of Sadie and what's best for all of us. The police will go digging. I know what they'll assume. That I was with Cass because we had a history, a more recent one than anyone knew. They'll suspect that something went south, and I took matters into my own hands. Whether intentionally or accidentally, the results will be the same.

I'm sickened that Cass is dead, but sometimes things get out of hand. People lose their tempers and erupt. It happens. And then a line is crossed. Some lines are pencil thin, so narrow they're nearly invisible. Others are broader and written in stone like the Ten Commandments. I'll never know now what else Cass meant to share. Never learn the whole truth and that makes my heart heavy. She never got the chance.

I didn't tell Sadie where I went late last night because the less she knows the better. It's safer for her than covering up secrets, because the more secrets you keep the harder they are to contain. People mix up their stories and make mistakes. And I don't want Sadie making *that kind* of mistake, the sort that could have her ripped away from Emma and landed in prison. Having me there will be bad enough, if it comes to that, and I hope it won't. Maybe Cass's death will be ruled an accident. That's my greatest hope.

I'm in my closet in an instant, hurriedly getting into my jeans, a T-shirt and a hoodie. Skip the socks and step into my boat shoes. I can't stay here and wait for the police. I have to retrieve the evidence that I stashed at our neighborhood playground and make it disappear.

I pull my backpack from our walk-in closet shelf and a wad of spare cash from our small fireproof safe. We keep our passports in there and other documents, like the titles to our SUVs. I leave those in place and close the safe, punch in a code so it locks.

Then I'm down the front steps and opening the drawer of the table in the foyer. I grab our spare key and shove it in my pocket, then I'm out the front door.

It shuts with a muffled click.

It's two a.m. and I'm back at Cass's creeping toward her deck door and through the shadows. I try the doorknob and the door opens. "Cass?" I call softly. "Cass, are you here?" I've texted but got no response. I pass through the kitchen into the darkened living room, and switch on a lamp. I stop short, my heart pounding. Cass lies stock still on the living room floor beside her coffee table. Her baseball bat's at her side and the color's drained from her face. She's ashen. I kneel and lean my ear toward her face, hear nothing. Hold my palm near her nose and mouth.

No breathing.

Cass is dead.

O'REILLY
THE COP

Before

Chief Claremont and I stand in the coroner's office. We're asking Libby McMann for her professional opinion. "Allen claims he hit and killed Cass with the baseball bat," Claremont shares, "but we've got our doubts. We want to be sure that cause of death is consistent with your findings."

McMann wears scrubs and a face mask. She tugs down the mask and pulls off her gloves. "I've been stewing over the whole baseball bat angle and here's why. Let's consider the position of the body when we found it. Cass was lying face up and not face down."

"Correct," Claremont says, "beside the coffee table. The bat was there too initially, but according to his statement, Allen took the bat and dumped it in the lake."

"Jail time for him?"

The chief shakes her head. "We're working out a deal. What we're trying to do is find the real culprit, the person who drugged Cass, and it couldn't have been Allen putting something in Cass's wine, could it? It wouldn't have taken effect that quickly. Sadie said when she arrived at six thirty, Cass was already stumbling around and acting drunk, and Allen had only been there twenty minutes."

"You make a good point," McMann concedes with a nod and then she continues. "If Cass was hit from behind with force, she would have more than likely pitched forward and landed on her stomach." McMann walks to the corner of her office and picks up a baseball bat. She's got all sorts of equipment lying around including some pretty gruesome-looking stuff.

"Blunt object, right?" she asks, waving the bat in the air. "Cass's coffee table had a curved lip and not a sharp edge so might have had the same effect. Stand here," she says to Claremont because she's shorter and the chief complies. We're used to McMann's demonstrations.

"Now say I'm Allen," McMann goes on, "or someone else intent on bludgeoning Cass. If I come up in front of her?"

Claremont peers skyward, assessing her view of the weapon. "You crush her forehead or maybe whack her on the side of her head."

"Against the temple would be good," McMann advises. "Bones are soft there."

"Okay." Claremont urges her along.

McMann passes me the baseball bat to hold and cradles the base of her skull with both hands. "But Cass's fracture was back here." She lowers her grip to her neck. "And here. Her spinal cord was severed."

"So someone hit her from behind," I conclude.

"Yeah, but they would have had to be a midget doing this." She takes back the bat and shoves it up toward the ceiling in short sharp vertical jabs.

"What are you saying?" Claremont asks.

"Allen's taller than Cass, so is Sadie. So are most people in general. Cass was on the shorter side. So someone hitting from behind wouldn't have whacked her from that angle."

"What if they took a swing at her?" I ask. "Batter up?"

"Possible but not probable from how the bones in her neck and head were crushed." She walks over to her desk and grabs a stack of books handing them to me. "Here, hold this."

"What's this?" I ask staring down at the pile of medical tomes.

"Cass's neck vertebrae of course." Claremont raises her eyebrows at me like I should have known that. She didn't know it either, come on. "Now hold on tight."

"Okay."

She takes the baseball bat and whacks into them.

"Hey!" I fall back a step and look down.

"What do you see?" McMann asks like a teacher in school.

"A bunch of the ones in the middle moved," Claremont answers.

"Very good." McMann nods. Then she grabs two more books from a shelf and compares them choosing the thicker one. "Fix those," she tells me over her shoulder. I realign the stack of books and hold it steady.

"Now let's try again, shall we?" She glances at me and Claremont. "Ready?"

I nod and she shoves the spine of a very thick book against my stack—with force.

The chief and I survey the damage. "Okay," Claremont says, "now fewer of the books in the stack have moved."

"Exactly," McMann says, sounding very pleased with herself. "The damage to Cass's neck and spine is much more in line with this"—she holds up the thick book—"than this." She picks up the baseball bat.

Holy shit. "So someone pushed her into the coffee table?"

"It's possible if you can match a suspect to her time of death, but my guess is Cass was so doped up she fell when she got up to go to bed. She was likely groggy when talking to Sadie, maybe dozed off for a bit then decided to get up and go upstairs. Only she didn't make it very far. The Ambien as good as killed her. If she hadn't been so unsteady on her feet, she never would have fallen and hit her head. And if she hadn't fallen and hit her head—"

"The drugs would have killed her anyway," Claremont finishes.

TERESA
THE EX-WIFE

Now

I'm sitting in a fucking holding cell on a *very uncomfortable* stone-cold cot that's chained to a cinder block wall, so I might as well be honest. The only thing I have to be thankful for is that I'm in here alone with ample time to think. Take it or leave it, that could be a good thing—or drive me batty. I'm saying *nothing to no one* until my counsel arrives. I broke down and phoned my asshat father, who has enough money in the bank to make this quietly go away. We'll see what comes of that. In the meantime, I've got my ruminations to keep me company.

So yeah, it was me that second night at Sadie's. I broke into her and Allen's house the night after Cass was found dead and Allen disappeared. The first night, I just skulked around in the backyard. I wanted to scare the daylights out of Sadie. Make her start to question everything, fret over who was out to get her and about what her husband had done. Had Allen killed Cass? Would he come for her next? I wanted her to fear that possibility thoroughly. I yearned to break down the relationship she and Allen shared, rip it to shreds—piece by piece—and leave it in tatters.

I didn't know if Allen had actually killed Cass before the sleeping pills took effect. Based on his unexplained disappearance, I calculated my answer, assuming yes. Whatever Cass said to Allen that night must have been pretty terrible. Maybe that she wasn't giving up and wanted him back. Maybe she finally told him about Bobby and threatened to tell Sadie too.

I knew Cass and Allen had a kid and the knowledge burned right through me, decimating my heart. They'd had a little girl, like I'd always hoped to have with Allen. Like Sadie also had with Allen. It was all so unjust. In this vast universe of stars and planets, how could I have been dealt this meteoric blow? Supernova-like in its strength, upending me and spinning me like a top. Making my whole world erupt in a blaze then suddenly go dark.

I didn't find out about Bobby until fairly recently. It was after Emma's kidnapping and her being found safe. The whole time Emma was away, Sadie kept talking about Cass being deranged. Said Cass had a dead son she believed was still alive. Sadie batted the name around: Bobby. *Bobby this, Bobby that.* The playdate that never happened. Blah, blah, blah.

What Sadie didn't consider is that I've got connections to Our Lady of Our Savior, the school where Cass Thomas taught, myself. Same place that Cass's supposed niece, but actual child, attends. Forrest is on a community soccer team and lots of his friends go to that school. You'll never guess who the new team coach is this year. Robin's husband, Leon Marconi.

Sometimes Robin attends the matches, and when she does, she brings her child with her. The likeness between the kid and Allen was so strong I found it impossible to ignore. The girl's name was Barbara but I heard her parents call her Bobby.

Then it clicked.

Maybe this Barbara/Bobby did come to play at Cass's sometimes. It wasn't implausible that Sadie had never seen her. Besides that, Sadie wasn't on the lookout for a little girl. She and the police assumed Bobby to be the boy Cass had lost in the auto accident along with her ex-husband, Richard, years earlier.

After a successful soccer match, I go to congratulate the coach on a game well played. I wait until Robin and Bobby are standing by his side.

"Great win!" I smile up at Leon. "Super coaching!"

Leon smiles. "Thanks, Teresa. Forrest did a bang-up job. All the kids did." He notes my gaze on his girl. "Oh hey," he says by way of introduction, "this is Bobby. You of course know Robin."

"Robin, hi."

The little girl stares up at me and a chill runs through me so deep it floods my veins like an icy river. There's no mistaking that this is Allen's child. She has his same exact nose and his deep-blue eyes, but Cass's plump round cheeks and mouth. I immediately feel sick to my stomach, and then I know. Bobby can't be Leon's little girl, and I doubt very much she's Robin's. Robin wasn't the one Allen fucked like a jackrabbit.

That was Cass.

Shit.

"Hi, Bobby." I smile politely. "How old are you?"

"Seven! I just had a birthday."

And the timing fits.

"How awesome! Happy birthday!"

She gives a little wave and I look at her parents, unable to take staring at her any longer. Now that I know, I can't unknow, and I hate Cass for it. Hate her for giving Allen what I couldn't. Then it dawns on me he doesn't know.

If he did, he would have found a way to become involved. Obliged to accept Bobby as a new part of his family. Squeezing out the half time he has for Forrest and reducing his affections and attention for our boy even more—from half time to a third. I fume at the thought of that happening. Of Allen further taking a wrecking ball to our lives.

I have to find a way to destroy his first.

KATE
THE EX-CON

Before

Shane comes to see me at my apartment later in the day. I'm still recovering from everything I learned this morning as well as my chats with my therapist and the police down at the station. His dark expression alarms me. He must have an update on what happened to my family. "Shane, what's going on?"

He wears a worried frown. "Unfortunately, I have news about your parents and sister."

I invite him in and we both sit down.

"What is it?" I anxiously search his eyes. "Have you learned something new?"

"Yeah, Kate, and I'm sorry. We analyzed the fingerprints on the gun and the timing of when everybody died and . . ." He heaves a breath and delivers the news. "It appears very likely that Diane shot both your parents and then took her own life."

My heart stays still for an extended moment and then it gallops. "Oh my God." I cover my mouth with my hands. "What about Diane's daughter? What about Nellie?"

"Your brother, Mark, has her in Florida. She'll likely stay with him and his family. He told the police Diane recently asked him and his wife to be Nellie's appointed guardians, if something were to happen to her."

"It's almost like she had a premonition," I say.

"Yeah." O'Reilly hangs his head and looks up. "In any case, I'm sorry about her and your folks."

"I'm not sorry about my folks—at all. In a huge way, I sleep easier knowing they're gone, and you want to know a strange thing?"

His forehead lifts. "What's that?"

"All these voices I was hearing in my head?" I make a motion behind my ear. "They've gotten really quiet lately."

"Well, that's good then." He appears genuinely pleased for me. "You're making progress."

"I am, yeah."

Shane smiles uncertainly then says, "There is one more thing."

"What's that?"

He shifts in his seat seeming ill at ease. "It's about our ongoing investigation into Allen. He's in police custody now, but we don't believe he murdered Cass."

"You're kidding. But who?" I freeze up suddenly. "You don't suspect Diane?"

"No. We believe your hunch was correct when you said she was more about blackmailing Cass than murdering her."

"So then?"

"I have an idea about what you saw at the coffee shop."

I stare at him wide eyed. "Teresa?"

"We think she may have put something in Cass's coffee cup, Ambien."

That's a shocker, even for me, and I've seen a lot in my time. "Oh wow."

"The problem is it's tough to prove it. We never found Cass's coffee cup and think she might have thrown it away somewhere, possibly in the dumpster outside her house when she got home, and before the trash truck came the next morning."

"I'm not sure why you're telling me this?"

His dark eyes sparkle so sweetly I want to fall back into them again, but I don't. Shane's with Val, and I've got other stuff I'm working on now. "I was hoping you could help the police confirm that Teresa did what we suspect."

"I'm not sure how I could do that. My back was turned. I honestly didn't see anything."

"Yeah, but." He pauses and grins. "Teresa doesn't know that."

I agree to help Shane catch a killer.

ALLEN
THE HUSBAND

Now

I'm in my hospital room waiting on Sadie. She texted they'll be here shortly. Emma is back from her spring break cruise and Forrest is staying with his grandma an extra week and completing his school assignments virtually. After that, he'll come home to live at our house for as long as needed.

I'm in a private room and doing decently well with my recovery, angled up in my bed in a sitting position and in no need of breathing apparatuses or any special machines. My midsection is bandaged where I took a minor hit to my stomach, but the wound wasn't critical thanks to the body armor the police suited me up with.

We talked about using blanks but needed my death to appear convincing to Teresa. Sadie agreed not to shoot until I got close enough for her not to miss or make a mistake—like accidentally shooting me in the head. Now that would have been lethal. The police guessed Teresa would only let her guard down if she believed I had died and that her secret would be buried with me.

If I were in custody, I could talk and share my side of the story. What if I denied putting Ambien in Cass's wine? Offered to take a polygraph to that effect? The police might start digging deeper into Teresa's story about having coffee with Cass, and she might ultimately fall under suspicion.

As a corpse, I'd been silenced and Teresa was free to go on about her life. So when Kate came to espouse her theory about Teresa putting Ambien in Cass's coffee at Café Latte, Teresa too easily dismissed her.

I'm really glad Kate's doing better. She was a sweetheart of a little girl. Despite her horrid parents, I always saw so many glimmers of goodness in her. It's awesome to see that part of her coming back into the light and learning to shine. Kate's paid for her part in Emma's kidnapping, and she went the extra mile in helping convict Teresa.

I don't like to talk about evening scores, but Sadie and I are at least in a good place with Kate, a better one than we ever could have imagined, and we do wish her well. It's very sad about Diane and her parents, but Kate's back in touch with her brother Mark, I hear, and he and his family can be there for her, like we are here for one another: Sadie and I and our kids.

We have three children now, because I've learned I have another daughter. Her name is Bobby and she's the child I had with Cass, the one I thought we'd lost. I now know that was the rest of the story Cass intended to tell me the night she died. She intended to share the news that Bobby was alive and well, and living at her sister's house, as Robin and Leon's child. I don't fault Cass for the choices she made. How could I? I've made loads of questionable choices myself.

And, in Cass's case, I trust her reasoning was thoughtful. She wanted the best life possible for our little girl and decided Bobby would have that with Robin and Leon. Sadie and I understand that too and we've worked something out with Robin and Leon, so we all can be open to keeping Bobby in her most stable environment, while helping to support one another.

Sadie told me about Bobby down at the police station. It was shortly after I'd been interrogated by Claremont and O'Reilly and right after I discovered that Sadie and I were off the hook as suspects. Our help was needed in catching the real killer. My heart broke when I realized that person was Teresa, but Sadie and I also both knew that the best way to get Teresa help was by bringing her to justice. That was the kindest way forward for her, and for Forrest, our precious son. And now I have, not one, but two wonderful daughters.

Sadie told me the news about Bobby being alive in private while we sat in Shane O'Reilly's office. She brought a nun from Our Lady of Our Savior with her, Sister Mary Catherine Ward, since she's the person Cass had confided in. I'm not ashamed to say that when they told me the truth I cried.

KATE
THE EX-CON

Now

Mark invited me down to Miami. I can't believe his *beautiful house*, his *beautiful wife*, his *beautiful kids*. A third child comes skipping toward me and smiles.

"Hi! I'm Nellie! Who are you?"

I'm not the weeping sort, honestly I'm not, but my eyes feel weirdly hot. "Hi, Nellie. I'm your auntie Kate." I stare at the other two children, a girl about Nellie's age and a younger boy. Mark introduces them and they instantly give me hugs. So does Elena.

"I'm so sorry for your tough times," she says warmly, and hugs me harder. "Things will get better."

"Thanks," I say and sniff. "They already are."

"And who is this gentleman behind you?" Mark asks heartily.

Oh fuck. I almost forgot. He's not here as my boyfriend, more like my supportive plus-one. But in the future? Who knows?

"Mark, Elena, kids." I turn and smile over my shoulder. "Meet Nick."

SADIE
THE WIFE

Now

I drive the girls to the hospital to see Allen. They're sitting in the back seat of my SUV chatting like they're old friends, but they only met this morning.

"I have a dog!" Bobby tells Emma. "His name is Migo."

I peer in my rearview mirror to peek at their sunny faces. "What's Migo?" Emma asks.

Bobby swings her ponytail, her blue eyes twinkling. "Migo means 'friend'!"

I chuckle to myself guessing she must mean *amigo*.

"I have a dog!" Emma rolls her big brown eyes. "But he's not real."

It's easy to see that they are sisters, but they don't know it yet. Allen and I talked things over and I discussed it with Bobby's folks. We're waiting until the girls are better acquainted to let them know they're related, so it won't come as too big a shock. With kids you never know. They could make the adjustment easily. In any case, Allen and I and Robin and Leon agreed to seek the guidance of a child psychologist in finding the best way forward.

Robin and Leon were more open to talking to me than I'd expected. It helped that Chief Claremont and Deputy Chief O'Reilly paved the way by explaining the situation first. They also spoke with Cass's parents. It seems Cass's family is grateful to me and Allen for helping catch Cass's real killer, and believes that, once the truth was out, Cass would have wanted Allen to be involved with his biological daughter.

Allen and I will also arrange counseling for Forrest. The poor kid has so much to cope with but we'll help him through it, the two of us together. As for us, Allen and I will go back for another round of couples counseling to work through our newest issues. He finally came clean with me about everything, including the two times he slept with Teresa during our marriage and the history of his affair with Cass. He told me about going to the hospital that night and about how he never knew about Bobby, and based on the corroborating story from Sister Mary Catherine, I believed him.

I guess I never really understood how much Allen loved me until he was willing to throw his whole life away just to protect me, when he thought I was the guilty one. At first, I was hurt he'd believe me capable of murder, but then he reminded me very gently I'd thought the same thing about him.

We enter the hospital parking lot and Emma kicks her feet against the seat. "We're here! We're going to see Daddy!"

No truer words.

"All right, girls, you ready?" I turn in my seat and Emma holds a homemade card. I promised the pair afterward we'd do something fun. We're going to get ice cream. I know it's a bribe, but parenting is hard work.

"Yay!" Emma cheers and Bobby giggles.

"I went to the hospital once," Bobby says proudly as I help them out of the vehicle. "Mommy told me. I was born here."

"Yes, you were. So was Emma." I smile down at the girls knowing in my heart there's room for one more. The more love you give the more your heart grows. I'm growing and learning each day.

I reach out my hands and latch on to each child and we parade toward the hospital.

"Mommy?" Emma says. "When is Daddy coming home?"

"Soon, sweetheart. Soon."

SADIE
THE WIFE

One year later

Allen drives us to New Haven Home. We ride in silence in our SUV, but I know what he's thinking. Why did this have to happen? Life sucks so badly sometimes, you can't control it. All you can do is put one foot in front of the other and move forward. That's what Allen and I are doing now with Forrest. He was traumatized by the revelation about his mom, of course, but he's made a lot of progress this past year and is back to doing well academically and in sports, has a tight-knit group of friends.

Forrest sits in the back seat staring glumly out the window. Each time we've come out here, we've asked him if he wants to see his mom, but he's always previously declined. This time, he said okay. He's a good boy, Forrest, and I'm so happy to have him living in our home. I take that responsibility seriously, like I do our relationship with Bobby. She comes to visit once in a while and plays with Emma. The two girls really get along. But there's nothing regular like a scheduled visitation.

Allen and I discussed it with her parents, Robin and Leon, and decided it's best for Bobby to stay rooted in the home she knows. Her aunt's death was jarring enough, along with learning she was adopted.

After we adults had consulted with the proper specialists, Robin and Leon gently told Bobby who her real mom and dad were because they were afraid of it coming out otherwise, and her finding out the wrong way.

We've been going to family counseling, Allen, Forrest, and I, and Forrest is doing so much better. We're all doing better, but this situation with Teresa is brutally hard. Because she confessed in the end, her lawyer was able to successfully argue she'd had a mental breakdown, and her mother lobbied to have Teresa institutionalized rather than put in prison. Teresa's rich father is footing the bill, although he hasn't visited once.

Teresa's mom drives down once a week, on Saturdays, from Northern Virginia. Afterward, she always comes by our place to have lunch with us and spend time with Forrest. She's a good grandma. He's lucky to have her and we're glad she's in his life.

It's a school day but still a special occasion, which is why we left for here shortly after Forrest got off the bus. Emma is playing at Bobby's and will have dinner at her house with Leon and Robin. It takes a village, truly, and we villagers are sticking together. Forrest is growing up and will soon go his own way, but he gets that we love him. We're his family. So's his mom. We make sure to emphasize that every day. Families don't have to live together for them to be whole, and his mom is in a place where she's getting the help she needs.

We drive past the high stone walls and through the iron gates of New Haven Home and it's like we've entered an enchanted land. The gates swing open and lush grounds expand all around us. Allen has a sensor clipped to the visor on his SUV that automatically lets us in. The long gravel road weaves through stately oak trees, their leafy branches curtsying in the breeze, and big puffy white clouds dot the Carolina-blue sky.

The facility crests before us, massive in its scope. It resembles an English manor house fashioned from limestone and is three stories tall with high-pitched gables and a tile roof. The pristine lawn's dotted with wildflower berms and elegant stone benches. Occasional fountains gurgle within stone surrounds. If I didn't know better, I might figure New Haven Home for a grand estate or a vacation locale like Biltmore House in Asheville.

People meander about enjoying the afternoon sunshine. Several look like patients, some are accompanied by staff. A nurse pushes a person in a wheelchair toward one of the many gardens. New Haven Home has twelve. We circle the building and park around back.

"Well," Allen sighs. "Here we go."

Forrest climbs from the back seat and Allen squeezes his shoulder. "You okay, buddy?"

Forrest nods, looking sad. He holds a store-bought bouquet of flowers in his hand. "Sure."

We find Teresa sitting in a sunny area of a place they call the dayroom, with huge arched windows overlooking the grounds. She stands when she sees us coming, spots Forrest at once and smiles in surprise.

"Forrest?" she asks weakly as we approach her. When her eyes water, so do mine.

He walks shyly toward her, his shoulders slumped. Then Allen warmly pats his back and he stands up straighter, suddenly looking like a man. He's changed his haircut and now wears his hair like his dad's, and he's dressed up for the occasion in a blazer, slacks and tie. I couldn't be prouder of him if he were my own. My heart fills to brimming and I count my blessings. Pray the heavens will grant my wish and ultimately bring Teresa home.

It won't be immediately, but someday. That would be good for Forrest, so that's what I want too. I love him as deeply as if he were my son, and he loves me too. He sends me a glance and a soft smile to let me know that I'm an important person in his life. He understands that I'm here for him through thick and through thin. But we're all very clear about one thing: who his real mom is.

"Mom," he says. His voice cracks unevenly. "These are for you." He hands her the flowers and my eyes grow hot. "Happy birthday."

ACKNOWLEDGMENTS

Huge thanks to my very kind and thoughtful acquiring editor, Alexandra Torrealba at Thomas & Mercer, for encouraging a sequel to book one, *The Last Morning*, as well as for approving the outline for this story, and to my terrific agent, Jill Marsal, for negotiating the deal. I had such fun revisiting these characters and giving them new challenges to face. I hope readers enjoy seeing them again too.

I owe an enormous debt of gratitude to developmental editor Clete Smith for his extreme wizardry in taking this manuscript from its initial messy pile of cool ideas and helping shape it into a cohesive and compelling form. Thank you, Clete! I couldn't have done it without you, nor without the much-appreciated contributions of Thomas & Mercer's vast and highly skilled editorial team.

When I first met my husband John many years ago, I was a struggling single mom trying to raise four children, mostly on my own. Describing me as a "tough cookie, a smart cookie, and just about every other kind of cookie I know . . ." John settled on calling me "Cookie" as an endearing nickname. As I thought that was awfully sweet (and that *he* was), I dubbed him "S.J." for "Sweetie J" or "Sweet John."

Now that we've successfully blended our families and are navigating the exciting road of our lives together, he's still the sweetest "J" I know. He fully supported the creation of this work, particularly during the deadline stages, by delivering endless gourmet and delicious dinners, and never once complaining when he had to ask a question twice. Or, okay, okay, maybe *three* times, since I was so deep in my authorial bubble the primary voices demanding my attention were those belonging to the characters in Chapel Roads.

So this one's for you, S.J.! It's been a really great ride and I look forward to our next adventures. The future's so bright, we're going to need sunglasses.

BOOK CLUB DISCUSSION QUESTIONS

1. In book one in the Chapel Roads series, *The Last Morning*, Allen's cast in a bad light. In this book, book two, *The Next Lie*, we learn more about Allen's past and present, and he goes to great lengths to prove to Sadie how much he loves her. By the end of *The Next Lie* she believes him. Do you? Why or why not?

2. Sadie has certain insecurities credited to her history of losing her parents early. In your opinion, do these explain her actions against Cass?

3. Teresa is an interesting and unapologetic character. Has she garnered your sympathy by the end of this story? Explain your feelings about Teresa.

4. From her rocky beginnings in book one, Kate Davis undergoes a transformation in book two. Are you satisfied with her outcome? Why or why not?

5. Diane made many tragic choices. Which details about her background helped you better process or understand them?

6. Who was your favorite character in *The Next Lie*, and why?

7. Compare your thoughts on who you believed killed Cass at the beginning of the book and then at different points in the narrative. Did you guess the real killer?

8. Two very different birthdays (Sadie's near the beginning and Teresa's at the end) bookend the story. A third birthday (Allen's) is described midway. Why do you think the author used birthdays versus other types of occasions to showcase

these particular characters' lives at those points in time? What do birthdays symbolize to you?

9. What was your biggest surprise in book two—was it about Bobby or something else?

10. What do you think? Did Allen kill his parents, yes or no?

ABOUT THE AUTHOR

Camden Baird writes fast-paced, emotionally gripping stories that keep readers up late turning pages. A *New York Times* and *USA Today* bestselling author, she's published more than forty works of fiction under different pen names. *The Next Lie* is the sequel to her debut psychological suspense thriller, *The Last Morning*. The author lives in North Carolina.